C000179464

LAST FERRY TO BUTE

MYRA DUFFY

To Bill and Morag,

Best wishes,

Myra Duffy

Published in 2011 by New Generation Publishing

Copyright © Myra Duffy

First Edition

The author asserts the moral right under the Copyright, Designs and Patents Act 1988 to be identified as the author of this work.

All rights reserved. No part of this publication may be reproduced, stored in a retrieval system, or transmitted, in any form or by any means without the prior written consent of the author, nor otherwise be circulated in any form or binding or cover other than that in which it is published without a similar condition being imposed on the subsequent purchaser.

British Library C.I.P.

A CIP catalogue record for this title is available from the British Library.

LAST FERRY TO BUTE

AN ALISON CAMERON MYSTERY

MYRA DUFFY

www.myraduffy.co.uk

http://myraduffy-awriterslot.blogspot.com

Characters in this novel bear no relation to any persons living or dead. Any such resemblance is co-incidental.
While a number of real locations have been used in the novel, details may have been changed for purposes of the plot.

Also by Myra Duffy

The House at Ettrick Bay

When Old Ghosts Meet

The Isle of Bute

The Isle of Bute lies in Scotland's Firth of Clyde, off the west coast of Scotland, a short journey from the city of Glasgow.

It has been occupied for over five thousand years but rose to prominence in Victorian days when its proximity to a major city made it a favoured spot for the wealthy to build summer houses and the not so wealthy to enjoy the delights of the seaside in the many rooms available for rent during the holiday season.

Bute is the ancestral home of the Stuart kings of Scotland and the 800 year old Rothesay castle (now ruined) was built by a hereditary High Steward of Scotland, from which the name is derived.

Today the island is a haven from the hustle and bustle of city life with quiet beaches, woodland walks and an abundance of wildlife, including seals.

For my family, with grateful thanks.

PROLOGUE

All day the mist had drifted in across the waters of the Firth of Clyde and little by little the mainland disappeared into swirling fog.

The last ferry from Weymss Bay loomed through the darkness, foghorn sounding in the eerie stillness, heading towards the island of Bute and a safe berth for the night in the main town of Rothesay. Cars crowded nose to tail on the car deck, hemmed in by heavy lorries transporting vital goods to the island.

Andy, the deckhand, shivered in spite of his thick oilskins. Not long now and he could head for home. Perhaps he'd call in at the Golfer's Bar, have a couple of pints and watch the end of the Manchester United game on SKY.

As the ferry swung into port, he watched his mate Sammie scramble up the ladder to the upper deck to join the extra lookouts, deftly unwinding the thick ropes and tossing them to the waiting crew on shore. The winches would keep the boat safe and secure until morning. Andy pressed the button on the control panel and the great ramp of the ferry juddered down. A signal to Sammie that they were berthed and one by one the cars and the lorries left the deck and bumped their way off on to dry land.

At the stern of the ferry the last car sat immobile. Andy cursed under his breath. If this was a breakdown it would hold them all up: the last thing he wanted on a night like this. He ran up and knocked on the car window, trying to see through the tinted windows. 'Problems?' he mouthed to the driver.

There was no response. He peered in, screwing up his eyes for a better view of the inside. The woman driver sat motionless, staring straight ahead.

This was the last journey the owner of this dark blue saloon car would ever make.

ONE

It all began with a phone call.

'Hello, Susie. How are you?' I glanced at my watch. Almost eleven o' clock. My friend Susie has been working in Los Angeles for more than two years, but still wrestles with the time difference and there was a pile of marking sitting reproachfully on the dining room table: my own fault for not making an earlier start.

'Susie? It's not Susie. Were you expecting a call from Susie? If so I can phone back later if there's a problem. It would be no bother. Or if you are going to be chatting for a long time I could phone in the morning though I expect it would have to be early because...'

'Hello, mum. No, it's okay. I thought it might be Susie at this time of night.'

'It's not late, is it? Were you off to bed? It's only....'

'No, no, it's fine. I'm always pleased to hear from you.' I paused, a sudden fear striking me. 'There isn't any difficulty about your holiday, is there?'

'No, no, I'm all set for tomorrow. I wanted to speak to you before I leave.'

My fiercely independent mother lives in a small flat in a sheltered housing complex, where she makes a good attempt to run everyone's lives. Fortunately it keeps her too busy to run mine: at least most of the time. My only sister, Caroline, had the sense to marry and emigrate to Canada many years ago. This

2

leaves her well out of reach for most of the year, but not entirely safe: my mother was about to descend on her for several months. 'No sense in going all that way for a couple of weeks,' she had said. I wasn't sure Caroline would agree. 'And it will be a chance to see Alastair.' I didn't bother to explain Canada is a very big country and the university where my son teaches is nowhere near my sister.

'I wouldn't trouble you, Alison, except that I seem to remember you said something about going to Bute? With some of your old friends?'

'Yes, that's right. We're having a reunion of my college year next April.'

'Ah,' she said with a long sigh. 'So you won't be going over for a while yet?'

'Not exactly.' I hesitated before saying any more, judging it best to find out what my mother wanted me to do before committing myself.

But the persistence which gave her the iron will to organise the sheltered housing complex was also evident in her dealings with me. 'What does that mean? Are you going over to the island or not?'

I couldn't bring myself to lie. 'I'm going over in a few days as it happens. Betsie's asked me to check out some of the hotels and the Pavilion, where we start the weekend.'

A pause. 'And what's wrong with Betsie? Why can't she do it? I thought you told me it was her idea. Really, Alison, I think you have quite enough to do without organising a big event like this. I scarcely see you for a start.'

No need to say this was because she was far too busy with whist drives, bus outings, film shows, tea dances and making the warden's life difficult to have time to fit me in, but all I said was, 'Yes, Betsie has already organised the reunion but she lives in France when she's not travelling round the rest of Europe because of her antiques business. When she contacted me about her plans for this reunion I volunteered to help with any last minute details.'

'You have plenty to do what with Deborah being home and...'

3

'Mother, is there something special you wanted to talk to me about or is this a general call before you go off to Canada?'

'No need to be cross, Alison.'

'I'm not cross, mother.'

'You only call me mother when you're annoyed about something.'

I took a deep breath and tried to bring her back to the main reason for her phone call. 'Did you want something from Bute?'

'No, no,' she said impatiently. 'Nothing like that, but I do want you to find something out.'

This was more interesting. 'What exactly?'

'It's all to do with Jessie. You remember Jessie McAdam, my old friend. She went to live on Bute a few years ago, went to that wee house in Port Bannatyne where her mother had once lived. I think it was a holiday home.'

'Yes, I remember,' I cut in, watching the hands of the clock move round to the half hour.

'Well, last year she fell and broke her hip and wasn't fit to look after herself. So she moved into the Hereuse Nursing home - you know that very expensive place out past Craigmore, overlooking the little bay? She has a lovely room right at the front. The view is spectacular I believe and so much better than the outlook here…'

I could feel the beginnings of a headache. Why on earth was my mother phoning me at this time of night to tell me this long story about Jessie?

'Mum, what do you want me to do?' I said patiently.

She seemed to recollect the reason for her call. 'It's the residents, you see. Jessie thinks items belonging to them are going missing. And what's worse, Jessie says they keep dying.'

What I was tempted to say was, 'Of course they keep dying, they're elderly.' Instead I tried to be tactful. 'We all must die sometime, mum.' I waited for her response, hoping my mother wasn't going to be depressed by this news from Jessie. I should have known her better.

'Not like this,' she snapped. 'Jessie thinks all these deaths in such a short time are suspicious and when you go over to Bute I

4

want you to go along to the Hereuse Nursing home and find out what's going on.'

My mother often surprises me but this request startled me. What on earth had Jessie been saying to her? This was hardly the time of night to be discussing Jessie's imaginings. What's more, if I didn't make a start soon, I'd have to spend most of the night marking essays.

Making an attempt to end this strange conversation, I said, 'I'm sure there's nothing to be concerned about. Jessie isn't used to living with so many elderly people.'

This response didn't satisfy her. 'She's not a woman given to exaggeration, Alison. She's very level headed and if I weren't off to see Caroline I'd go myself. I can't leave it till I come back: I'm far too worried about Jessie for that. I thought if you were going to be on the island anyway, but if it's all going to be too much trouble…'

I interrupted her. Sometimes it's easier to agree and even if she wasn't going off on holiday, it wasn't a good idea to have her rushing into this nursing home, accusing them of harming the residents.

So I took a deep breath and said, 'Fine, I'll go along, but don't expect too much from what I find out. Those who've died were probably ill or had serious health problems. That does happen in a nursing home.' I didn't want to raise her expectations and said, 'Anyway, apart from that difficulty with her hip operation, I thought you said she was in good health?'

'No, Alison, you don't understand. It's much more serious than that. Jessie thinks she'll be next to die …and she thinks she's going to be murdered.'

TWO

Simon was propped up on a bank of pillows, engrossed in a thriller, when I eventually made it to bed.

'That was my mum on the phone,' I said and gave him a brief account of what had happened.

'Your mother muddles everything up,' he said, putting his book down on the bedside table and reaching for the lamp switch. 'Best not to have anything to do with this.'

'I know, but she sounded really concerned or at least she did when she got to the point.'

He sighed. 'Alison, I know you become involved for the best of reasons, but don't you think you're busy enough?'

I attempted to make light of the situation. 'Well, I'm going over to the island for a few days later this month - remember Betsie asked me to help with this reunion? There would be no harm in visiting Jessie. I'm sure she doesn't have many visitors and once I've seen her it will stop all this nonsense.'

Simon said no more, but contented himself with sighing and burrowing his head under the duvet.

I opened my book, but my mind kept drifting back to the conversation with my mother. I wanted her to enjoy this trip to Canada. Caroline hasn't been back to Scotland for several years and my mother was desperate to see her first great grandchild, a little boy, courtesy of Caroline's only daughter, Leana. A visit to Jessie would take a couple of hours at most and everything else I had to do on the island would be straightforward, thanks to Betsie's hard work and her explicit instructions.

Though I was confident about my trip to Bute, what was happening at home was a different matter. Next morning, as I was putting the hastily corrected exercise books into my briefcase, ready to leave for Strathelder High School where I teach, Deborah came rushing into the kitchen.

'You're up early,' I said, glancing at the clock.

'Mmm,' she said through a mouthful of toast, lifted from Simon's plate before he could stop her. 'Didn't I tell you? I have an interview for a job today.'

Of course, that was why she was looking much smarter than usual. Her long dark hair was neatly tied up on top of her head and she was wearing a blue skirt of a respectable length topped by a cream jumper. She suddenly looked much more grown up, partly because she had toned down her normal heavy makeup to a smudge of eye shadow and some mascara on her dark lashes.

My heart gave a leap. After so many false starts, was Deborah at last about to find a job she liked? 'What sort of job is it?' I asked, putting my briefcase beside the door and turning away to start loading the dishwasher to disguise my interest.

She waved the remains of the slice of toast at me as she sat down opposite Simon, dislodging Motley, our long suffering cat, in the process. He stalked off, tail in the air, meowing in protest. 'I knew you would come up with a whole lot of questions - that's why I didn't tell you earlier.'

Simon intervened. 'We do have your welfare at heart, Deborah.' Perhaps this air of pomposity was something to do with his recently acquired beard, of which he was inordinately proud.

She stood up, flicking crumbs from her skirt. 'It's a job in the Regius Gallery: they're looking for an assistant who knows something about art.'

Simon and I exchanged a glance before he frowned and said, 'Isn't that a bit low level for the qualifications you have from art college?'

'Granted it doesn't pay much,' said Deborah, airily dismissing his concerns, 'but it will give me lots of chances to become involved with the art world and to do some travelling. Sylvester works out of his main gallery in London but he wants to recruit some people locally to expand his business.'

'Sylvester?'

7

'Yes, Sylvester de Courtney. He owns the Regius Gallery. You must know about him.'

Simon said bluntly, 'Never heard of him' but the name seemed to ring a bell with me. I had heard of him somewhere, but for the moment couldn't think where that would be.

I frowned, willing Simon to keep quiet. This might be the chance Deborah had been searching for. She had drifted from course to course, job to job, so hopefully, if she made it through the interview, she would stay with this one for some time.

'Well,' she said, 'you soon will have heard of him. He's going to be BIG. And besides,' she added, with a sigh and an enigmatic smile, 'he's really hot.'

Not the best incentive for applying for a job, but I started the dishwasher in silence as Deborah grabbed another slice of toast.

'Anyway, must be off. Wish me luck.' With that she whirled out of the kitchen and the front door banged shut.

'This might be the great opportunity?'

'And it might be another false start.' Simon wasn't as easily convinced.

'I have to make tracks as well,' I said, yawning.

Simon continued to sit at the table, reading the paper.

'Aren't you heading off?' He usually leaves for college well before I've managed to finish my first cup of coffee.

'Later,' he said. 'I've a meeting in Perth at eleven so it's hardly worth while going in to the department first. I'll do some work here before I leave.' With that he went back to reading his paper.

Simon is head of a department in the local further education college which has thankfully survived financial crises, threats of mergers and several possibilities of closure. 'The only good thing about the recession,' he now said with alarming frequency, 'is that education proves a popular option.'

College numbers were healthy, very healthy indeed. This was good for both of us, though I still kept my part-time teaching job at Strathelder High.

I set off for school in good spirits, looking forward to the trip to Bute at the end of the month and even the visit to see Jessie. Though it was some time since I'd met her, I remembered her as feisty, with interesting tales of her time as a young woman in India.

How wrong I was about everything.

THREE

It was too cold to join the few hardy souls hunched outside on the seats on deck as the ferry swung round, away from Weymss Bay and out into the open waters of the Firth of Clyde, gathering speed as it ploughed through the waves.

I thought back to the events of the past few weeks. Was Simon right and had I taken on too much? I gazed out of the window and thought about my list of tasks. When I had volunteered to help Betsie with the reunion, it had all seemed so simple, but every day now brought fresh instructions. I'd have to do as much as possible on this trip to Bute and hope the rest could be finalised by e-mail and phone.

Betsie had sounded so grateful. 'I have this big antiques fair in Germany to attend in March, Alison. It's going to take all my time and energy to organise myself for that.' Yet again she assured me most of the arrangements for the reunion were in hand, but not quite finalised, as I was now discovering.

At home, Deborah was still waiting for the result of her interview at the Regius Gallery, but she was as optimistic as ever. 'Fingers crossed,' she said. 'The interview went really well and I am sooo... keen on this job.'

To make matters worse, a colleague at Strathelder High had gone off on long term sick leave. 'Please, Alison, if you could help out for a few weeks?' the head of the English department had pleaded. My free time was looking very limited.

'Tell her you can't do it, mum,' Deborah said, when I asked her for help in tracking down some of the more elusive members of our old college group. 'Tell Betsie that when you offered to help you didn't know how much work you'd have on. I know it seemed a good idea, but it's taking up all your time.'

The phone calls and the bills were mounting up. What's more, I suspected some of my old classmates had gone to ground, realising the idea of a college reunion had been Betsie's. Her larger than life personality didn't appeal to everyone.

We'd only met once since leaving college. On one of her very rare trips to Britain she had made the journey north and we met in a café in Glasgow's West End where she outlined her ideas about the reunion. As big and blowsy as I remembered her, she still overwhelmed me. I was happy to nod agreement to everything she suggested: after all, at that time, the very beginning of the year, I had little involvement in her plans.

I should have been more aware, guessed she was dropping hints, hoping I'd offer to help. 'I'm determined to organise this reunion,' she said, taking another sip of her extra large cappuccino. 'It'll be tough going though,' she added, coughing loudly. 'I can't seem to get rid of this dreadful cough and on top of my diabetes, it's as much as I can do to keep the business running. All this travelling is becoming too much.' Years of smoking had made her voice gravely, rasping. She paused for a moment while she popped a large piece of the carrot cake she had ordered into her mouth. 'But thirty years is an important landmark, don't you agree?'

'Can't you find another job? Something with less travelling?'

'The antiques business is all I know. I never did get round to using that teaching diploma. If my father hadn't died so soon after I qualified I might have taken a different path. I couldn't let the family business go, could I?'

'Why did you decide on Bute? We were all at college in Glasgow and surely that would have been more convenient?'

'It will give everyone a chance to have a proper break, away from the city.'

'Mmm…suppose so,' I replied doubtfully, not entirely convinced.

She shook her head vigorously, dislodging one of the hairpins that kept her hair piled on top of her head, ignoring my concerns. 'It's good to talk to someone who understands,' she said as she chewed on the last of the cake defiantly saying, 'Carrots are good for you.'

If you would eat less and give up smoking, your health would improve no end, I thought, but said aloud, 'If you need help, let me know. I could give you some assistance if you're really in difficulties.' How foolish: as soon as the words were out of my mouth I regretted them.

She waved my offer aside. 'I'm sure it will be fine. But thanks for volunteering. I'll bear it in mind.'

I forgot all about the reunion until she phoned me in late October, pleading for the 'help you promised.' How could I refuse? At first it didn't seem like much work: in the beginning all she wanted was help in finding some of our more elusive classmates, but little by little other tasks were added.

Even the hours searching for these people from the past consumed more and more time. No wonder Betsie had passed this job on to me. Fortunately Deborah was on several social networking sites but, while finding the men from our class was fairly easy, we sometimes drew a blank searching for women who had married and changed their names - often more than once.

'Are you sure you're up for this?' said Deborah after one particularly fraught session where a couple of hours on the internet had produced exactly one lead.

'I sort of drifted into it,' I apologised lamely, not wanting to admit the full extent of my cowardice.

'Are you still working on the reunion?' said Simon, coming into the room. 'Looks like a packed weekend. Do you want me to come along to all these events?' he said, peering over my shoulder to examine the programme we'd now produced.

'I thought you might like to be there for the gala dinner. It's at Mount Stuart House and should be very glamorous.' At his startled look I hurried on, 'Most spouses or partners are being selective. Perhaps the ceidlih?'

'Sounds okay. I'm always ready for a break away from Glasgow.' Then he added, 'How many of your ex-classmates have you managed to track down so far?'

I ran my finger down the list. 'Of the thirty I think I've managed to find about ten and Betsie says she has another twelve or thirteen. That leaves seven still missing and then there's Susie and me, which leaves five. Of course Andy may not come. I think he's in some tax haven or other - Switzerland or Monaco or somewhere.'

'No difference,' laughed Simon. 'Too grand for you all now I expect.'

Andy had been the most successful of us all only because he'd decided to abandon the joys of teaching for setting up a mobile phone company at a time when it was still a new venture.

'We won't miss him. We've plenty of people coming,' I said. 'You can't expect that after all this time everyone would be available.'

There was a little niggling doubt because, although between us Betsie and I had tracked these classmates down, persuading them all to agree to a three day reunion on the island of Bute would be quite another matter.

I persevered, adding to the list as best I could, checking names against addresses, trying to second guess those who would be easy to convince this was a great idea and those who would need several pleading phone calls. And now I was off to Bute for a few days to finalise all the arrangements.

We had now passed Toward, the lighthouse surrounded by a cluster of whitewashed houses edging the shore and soon we'd be berthing at Rothesay. This reunion might be a terrible mistake. Would everyone have changed much? Would we all recognise each other? If I lost a bit of weight and had my hair done in a new style, or maybe even had those lowlights some people talked about... and then there was the question of what to wear.

I stole a glance at my fellow passengers on this journey to Bute. Some would be regular commuters, others day trippers. The elderly couple opposite were most likely going on holiday, their long relationship evidenced by the single suitcase. In the far corner sat a woman of a certain age, her curly hair bleached blonde, a tan tending to orange, fashionable oversized spectacles and a black PVC raincoat. An attempt to keep the years at bay and almost succeeding.

The voice of the captain, advising passengers to return to their cars, boomed from the tannoy, startling me from my perusal of my fellow travellers. I jumped up, hastily retrieving my scattered belongings and went through the passenger lounge to come out on deck and down the outside stairway as the ferry swung round into the curve of the bay at Rothesay.

The buildings along the front - large semi-detached houses, tenements, elaborate flats ranging in style from Victorian to very modern - hugged the shoreline, sitting cheek by jowl, while their neighbours in the streets in the hills above appeared to be peeping over their shoulders for a better view.

I returned to my car, still thinking about what new clothes to buy. Unfortunately what to wear turned out to be the least of the problems about the reunion on Bute.

FOUR

On the island it was a day of soft rain, no more than a smirr. Enough to warrant an umbrella, as without one the tiny droplets of rain would cling to everything. Thank goodness I'd bought a new umbrella, I thought, as I drove off the MV Argyll and down in the line of cars towards the only set of traffic lights on the island.

The new CalMac ferries were in many ways much more comfortable, especially in winter weather, than the previous 'streakers' but many of us missed the informality of those boats. No doubt people of my mother's generation had similar feelings about the old paddle steamers that once plied the route. Only one of those now remained, The Waverley, taking tourists up and down the Clyde during the holiday season.

The sleek replacements, twice the size of the old ones, boasted large airy passenger accommodation, the panoramic windows taking full advantage of the magnificent views of the Firth of Clyde as the ferry sailed towards the pier at Rothesay. I'm sure it was all much more efficient, but a strange nostalgia for the old boats lingered. Perhaps the reunion was affecting me, making me remember the old days with an affection they didn't deserve.

A trio of seagulls perched on the seawall unperturbed by the light drizzle, their white plumage ruffled by the wind. Beady eyed, they scanned the visitors frequenting the island at this time of year, hoping for some discarded food.

Sadly for them, any visitors were more interested in taking photographs of the remaining few yachts swaying gently in

Rothesay marina, most being berthed further up the Clyde coast for the winter or sailing in warmer climes.

It was good to be on the island of Bute again. I hadn't been back here since my involvement with Susie and her house at Ettrick Bay, but the problems we'd had then were forgotten in my pleasure at returning.

As I accelerated through the green light I felt happy, knowing that after dealing with everything Betsie had requested and visiting Jessie, I could treat myself to a well deserved coffee and cake at the Ettrick Bay tearoom and a brisk walk along the shore to Kirkmichael, though not necessarily in that order.

There was a free parking bay in Guildford Square where I could sit and check my list of tasks. The square was busy with pedestrians heading for the main street, but my Christmas shopping would have to wait till later. The first stop had to be the library in Moat Street to confirm arrangements for hosting the talks Betsie had included in the weekend events, though from brief description she had given me, it was no more than a way of catching up on those who had made a name for themselves. Perhaps it wasn't too late to pick up a few ideas.

I decided to stop off to buy a sandwich at the Electric Bakery. Little knots of shoppers thronged the pavements in Montague Street, the gossip as interesting as the Christmas purchases. The main town on the island, Rothesay, is one long street with several smaller streets off and today this area was even more crowded than usual.

The town was in festive mood and I stopped more than once to admire the tempting, glittering window displays in the Bute Tool Company and the various gift shops, the Christmas lights lending an air of frivolity on a gloomy afternoon. Even the fishmonger's had sprigs of holly carefully placed among the display of plaster crabs and fish.

I shivered in spite of being warmly wrapped up. The north wind off the sea whistled through every nook and cranny, the low rise buildings offering scant protection to the shoppers. Little swirls of late autumn leaves that had escaped the attentions of the street cleaners swirled round my feet in a mad dance, settling in the already clogged gutters.

There was no need to take the car for such a short distance and I walked briskly up the High Street, past Rothesay castle, towards the Moat Centre. The library was busy, a good refuge for a damp morning. Several people browsed quietly among the shelves and in the tinsel decked corner at the children's section there rose and fell the sounds of a group of tiny tots singing: the choice of Incy Wincy Spider appropriate for a day such as this.

There was one librarian at the desk, stamping the books of an elderly man. From the pile of books in front of him it looked as if he was set for a relaxing afternoon's reading and I felt a sudden pang of envy. As soon as he left, books safely stowed in a large plastic bag, I explained the purpose of my visit.

'I'll find out what we have booked in,' the librarian said and disappeared into a back room. He emerged a few minutes later, smiling. 'Yes, it's all arranged. If you want to check the details?' I felt a sense of relief, sensing a good omen for the rest of my visit.

A queue began to form behind me, 'Thanks for your help,' I said, mentally ticking off this item from my list.

I came out of the library into a lightening sky, little shafts of sunlight peeping through the clouds and glistening on the wet pavements, inviting me to stand for a moment, drinking in the clean air.

One of my tasks was to check the hotels listed by Betsie as possibles for the reunion delegates, as well as go along to the Pavilion to discuss the options for the first day's meeting and the Sunday evening ceidlih and then head out to Mount Stuart to discuss menus for our gala dinner. As I was in the centre of Rothesay, only a few moments drive from the Pavilion, it made sense to start there before going over to the Hereuse Nursing home to see Jessie.

The more I thought about Jessie, the more I was certain Simon was right: my mother was worrying about nothing. The idea that a respectable nursing home wouldn't care properly for the residents was absurd. Was it possible poor Jessie was missing her own house and resented being in a care home?

My trip to the Pavilion, on the edge of the town, wouldn't take long. I drove past the frontage and round the corner to squeeze into the little car park at the back. The plaque on this Art Deco building proudly proclaimed the building had been completed in 1938: a time when there was little need for a large car park as most people still walked everywhere or used public transport, a reminder to check out the arrangements for transporting the delegates to and from the various venues. Few people coming to the reunion would want to drive.

The main doors were at the side of the large bow fronted window projecting from the first floor of the main building. The curved sweep of the windows on both levels of this square set, flat roofed edifice had been designed to make the most of the views over Rothesay Bay and the long low balcony to the right would be a good place for people to come outdoors and relax between events. In spite of my reservations about the reunion, Betsie had done well to select this as one of our venues. I pushed open the iron framed door. Under the covering of blue paint, a little bit of rust came away and stained my hand: one of the problems with buildings of this period, especially in the bracing sea air of the island. There were rumours this important local building was in line for a grant for refurbishment and not before time.

I crossed the Art Deco floor, strikingly tiled in a geometric pattern of green, cream, red and gold, pushed open one of the sets of double doors opening into the carpeted hallway and stood looking about for a few moments, uncertain where to go next. There were several rooms leading off this entrance and a semicircular wooden box office against the wall in the far corner, but all was quiet and there was no one in sight. The nearest door was marked Private and as I knocked it sprang open, taking me by surprise.

'Hello, there. How can I help you?'

Surely this young man couldn't be the manager? His dark gelled hair, quiffed at the front, only added to his good looks. His attire of tight jeans, a shirt in a brilliant shade of blue and a jumper draped across his shoulders had probably been chosen to make him look deliberately casual.

'I'm Alison Cameron. I'm enquiring about booking this venue.'

He grinned, showing a set of very white teeth. 'Hi, Alison, I'm Jason Wistman. I was about to have some coffee. Care to join me?'

'Coffee would be great.' No point in offending him by saying this would be my fourth cup of the day and it was only half past ten.

'You're the manager here?'

Jason lifted an eyebrow. 'Good heavens, no. I work here part-time but I'm filling in today because the manager has had to go off the island for a hospital appointment.'

'Nothing serious I hope?'

'A run in with a shinty stick,' said Jason. 'He'll be back tomorrow.' He stopped abruptly, so that I almost bumped into him. 'If you'd rather wait...?'

I waved my hand. 'No, no, not at all.' The idea was to check the Pavilion out as quickly as possible and move on to the next place on my list.

'Let's have that coffee and you can tell me how we can help you.'

I followed him upstairs, slightly out of breath in an effort to keep up with him as he bounded ahead. He made towards the room on the right and pushed open the door. This was the café and he directed me to a table by the window, commanding a view right round the bay towards the sweep of Craigmore. I bravely declined the offer of one of the cakes set out temptingly under glass domes on the counter.

'So, Alison, what can we do for you?' He stirred his coffee, looking at me expectantly.

'I'm here to have a look at this venue for our reunion.'

'A reunion? Cool or what?'

I was amazed he knew what a reunion was, considering his age. 'I think you might have some rooms that are suitable?'

'Of course, of course.' He drank down his coffee hurriedly and sprang to his feet. 'Come on, let's have a look.'

We went back out into the upper hallway and as he pushed open one of the pairs of doors facing us, I found myself in an enormous hall with a slightly raised platform round all sides and a stage at the far end. White pleated material hung in swathes from the ceiling, forming a canopy that soared in the middle to a central ruche. The room was imposing, dramatic. What could I say? 'It's wonderful, but perhaps a bit big?' It was an impressive space, but would it be suitable for our numbers? We'd need a lot of people to fill this.

The look on his face showed his disappointment at my reaction. 'Won't you be having a dance one of the evenings? This place has seen some of the best dances in the country. Look,' he gestured over to the corner, 'you even have your own bar all ready.' A long bar ran along one side of the room on a raised platform, well back from the central space.

I blustered, 'It is a wonderful room. Maybe we could alter it in some way? Make it more suitable for a smaller group?'

This attempt only made things worse, as he was now looking thoroughly alarmed, 'Oh, I don't think there's any way you could begin to alter this place. It wouldn't be allowed,' he replied, frowning.

I contented myself with looking round, adopting a suitable expression of awe and trying to dispel his concerns. 'Of course, of course. I'll have a think about how we could use it. It would be a pity not to.'

Jason shuffled his feet: standing here gazing at the draped ceiling wasn't helping us make progress. He nudged my elbow. 'If this doesn't suit, then perhaps we could have a look at other options?'

I trotted behind Jason back into the smaller hall that was the café. This was much more what we needed. In the distance the ferry was sweeping in to berth deftly in the calm waters of Rothesay Bay, a view that would delight the reunion delegates.

Jason grinned as he saw the expression on my face. 'So this is more what you had in mind? We can certainly re-organise this place. We often do.'

'This would be ideal for some of the events and perhaps if we have enough people coming we could use the main hall for the ceidlih,' I said, trying to remember exactly how many people were attending.

Jason seemed relieved at my approval. His eyes lit up and he smiled engagingly at me. 'Great. We can sort out all the details when we go back to the office.'

As we made our way down the marble staircase, I ran my hands along the sweeping iron railings. This Art Deco building would be a superb place to hold some of our events: everyone was sure to be impressed. 'Have you always lived here on the island?' I said by way of conversation.

'Uh, uh,' Jason replied. He laughed. 'Believe it or not I only came over because of my girlfriend.'

'That doesn't surprise me. Would I know your girlfriend?'

He shook his head. 'I don't think you'll have come across her. She works out at the nursing home past Craigmore, is one of the carers there. I came here a couple of years ago and I love being on the island - it's a great place to live.'

I had to ask. 'Not the Hereuse Nursing home?'

He looked surprised. 'You know it then?'

'A friend of my mother is there. I'm going over to see her later because my mother's a bit concerned about her.' As soon as I spoke I realised my mistake. 'Probably needlessly,' I added quickly, in case he thought this was a criticism of the place where his girlfriend worked.

Jason turned away suddenly and it was impossible to see the expression on his face. Surely my comment couldn't have offended him so much?

We went into the office and sat down. Jason pulled out a large diary from the drawer in the desk. 'Now when were you thinking of having the reunion?' He was brisk, business like, his earlier friendliness gone.

'Well, the middle weekend in April, when most people are on holiday.' This was strange. Surely it was all arranged?

He flicked through the pages. 'So sorry, we can't do that weekend. There's already a party booked in and an art exhibition in the foyer.' He peered at the entry. 'The Regius Gallery is organising that.'

I laughed. 'I'm confusing you. I should have explained more clearly. The person who made the original arrangements is Betsie

O'Connor and that weekend you have booked in April will be ours?'

Jason stared at me. 'You know Betsie O'Connor?'

'Why, yes. I'm helping her out with the final arrangements as she lives in France and is too busy with work at the moment to make the trip herself.'

He didn't reply and I fidgeted with the strap of my handbag in the silence between us.

He shut the diary quickly. 'I'll let the manager know you came and what you want. I'm sure it will be fine if Betsie arranged it. Just give him a call.' He stood up, dismissing me.

I wanted to ask him if there was a problem but had the distinct impression more questions would not be welcome, though I didn't know why. After all, what did it matter to Jason? I said thanks and left hurriedly, but I could feel he was standing there, looking after me. Was there something Betsie hadn't told me?

FIVE

Any questions about Jason's strange behaviour would have to wait. With a sense of unease, I left the Pavilion, pausing to take in deep breaths of the seaweed smelling air. The rain had stopped, but the wind had sprung up. I caught a faint whiff of smoke from a distant chimney, where someone had decided the day was far enough on to light a fire. There was no time to linger: the sooner I could complete the business at Mount Stuart, visit the Hereuse and check the hotels, the sooner I could head for Ettrick Bay. At this time of year, when the days are short, I wanted to catch the last of the light.

My appointment at Mount Stuart was for eleven thirty and then I'd call in to see Jessie, leaving me plenty of time for the visits to the hotels Betsie had asked me to view before catching the ferry back to Weymss Bay.

Heading back through Rothesay, out by the shore road, it was difficult to concentrate on the driving rather than the view. The ferry swung out of the bay and sailed alongside me for a few moments, disappearing from sight into the open waters of the Firth of Clyde as I headed towards Mount Stuart.

An hour later, equipped with enough information to please even Betsie, it was time to visit the nursing home, after a quick stop to eat my sandwich at one of the little grassy verges overlooking the water.

Engrossed in thought about which menu we might prefer for the gala dinner, I almost missed the turn off, despite the sign HEREUSE NURSING HOME in gigantic letters at the front of a large pair of wrought iron gates.

The gates swung open automatically on my approach and I edged my way up the long drive, shaded on either side by regimented lines of ancient trees, gnarled and distorted by years of winter storms. The stone Victorian house that rose before me was one of the many old family villas that had been built on Bute, a relic of a time when rich Glasgow merchants came down, or decanted their families for the summer, to escape the fetid air of the city. While the original house remained, stolidly built, adorned with ornate balustrades and wrought iron windows, there was evidence of more modern additions, one on each side of the main house. It gave the place a curious look because there had been no attempt made to blend the old with the new and the result made me think of a solemn dowager attended by a couple of flighty girls.

I pulled up immediately inside the gates, my tyres scrunching on the golden gravel covering the original front lawn and sat for a few moments wondering how best to approach this task my mother had given me. I knew Jessie only slightly: she was my mother's friend, a friend made in her later years through some club or other my mother had joined. I racked my brain for topics of conversation, wondering how short I could respectably make this visit.

'Try to bring the conversation round,' my mother had said. 'Don't ask her outright.'

As though I would march in to Jessie and say, 'I hear you are think you are about to be murdered.' On the other hand, it was difficult to come up with an opening to our conversation that wouldn't be too obvious and would give me a reasonable explanation for my visit.

Deciding there was no point in sitting any longer, I turned the car further up the drive, suddenly remembering it would have been a good idea to buy flowers or chocolates while I was in town. Ah well, too late now.

I drove past the main door and parked alongside a large white van labelled Independent Caterers Limited. Several people were clustered round the van, no doubt taking away the various food receptacles from lunch, all well covered up. One of the men loading up walked round from the back of the van, climbed into the driving seat and started up, accelerating past me and out through the gates. From the size of the van it would appear they had a lots of customers here on the island and the residents of the Hereuse Nursing home might no longer have food prepared on the premises: not necessarily bad, merely more efficient. It could be a source of Jessie's complaints however.

I locked up the car, though there was no need to do so and walked up the path bordered by shrubs and little hedges chosen for ease of maintenance rather than appearance. I took a deep breath on approaching the massive oak front door and rang the bell, listening to it echo inside. As I was about to ring again, the door opened and an elderly woman in uniform directed me to the large wooden reception desk, flanked on either side by a Christmas tree whose lights flickered on an off in a most annoying way. The sound of carols, much muted, filled the air and the windows were adorned with fake snow stencils of Santas, reindeer, angels and stars of all sizes.

The receptionist was smartly dressed in a navy blue suit which was a fraction too tight and when she moved to greet me, the bulges rippled under the constricting cloth. She was expertly made up, her face almost a mask and a deep fringe of auburn hair completed her doll like appearance. She smiled in greeting at my approach, the make up forming tiny fissures in her face. 'I'll find someone to help you,' she said and lifted the internal phone.

I walked around while waiting for her to complete her call. Though the home was well kept, it betrayed its age in all sorts of ways: the elaborate cornicing was broken in places and the windows were decidedly ill fitting, judging by the chill in the air in spite of the many radiators lining the walls. Through an archway I could see into the east wing, where the plush carpets of the old building gave way to thick lino and the aroma of fresh lavender was overtaken by the smell of floor polish and air freshener, scarcely disguising the sting of cleaning fluids and the faint smells of lunch. A few residents wandered slowly along the corridor and all the doors were closed, shut tight, carefully numbered. A small nameplate with a slot for a name written on card was fastened at eye level beside each door: none of these residents would require anything more permanent.

The only open door led to a large lounge and I peered in, wondering if Jessie might be here. It was an airy and blandly cheerful room, the walls decorated with prints and vases of flowers on the many small tables. Everywhere there were yet more signs Christmas was approaching: the large tree that filled that whole corner from floor to ceiling, the tinsel on every picture, the swags of greenery on the mock fireplace where cherubs lurked among the fake poinsettia.

In the corner, a small white haired lady had her back to me, talking animatedly to a man who seemed to be paying her not the slightest bit of attention, but tapping his walking stick rhythmically on the floor. There was no sign of Jessie. The white haired lady turned round and stared at me. 'Sorry to disturb you,' I said, backing out.

'You're welcome to come in,' she replied but I waved and hurried back to the reception area.

Suddenly a voice beside me said, 'How can I help you?' Her badge proclaimed her as 'Sharon: Senior Care Assistant' even though she looked far too young to be a senior anything. Her severe hairstyle of pale brown hair swept up in a bun and a complete absence of make-up made her appear as if she was a lot younger than Deborah. Her unlined face was devoid of much expression though her very arched eyebrows made her look permanently quizzical. If this was Jason's girlfriend, she was as plain as he was handsome.

'I've come to see Jessie McAdam,' I said.

Sharon, trim in the purple uniform of the home, tucked a stray lock of hair behind her ear. Her smile faded. 'Oh, well...'

'Surely there isn't a problem,' I interrupted, ready to stand my ground should there be any difficulty suggested about my visit to Jessie.

'No, no, it's not that.' She gripped my elbow tightly, steering me out of the lounge, back into the main building and across the hallway towards a door leading into a small room. 'If you would wait here, I'll ask Sister Mackie to come and have a word with you.'

As she turned away, I sat down on the nearest chair. The room was small but comfortable, with several easy chairs randomly placed round the walls, a deep pile carpet and a large mirror adorning the wall opposite me. Apart from a vase of real flowers on the one low coffee table, there was nothing else in the room, not even a brochure or a magazine and strangely none of the signs of Christmas so evident in the rest of the home. This room had a strange feeling about it, a sombre, almost expectant air. What was going on?

A few moments later Sister Mackie came bustling into the room, closely followed by Sharon. She was small and slight, her cap showing little of her severe hairstyle and from the set of her face it appeared the news she had to tell me was not good.

'Is there something wrong with Jessie?' I said, standing up, dreading her answer. Perhaps she had become so ill she wasn't being allowed visitors and my first thought was selfishly not for poor Jessie but about what to say to my mother.

There was no welcoming smile as Sister Mackie said, 'I think you should sit down, Mrs Cameron. I'm sorry to tell you that Jessie passed away early last week. It was sudden, but peaceful.'

My first reaction was one of amazement. 'Why weren't we told?'

A pause, then, 'We found it impossible to trace any relatives,' said Sister Mackie defensively.

This was hard to believe. 'You must at least have known that she had friends? You could have called us.'

None of this made sense. Surely Jessie had nominated someone as her next of kin? All these thoughts flashed through my head, but before I could say anything more Sister Mackie went on, shaking her head in response. 'In a place like this death happens all the time. If there is no obvious next of kin, we take charge of the funeral arrangements.'

As she saw the look of disbelief on my face she went on, 'It was all certified by the local doctor. It was no more than old age. Her heart gave out.'

'And what were the funeral arrangements?'

Sister Mackie avoided my gaze. 'She was cremated in accordance with our policy.' She must have registered the look of horror on my face, because she continued swiftly, 'We had a good representation from here, you know. We do give residents like Jessie without any relatives a proper and decent funeral.'

It was all too neat somehow, especially when I thought about what Jessie had said to my mother, the fears she had expressed. How I wished I'd made the effort to come over to Bute sooner. 'Who's the person in charge?' Sister Mackie wasn't going to give me any more information, that was for sure.

For a moment she looked fearful. 'Mrs Bradshaw, but she won't be able to tell you any more than I can.'

I would like to speak to Mrs Bradshaw,' I said, firmly.

Sister Mackie hesitated. 'I'm afraid it's her day off.' She stood there, looking as if she was waiting for me to make the first move.

'But she lives here, on the premises?'

'Yes, she lives in one of the staff houses at the very back of the old building...' Sister Mackie stopped abruptly, realising she had said too much. 'If you want to make an appointment?'

'I'll go and see if she's at home,' I said, making for the door.

Sister Mackie moved swiftly to bar my way. 'You can't do that,' she said. 'Now, I can, as I said, arrange an appointment...'

'Watch me,' and I pushed her aside and almost ran down the hallway, out of the front door past the receptionist and an astonished Sharon.

I banged the front door behind me and scurried round to the back of the building, in case Sister Mackie decided to pursue me. I was determined to have some answers from Mrs Bradshaw about what exactly had happened to Jessie.

It was only as I hurried along, hoping to reach Mrs Bradshaw before Sister Mackie alerted her that I thought about what had been said. '...residents like Jessie without any relatives...' Exactly how many residents like Jessie had died recently?

SIX

The house was one of a terrace at the bottom of the expansive gardens behind the main buildings. Originally rough dwellings for the stable hands or grooms on the estate, these outbuildings had been converted into tiny houses for staff. The conversions were stylish and four little houses clustered together, each distinguished by a differently coloured door. Mrs Bradshaw's domain was at the near end of the row, the prime location. The tiny front garden was crammed with ornaments: cheerful gnomes in rows, a small pond, guarded by a leggy plastic heron whose beak was damaged at the end, an imitation bronze birdbath and a solitary tree bedecked with wind chimes and Christmas lights.

She must have been warned of my approach by someone in the nursing home and, as I lifted my hand to the highly polished brass knocker in the shape of a lion, the door suddenly opened and Mrs Bradshaw stood on the threshold, her massive bulk completely filling the space. She was indeed a force to be reckoned with from her tightly permed grey hair to her stoutly corseted figure and, even off duty, her clothes were plain, severe. No jewellery graced her outfit and her feet were encased in old fashioned brogues.

She peered at me over her glasses, a grim look on her shrewd, weathered face. 'If you are looking for the entrance to the care home it's round the other side of the building. These are private quarters.'

She made to shut the door but I moved forward, not quite jamming my foot in it, but coming pretty close.

'I want to speak to you about one of the residents,' I said.

She glared at me, pulling off her glasses for a better look. 'Then you should make an appointment at reception in the main building.'

'I'm only here on the island for the day,' I said. 'Goodness knows when I'll be back.'

For a moment I thought she was going to dismiss me, to slam the door in my face. I refused to be intimidated by this fierce woman and she suddenly realised I wasn't going to budge because she opened the door a fraction more and said, 'You want to talk to me about someone at the Hereuse?'

I nodded, but said nothing, deciding to wait until I was inside before telling her about my concerns. The problem was, all the adrenaline had dissipated and I wasn't too sure why I was here. In fact the longer I stood on the doorstep the less sure I became. Jessie had been old and ill, so what other explanation could there be for her death except old age? And yet, and yet. A little voice in my head was nagging me that Jessie had been afraid, very afraid.

Then there was the problem of my mother. I didn't want to let her down and if nothing came of this visit to Mrs Bradshaw I could at least tell her I'd tried my best. I said, 'I wonder if I could come in for a few moments. It's a bit public standing here.'

I think she found this request so unusual, so unlike the way most people treated her, that she held the door further open without a word and I stepped inside quickly, concerned she might suddenly change her mind.

'I don't usually deal with enquiries in this way,' she said grudgingly. 'But,' no doubt realising I wasn't to be easily deterred, 'as you are only here for the day what is it you want to ask?'

Oh dear, was I going to have to make up yet another lie. Could I risk claiming to be a relative? Fortunately she didn't ask for further details.

She ushered me down a long thin hallway and into the front room. 'Please sit down,' was not so much a request as a command and I looked around, opting for the chair nearest the door. That way, if everything went wrong it would be easy to make my escape quickly.

More surprises: although the room was small there were a number of ornaments and clocks which looked even to my unpractised eye as if they were antiques of some value, sitting side by side with ornaments which were most certainly not valuable. It was a strange mixture.

Mrs Bradshaw sat down heavily on a chair opposite me in silence, waiting for me to begin. I shifted in my seat, not through nerves. Unfortunately this chair was mock Victorian, as was most of the rest of the furniture in the room and its straight back and spindly legs made it most uncomfortable. How best to begin without raising her suspicions about the real reason for my visit? Finally I could stand the silence no longer and blurted out, 'I'm here about Jessie, Jessie McAdam. She died recently....' My voice trailed away as the expression on her face become glacial.

'Yes, indeed. Most unfortunate. We are always sorry to lose any of our residents. But you must expect that with elderly people.'

She glared at me and folded her arms across her ample chest, as though daring me to challenge her statement of fact. 'She had no relatives so we had to arrange the funeral, a cremation, exactly as she wished.'

I hesitated. This was the same story Sister Mackie had told me but Mrs Bradshaw's unhelpful attitude made me cross. 'As far as we knew there wasn't anything much wrong with Jessie and she wasn't that old, not by today's standards.'

Again the icy stare. 'Are you some kind of medical adviser, Mrs Cameron?' Without waiting for a reply she went on, 'If not, I suggest you know very little about the kind of ailments that can afflict old people and how suddenly they can deteriorate.'

She leaned forward and I could almost smell the suppressed anger. 'The trouble is, people expect their dear ones to live forever.'

'Not forever,' I replied, 'but we were surprised the funeral was so quick and that no one was contacted.'

'That is our usual policy where there are no immediate relatives. We do make some investigations but if we can't track anyone down, we make the arrangements accordingly. She had no regular visitors. You didn't visit, did you?'

31

She sat back triumphantly, sure she had put me in my place. If Mrs Bradshaw thought that would stop me in my tracks and cower me into leaving, she was wrong. My mother hadn't visited, but she had kept in touch. I was more convinced than ever that there was something strange happening, something she was trying to cover up.

'I don't know why you didn't contact my mother,' I said. 'I would most certainly have come over. Jessie must have talked about us at some time.'

Mrs Bradshaw shook her head. 'She didn't mention anyone we might contact. We do have to respect residents' wishes. And the dear soul's last wish was to be cremated.' Her look dared me to contradict her.

By trying to pursue this line of enquiry I'd have to confess to being no more than a friend - or rather that my mother was a friend. If Jessie had any relatives they were long deceased. She often said we were her surrogate family: an only child of parents who were also only children, any relatives would be very distant.

Mrs Bradshaw stood up, bringing this interview to an end. 'I hope that I've helped you, Mrs Cameron and that you're satisfied that we at the Hereuse Nursing home have done everything possible to make certain that we offer the best care to our dear residents.'

Her words sounded hollow, mocking, but there was nothing else to be said at the moment, not until I had the opportunity to think everything through. That Mrs Bradshaw had obviously had enough of my company was clear in the way she almost propelled me back down the hallway.

As she opened the front door, a sudden thought struck me. Jessie must have had a sizeable bank balance. The house she had sold in Glasgow's West End must have fetched a large sum and her house on Bute had been her mother's. Even with the steepest of nursing home fees at the Hereuse, she must have left money, a lot of money. 'Did Jessie leave a will?' I said.

For the first time in our discussion Mrs Bradshaw looked uncomfortable. 'I'm not sure it is of concern to you,' she replied, 'but yes, she did leave a will.'

I steeled myself for the follow up question. 'Who was the beneficiary?'

For a moment it seemed Mrs Bradshaw wasn't going to reply. Then she said, 'If you must know she left everything to the Hereuse Nursing home,' defensively adding, 'And in case you are wondering why, let me tell you that she was so pleased with the care she received here that she wanted us to benefit.'

I was lost for words. My impression was that Jessie was far from being happy with the treatment she was receiving. If she had left all her money to an animal charity or to the local hospital that would have made a lot of sense, but not this, not leaving it all to the nursing home.

'What happened to her personal items?

'They are stored in case anyone comes forward at a later date,' she said. A pause, then, 'If you can prove your identity I'm sure we could release them to you, though there is nothing of value in them.'

I'm sure there's not, I thought grimly. Mrs Bradshaw's explanations were far from convincing and this trip to see Jessie at my mother's request had taken on a different aspect altogether. There was something very wrong here and I was determined to find out what it was.

SEVEN

Simon was downbeat when I phoned to tell him about my visit to the Hereuse Nursing home, using all his powers of persuasion to dispel my fears. 'This Mrs Bradshaw was probably right. The elderly do get confused and Jessie sounds as if she was becoming muddled in the time before she died. Don't feel guilty. You've done what your mother asked and it's not really your responsibility.'

'I suppose so.' I wasn't completely re-assured, though it was difficult to imagine what else could be done. 'But what if there is something going on at that nursing home?'

'You have plenty to do sorting out the reunion. I'm sure there's nothing sinister about these deaths, no more than old people dying of natural causes. We'll talk about it when you come home. What have you left to do this afternoon?'

'Visit the last couple of hotels and,' looking at my watch added, 'that shouldn't take me long, though I'd forgotten how early it gets dark at this time of year. I'll try to catch the quarter to five ferry.' My walk at Ettrick Bay would have to wait until another time.

'I'll sort out something for dinner when I come in from college. I don't expect to be late tonight. I'm only sorry I can't give you more help with the reunion.'

He was right. No matter how supportive he was, these arrangements were something I had to sort out on my own. 'Fortunately Betsie has been very organised and so far it's all going like clockwork.' I didn't mention my curious meeting with Jason at the Pavilion.

'I've also some good news,' he went on. 'Deborah has had a phone call this morning. She's been offered the job at the Regius Gallery. Even better, she was asked to come in straightaway. They called just after you left this morning.'

I felt immensely cheered as I said goodbye to him, my fears about Jessie groundless and my hopes for Deborah's future much improved. I shut my mobile down and was still staring at it when it rang again, startling me. This time it was Betsie. 'Hello Alison, how did it all go?'

'Hello, Betsie, I'm fine thank you,' I said.

'Oh, no, am I in trouble again? I thought I was saving you time by being so direct.'

No point in arguing with someone like Betsie, better to bring her up to date as quickly as possible, laying emphasis on the '…and that's everything confirmed with the Pavilion and the arrangements with Mount Stuart.' I added, 'And I've checked out most of the hotels: you appear to have made good choices.'

She sighed. 'Yes, but…'

'What is it Betsie? Tell me.'

'I've had a bit of a surprise, really,' she went on, 'since last time we were in touch… '

My heart sank: what was she going to say?

'…the numbers have increased rapidly and I wondered if we might now need the bigger hall in the Pavilion for some of our meetings. We have a number of partners and a few other family members coming, more than originally thought.'

'But the hall is huge,' I protested, thinking of all the vast space only made to appear slightly smaller by the draped canopies covering the ceiling. 'We would need lots of people to fill that space.' In spite of my misgivings she'd evidently been able to persuade lots of people to make the journey to Bute for this reunion.

'Who exactly have you been inviting?' As she prattled on, it sounded as if our original group was to be joined by others with only the slightest of connections: not quite the cosy occasion we had had in mind originally.

Betsie started again. 'So, Alison, if you could…'

'Wait a minute, Betsie, I'm on my mobile and I think I'm running out of credit. Why not e-mail me and I'll do what I can?'

'I'll do that right now. I'm sure you'll be fine,' she said in a wheedling tone of voice.

Resigned to carrying out her instructions, I said, 'Don't blame me if it all goes wrong.' I'd no intention of going back to the Pavilion and a phone call would be sufficient to make any new arrangements.

'Of course not. Anyway, what is there to go wrong? You're so good at this kind of thing. Keep me posted and I'll go and e-mail you right now.'

She rang off abruptly, no doubt worried I might change my mind, leaving me staring at the phone. But not for long. This time it was Deborah.

'Delighted to hear your news,' I said.

'Yes, isn't it great!

'Good first day?' My response was automatic.

'Brilliant, actually, though it was really just an introduction. I start properly next week. And hey, guess what? You know this reunion of yours on Bute?'

'Mmm,' seemed more than enough to say.

'Sylvester has booked space in the Pavilion for an art exhibition at the same time. He thinks your reunion would be a cool opportunity to showcase some local talent and I'm sure there will be plenty of people there happy to buy.'

She sounded so pleased, so excited, I didn't have the heart to tell her I already knew about the exhibition . . .or that not many of the people coming to the reunion, even the most successful, would be willing to spend a lot of time or money on buying pieces of art, though I could be wrong. I hoped for her sake that I was.

'So I'll be there at the same time as you. Perhaps you can rustle up some of the people you know - the rich people.'

'I don't know any rich people.' This came out much more crossly than intended. I was still considering my conversation with Betsie and how to sort out the challenges of the Pavilion venue. Then thinking there was no sense in disillusioning Deborah so soon, I said quickly, 'On the other hand perhaps

Betsie will have contacts. She must have plenty in her line of work, being in antiques.'

'Thanks, mum. This could be make or break for me.' Anxious as Deborah was to succeed in her new post, there was a limit to how much help I could give.

I had to ask her. 'Why did Sylvester choose Bute?'

'Oh, he travels all over the country - all over the world actually - but this year he's decided to concentrate on Scotland and on the islands in particular.'

Would Betsie be happy with this proposal, happy with sharing the limelight with Sylvester's art exhibition? That was very doubtful. What had started out as a small reunion of a few old college friends was rapidly turning into a Hollywood production. It was becoming all too much responsibility yet there was no way to back out and if it would help Deborah in her career, then what else could a mother do?

'Oh, by the way,' Deborah added with a studied casualness, 'Sylvester's set up a meeting next Wednesday night to discuss the details of the Bute exhibition. You'll be at home, won't you? I thought we'd drop in to say hello.'

My heart sank. Wednesday was my busiest day at school and I'd have to make a special effort to make a meal for a guest.

'Will you want dinner?' I asked, fearing her reply.

'No, no,' she said airily. 'We'll eat out before we come. We won't stay long, but it'll be a good opportunity for you to meet him.'

That was next week's problem. There were still several hotels to check out before heading back to Glasgow. While Deborah was enthusiastic about her new job, I hoped she wasn't going to become more than enthusiastic about Sylvester. The omens weren't good and, given her past experiences, I had cause to worry. Was this going to develop into more than a working relationship? I sincerely hoped not.

NINE

Storms on Bute: I was trapped. It was my own fault for returning to Mount Stuart, but in my haste to fit in a trip to the nursing home, I'd left my brand new umbrella there so back I went, thinking there was plenty of time before heading up to Glasgow on the ferry.

The member of staff on duty greeted me warmly and we had a long chat. Unfortunately, while I was indoors, protected from any change in the elements by the thick walls of the building, the wind had swung round to the north and the gentle smirr of rain became torrential. By the time we said goodbye and I headed down to the ferry, the waves were battering across the esplanade, rising and surging like wild horses.

Now it was evening, dark and dismal: puddles glistened under the streetlights. I should have remembered that in a couple of weeks it would be the shortest day. Why had I not made straight for the ferry terminal from the nursing home and picked up my umbrella on my next visit? It would certainly be of no use in these winds.

As I drew up to the deserted car lanes at the pier, to my dismay the illuminated sign read, 'Ferries cancelled until further notice' and as I sat there pondering what to do, the wind increased yet again.

There was no option: I'd have to stay overnight. My hope was that the Discovery Centre was still open and abandoning my car outside the entrance I fought my way through the wind into the safety of the building, in the nick of time. 'We were about to close,' the girl behind the counter said when I told her of my plight. 'You were lucky. Let's see what we can do.'

The small hotel she'd suggested in Rothesay was called Mon Repos but in spite of its name it didn't appear there was anything restful about it.

'More bad weather on the way,' said the owner, Malcolm, as I checked in. His long gloomy face spoke of many years of seeing the worse side of life. 'Though I think there might be a window of calm tomorrow morning early.' He seemed less than pleased at this prospect, his sad outlook on life enhanced by his funeral guest clothes of black trousers and jumper.

'I'll catch the first ferry out tomorrow,' I said, 'and hope to be up in Glasgow before the weather closes in again.'

At this he looked even gloomier. 'If you have a pressing need to be back, you'd have been better going tonight.'

'But the ferries aren't running,' I protested.

'The Weymss Bay ferry is off,' he agreed. 'You're well and truly stranded here until this storm blows over unless you want to try the Colintraive - Rhubodoch ferry?' Did a ghost of a smile flicker over his face as he said this?

'I think I'd be better staying over,' I said, unwilling to take the long road back to Glasgow over the Rest and Be Thankful in this weather.

Tired out by my experiences, I went to bed immediately after dinner. I had a good book and sitting in the lounge, worrying about the storm, had no appeal. Exhaustion and the sea air overtook me before I'd managed even one chapter and by ten o'clock I was sound asleep. Several times during the night I was vaguely aware of the sound of the rain battering against the window, the tree branches tapping out a ghostly message, but only registered it for a moment before falling sound asleep again, until startled by the shrill noise of the radio alarm clock.

I sat up in bed and fumbled around in the eerie darkness, groping about until I found the light switch on the bedside lamp, listening to the rain strike unceasingly against the windows. It seemed the fierce winds had if anything strengthened overnight and if it continued to be as stormy as this the first ferry from Bute, if it ran at all, would be diverted to Gourock: a nuisance, but not a major disaster.

Once showered and dressed I headed downstairs, ready to grab a quick bite to eat before heading for the ferry terminal.

The dining room was at the back of the hotel overlooking the garden and here the noise of the storm seemed less, something that gave me hope, though a glance out the window at the battered plants and broken flowerpots showed how violent it had been during the night.

In keeping with the rest of the hotel the décor here was firmly stuck in the nineteen seventies and the swirly wallpaper in lime green and orange with a mismatched but equally swirly carpet in brown and gold made me feel almost queasy. Never mind, I'd soon be on my way. A tantalising smell of bacon drifted in from the adjacent kitchen as I sat down at one of the only two set tables, deliberately choosing the one in the far corner. Malcolm was busy with the only other guest. Visitors to the island being few and far between at this time of the year, we had his undivided attention, not necessarily a good thing.

He lumbered over, clutching a pen and paper though with so few guests this was surely unnecessary. 'I hope you're not thinking about catching the ferry?' was the way he greeted me.

'I am,' I replied, determined not to be deterred by his tone of voice, keeping my eyes fixed on the menu.

He shook his head. 'No chance of that, I'm afraid.'

I looked up to meet his sorrowful gaze. 'A bumpy crossing doesn't worry me,' I said with more conviction than I felt. Though it takes no more than thirty five minutes to sail from Rothesay to the ferry terminal at Weymss Bay it can be a taxing journey if the weather is bad.

'It's not so much a case of a bumpy crossing as no crossing, not unless you want to try to swim of course.' He chuckled at his own wit, his face creasing as he did so. 'There won't be any ferries today. Perhaps not even tomorrow.'

My heart sank at this terrible news. Even with a few days off school, I didn't want to spend my time here alone on the island in this storm. 'Surely if the weather improves the ferries will run? Don't they divert to Gourock?'

'Have you had a look outside, Mrs Cameron?' With a flourish he pulled back the curtain at the window in my corner of the room to give me a better view. Little clouds of dust flew out, making me sneeze, but Malcolm ignored this slight problem with his housekeeping arrangements. 'Look, it's as I told you. Because you can't hear it as well in this part of the house, it doesn't mean it's not happening.'

A closer inspection revealed the garden was almost a quagmire, the few straggling plants lying prone, buffeted by the wind, the tree at the far wall creaking as it leaned over perilously. The window started to steam up as we watched the rain renew its force and come battering off the panes of glass.

'And have you looked out at the front? It will be amazing if the seawall holds.'

I hadn't yet looked out of the front door, but was less than happy with his unhelpful predictions and was even considering the Rest and Be Thankful road if it was the only means of returning to Glasgow.

'I suggest you do that before you think about when you might leave the island. In the meantime I'll bring through your breakfast. The full works, a full Scottish breakfast, is it?' Now that he had convinced me I was captive in the hotel, he seemed to cheer up. Probably he liked company, any company, at this lean time of year.

I had intended to have a coffee and some toast but, trapped here, might as well do as he suggested. If nothing else it would pass the time so while Malcolm lumbered off to the kitchen to tell his unseen wife of my order - and no doubt of my lack of understanding about the weather - I went to the front door. Not only was the rain coming down in torrents, unceasingly from a lowering grey sky, but the waves were pounding up against the seawall and coming over in vast sprays and plumes of water, like some demented animals. Not so much white horses as wild and untamed horses.

Malcolm was right. In the far distance the ferry was tied up at the pier, riding the huge waves bravely, but not bravely enough to set sail. Even looking at it made me feel glad to be on dry land. Perhaps it was better here at the Mon Repos after all. In the marina at the Rothesay pier a few boats were still moored and as they rose and fell, pummelled relentlessly by the waves, at least one of them had its mast lying askew across the deck, damaged beyond repair.

I shivered, closed the door and went back inside to find Malcolm was again in conversation with the other guest who looked as if all he wanted was peace to eat his breakfast, something Malcolm didn't seem to understand. He turned his attention to me and the other guest rose abruptly and made good his escape though, like me, he would have little choice about what he would do today.

Malcolm's silent wife came through with a plate laden with bacon, sausage, egg, beans and some fried bread for good measure. As I'm not an early morning eater, I regarded this huge plate of food with some concern, trying all the while to look delighted.

Fortunately Malcolm said, 'I can't stay chatting all day. I have to get on,' as though I'd been detaining him

In the event, I ate most of it. It must have been something to do with all that fresh air, because I was much hungrier than I had thought.

Anticipating no more than a day trip to the island I had brought only one book with me so it would be a case of trying to scout around the hotel and find something else to read. Either that or a diet of daytime television. By now it was almost nine o'clock, time to phone Simon and tell him it might be some time before I was home.

He wasn't happy. 'I thought we were going out to the cinema tonight? You've wanted to see that film for ages.'

'Well, we can still go,' I said with an attempt at humour, 'I can go here and you can go in Glasgow and then we can compare notes.'

He laughed. 'Let's hope it doesn't come to that.'

'I'll keep in touch and text you when I know what's happening.'

There was a grunt of acknowledgement at the other end of the phone. There was no option until the weather abated and the ferries started running again. What was I to do with my time here? I didn't fancy staying in the hotel with the lugubrious owner but it was scarcely weather for a walk at Ettrick Bay.

Malcolm came into the room, ready for a chat and my mind was made up. 'If I could settle my bill,' I said, 'though if the weather doesn't clear up I'll be back tonight if that's okay?'

He looked astounded. 'You're not venturing out in this weather? Where are you going?'

I don't know why, but I said the first thing that came into my head, 'The Hereuse Nursing home.'

He looked puzzled. 'Do you have a relative there?'

'No, but one of my mother's friends who was there died recently and I'm going over to collect her effects.' Even as I said this, his expression changed.

'We had some trouble there,' he said darkly. 'My wife's uncle went in to the Hereuse last year. He was in good health, just a bit frail. Next thing we knew he had died.'

Surely this wasn't another unexplained death? I stopped. 'Was there a problem with that?'

He laughed. 'Mmm…my wife wasn't too pleased he had left everything to the Hereuse.' Then as though he realised he had said too much, he continued. 'Take care in this weather. The roads will be treacherous.'

'I'm sure I'll be fine. Your wife's uncle - what did she do about it?'

But he wasn't willing to say any more. 'It's all over with,' he replied, tight lipped. 'Are you sure you want to go out?'

Before he could launch into a long story about why I should stay in the hotel, I grabbed my coat.

'Be careful,' he called as I wrested open the door against the wind.

'I will,' I mumbled from behind the scarf now covering the lower part of my face. Once outside the little shelter afforded by the hotel, the wind took my breath away and I had to hold onto the fence at the side of the path as I made my way to the gate. Why had I suddenly had this mad idea of going back over to the Hereuse? Then I consoled myself that in this foul weather there was little else to do and I could stop off in town for some lunch and a magazine or two.

My car was parked directly outside the hotel, in a standing area carved out of the original garden, offered some protection by ancient shrubs and bushes bending ominously in the wind. The waves had strengthened in the northerly gale and were crashing over the sea wall in a fierce swell, sending plumes of water high into the air. It was a struggle against the wind to open the car door, but once inside, I shrugged off my scarf, soaked through from my brief scuttle between the hotel and the car. I turned on the engine, set the heater to its highest and sat for a few moments to dry out before putting the car into gear and starting off cautiously, mindful of the buffeting effect of the wind on my small vehicle.

Round the corner, out of the worst of the wind, the road was badly flooded and I tagged on to the few cars in front, slowly snaking their way through the deep puddles. For a moment I thought about turning back but then remembered Malcolm: that was enough to spur me on.

The journey to the Hereuse was much longer than usual as everyone was driving very slowly to avoid the flooding. I kept to the middle of the road, watching for spumes of spray and fallen tree branches. At Ascog a large tree had come down and lay diagonally across the road, but there was enough space for one car to creep past cautiously.

Finally I drew up to the gates of the Hereuse Nursing home slightly shaken by the journey, unhappy about meeting Mrs Bradshaw again, especially with everything else that was happening, but this seemed too good an opportunity to let slip. She had said I could take Jessie's remaining few possessions, though I'd rather not see her at all. Probably all that was left was what they couldn't sell, I thought uncharitably, vexed that in my rush to escape from Mrs Bradshaw I'd neglected to return immediately to the nursing home to collect them.

There might be one or two items that would be of sentimental value to my mother, but apart from that, the rest would go to the charity shop. It wasn't a task I was looking forward to, but one that had to be done and it would be a conclusion to this sorry episode, a good outcome for everyone.

I should have phoned the home in advance, but sometimes the best way to approach things is to maintain the element of surprise. Hopefully Mrs Bradshaw might be engaged on other business, leaving me free to ask around. I still had that niggling curiosity about what Jessie had said to my mother. I slowed to a crawl as the main door came into sight, thinking all the time about turning back, saying to my mother there was nothing left, the nursing home had disposed of everything, but guilt wouldn't let me. Besides, she wouldn't let it rest at that: she would phone them and then my falsehood would be well exposed. I feared Mrs Bradshaw, but feared my mother even more.

I took a deep breath as I came out, locked the car and headed for the front door. On this more sheltered part of the island the winds were not as fierce, something that gave me hope that the ferries would be sailing this afternoon.

A figure came hurrying out. I recognised that quiff of gelled hair. It was Jason, from the Pavilion, today dressed dark leather trousers topped by a biker jacket and carrying a helmet, most suitable attire for the weather. 'Hello, Jason,' I said, smiling at him, 'visiting your girlfriend?'

He stared at me, but gave no sign of recognition. I tried again. 'It's Alison, Alison Cameron. I met you at the Pavilion.'

This time he gave a nod and mumbled something before hurrying off. A few moments later there was the noise of a motorbike and he came whizzing round the corner and down the drive, head bowed into the heavy rain.

Did he genuinely not recognise me? I shrugged. Or did he object to the question about his girlfriend? With more to concern me at the moment, I dismissed his strange behaviour from my mind.

There was nothing else for it now: I rang the doorbell cautiously but needn't have worried. Sharon answered the door. 'What have you forgotten?' she said crossly, then blushed deep red as she realised it was me. Ah, so Sharon was Jason's girlfriend? Strange I wouldn't have thought this pale, mousy girl would be Jason's type at all.

She attempted to cover her confusion. 'Sorry, sorry, I thought you were someone else.'

This worked to my advantage. She ushered me in without another word.

'I'm not sure I can hand everything over,' she said when I made my request.

'Oh, I'm sure it will be fine,' I replied airily. 'Mrs Bradshaw knows all about it. She was the one who said I could collect Jessie's few remaining items.'

Still she appeared uncertain, unwilling to do anything that might cause trouble for her. Then she seemed to think it would be best to get rid of me as soon as possible. 'I suppose it will be okay,' she said. 'There's very little left.'

As casually as possible I said, 'I don't suppose you've been able to trace any relatives yet?'

'Nooo...'she admitted. She looked up at me. 'There's nothing here to say what should be done with Jessie's belongings.' She frowned as she again consulted the large blue book she had extracted from under the drawer in the hall table, running her finger down the page in concentration. 'Perhaps I should phone Mrs Bradshaw.'

'I'm certain there's no need for that,' I persisted, anxious not to lose the advantage gained. 'After all, it's only personal effects that we'll get. I'm sure there is nothing of real value. My mother and she were friends for a very long time: it's a sentimental thing really. It's all been arranged.'

'I suppose so.' She still wasn't entirely convinced. 'Though Mrs Bradshaw would like to have the last word.'

I'm sure she would, I thought. I didn't know if I could face Mrs Bradshaw, even though I was legally there and if Sharon insisted on tracking her down, I would leave, with or without Jessie's possessions.

She leaned over to the desk and quickly dialled a number. I saw her frown when there was obviously no reply. 'I think she must have switched her mobile off. She's off the island today so perhaps she's somewhere where the reception isn't good.'

I could see she was torn between agreeing to my demands and worrying about facing the wrath of Mrs Bradshaw if she made a mistake. 'Tell you what,' I said. 'How about I take Jessie's few belongings and then if there is any problem, I'll bring them all back?' I fished in my bag, rummaging through old receipts, bits of makeup and money off vouchers. I must be able to find something. Fortunately our latest gas bill was there. 'Look, here's my address if you want to take a note of it and I'll give you my mobile number.'

For a moment she hesitated, then seemed to come to a decision. 'All right, I guess there's no harm in it. And you're right. There are very few items left.' She took the gas bill from me and slowly wrote the details down as I tried to squint at it, wondering if it had been paid.

As she handed it back to me, 'I'll sign for everything,' I said eagerly.

'Wait there a moment.' She disappeared off down the corridor, her footsteps muffled by the thick pile carpet. There was the sound of a door being opened in some distant cupboard.

I tapped my feet impatiently. In spite of the Sharon's reassurances, I expected Mrs Bradshaw to come round the corner any minute, breathing fire. A few minutes later, when I had almost given up hope of her returning, Sharon came back, carrying a brown cardboard box.

'Here you are,' she said as she put it down on the counter with a thump. She looked at me anxiously. 'Will you manage it?'

'I'll be fine,' I said brightly. I would have coped with a box three times as large if it enabled me to leave the Hereuse before Mrs Bradshaw returned. I slung my handbag over my shoulder and, heaving the box up as high as possible, said, 'How well did you know Jessie?'

She eyed me warily. 'Not very well. She was one of the newer residents. Though,' in case she was upsetting me, 'she was a lovely person.' She made it obvious that was the end of the conversation as far as she was concerned.

'If you would be so kind as to open the door?'

Sharon made to do so then suddenly she said, 'I think you had better do as you suggested and sign for this in case of any problems.'

She meant problems with Mrs Bradshaw, because no one else would be interested in poor Jessie's possessions. I put the box back down on the counter with some difficulty and muttering under my breath, dutifully signed the book she thrust towards me, trying to make my signature as difficult to read as possible.

'Sure you don't need any help?' She looked at me anxiously. 'I could call one of the porters to assist you.'

I shook my head. 'I'm absolutely fine,' and left quickly before she took matter into her own hands and summoned help. All I wanted to do was make a hasty exit.

I loaded the box into the boot and sped off at more than the '20s Plenty' indicated on the signs in the driveway, but I was in no mood to follow rules on this occasion. My only concern was to put as much distance as possible between me and the Hereuse Nursing home.

I pulled over outside the Craigmore tearoom, trembling from head to foot and had to sit for a few minutes to try to calm myself before driving on. What on earth was wrong with me? All I had done was rescue a few of Jessie's possessions from the nursing home where she had spent her last days. Now my final task was to deliver them to my mother and let her decide what would happen next. That would be my part in this affair completed, over with.

First I had to try to contact my mother, let her know about my visit. The mobile reception on the island can be tricky at times so if the conversation became too difficult, I could end the call. Cowardly, I know, but it would be easier to talk to her later once back on the mainland. I checked the time difference on my mobile then called her, waiting patiently for her to pick up her phone, watching a wooden boat with billowing sails make its way unsteadily towards the Rothesay harbour. The wind had died down, but still the boat leaned over, those on board pulling hard on the mainsail ropes.

As I expected, the conversation with my mother was difficult, not only because of the subject of poor Jessie, though that was bad enough, but because the mobile signal kept dropping.

Her response wasn't at all what I expected. 'What happened to Jessie's money?'

'I guess there wasn't much left at the end,' I responded crisply. Strange we both had the same idea but it wasn't a good idea to tell my mother what Mrs Bradshaw had said.

She didn't pick up on this but went on, 'She was a wealthy woman. Her husband left her very well provided for and then of course she sold that place of hers for a tidy sum, not to mention the valuables she had. Some of them were worth a lot.'

'Probably all went on nursing home fees,' I replied vaguely, continuing to watch the small boat as it fetched about, riding the strong waves.

'Nonsense.' My mother's voice was so loud I had to hold the phone away from my ear. 'She wasn't in that nursing home long enough to eat up all the money she had.'

'Well, there's not much we can do about that and it is a very expensive place.'

My mother was not to be put off. 'She had absolutely no relatives as far as I know. Can't you find out what happened?'

I couldn't keep up this pretence this any longer. 'I think any remaining money went to the Hereuse Nursing home' and held the phone away from my ear, dreading her reaction.

There was a crackling and the signal faded only to return with my mother saying '...and the jewellery she promised she would leave me.'

I bit my lip. Had it been wise to tell my mother the full story? That Jessie had apparently left everything to the Hereuse Nursing home? 'It's none of our business,' I said feebly, knowing my mother would not be dissuaded.

'Alison, I know Jessie was worried about something. She would never have decided to leave everything to that nursing home, not unless she was under some kind of compulsion.'

'All right,' I said. 'If it will put your mind at rest I'll try to check out some details for you.'

'No need to check them out, because I know that...'

At this point the signal faded completely and, in spite of dialling again several times, I couldn't get through.

I was annoyed with myself for being so weak willed. Now I'd be off on some wild goose chase to find out what Jessie had done with her money, if there was any money, that is. My mother's idea of lots of money might not be in line with today's high prices for nursing home care and what she had left to the nursing home might have been no more than a paltry sum. If she had any jewellery, why did my mother think she would inherit it? Jessie might have said something at one time, but it was quite likely she could have changed her mind.

Once back home in Glasgow, I'd make some desultory enquiries about Jessie's will, but further than that wouldn't become involved. I had plenty to do between my teaching job and trying to keep the house in some kind of order, a task at which, alas, I often failed. Put it on the list, I said to myself.

But would I be able to let it rest there, with this nagging doubt about the circumstances of Jessie's death? I hoped that somewhere in this box from the nursing home there would be a clue about what had really happened to her.

TEN

It was difficult to say what made it so hard to warm to Sylvester de Courtney. He was tall and good-looking in a foppish way, thin featured with bushy eyebrows and a small goatee beard only a shade darker than his blond hair. Perhaps it was the way he was dressed? Someone who wore a cravat, teamed with a pale cream suit (especially at this time of year), gave the impression of trying too hard. Or was it because he dyed his hair? On close inspection those pale blond streaks appeared to owe more to the skills of a hairdresser than to nature. And I still had this nagging feeling I'd heard about him, read about him somewhere.

Then again he was so charming, professing great pleasure in meeting me. 'Deborah has talked so much about you. You are every bit as lovely as your daughter.'

If he was attempting to flatter me, he had gone the wrong way about it. 'And Deborah has told us about you,' I replied, annoyed with myself for sounding so abrupt.

He appeared not to notice. 'All good, I hope,' he said, winking at Deborah, who blushed.

Unfortunately Simon had a college meeting this evening, leaving me to cope on my own. What he had actually said when he heard Deborah was bringing Sylvester home was, 'Is that his real name? Surely it's made up?' He added for good measure, 'I may be back in time to meet this new chap of Deborah's, but then again I might go to the pub with the others.'

'You're not leaving me all evening on my own?' I protested. 'Deborah is bringing him specially.'

'I can't be expected to meet every new boyfriend of Deborah's,' he growled. 'Some of them only last ten minutes.'

'He's not a boyfriend, he's her boss.'

'That doesn't make any difference. You know what Deborah's like.' Then he relented and smiled. 'Okay, don't worry. If I can leave early, I will try.'

I fretted about what I should offer: a drink, tea and a sandwich? Or would Deborah expect me to produce something more substantial later? As it happened, there was no need to worry. They arrived well after nine o'clock, refusing all offers of food or drink.

'We're only passing through,' said Deborah. 'Sylvester wants to hurry back to the Glasgow gallery. One of his artists has a new exhibition and it's really well attended. There are loads of people there.'

She rolled her eyes at Sylvester, who acknowledged her comment with a regal nod of his head. 'I'm pleased to say everything is going very well indeed, in spite of the recession.'

He had a smug air, a self satisfied way of talking, but my own feelings had to be disguised for Deborah's sake. It meant a lot to her that she was employed again after yet another spell of idleness.

'You specialise in paintings?' I enquired politely. Topics of conversation were scarce and I kept sneaking a look at my watch, wishing Simon would arrive.

'I wouldn't exactly say specialise. I do try to work with as many painters as I can, nurture young talent, but I do have other interests, I ...'

Deborah broke in. 'Sylvester has such an extensive knowledge. He knows all about all kinds of paintings ... and antiques.'

'And you do that from the Regius Gallery?'

He shook his head. 'No, I have other galleries for those. I work mainly in London, though of course I have an interest in antiques from all around the world.'

Deborah added. 'I told Sylvester about your reunion plans. Bute will be most definitely be one of the islands we'll be taking in.'

'That sounds good,' I replied, trying to inject a note of enthusiasm into my voice.

'You remember what Sylvester is planning to do?'

I made a vague, non-committal noise. 'Yes, but not the specifics. Tell me again.' This would pass another few minutes as he elaborated on his plans.

She glanced at Sylvester who gave her a wry smile of approval to continue. 'Sylvester has managed to find funding to take a touring art exhibition round some of the major Scottish islands. The idea is to exhibit some well known paintings together with paintings by local artists. Bute, for example, has a thriving art club.'

I frowned. 'But don't they already have an exhibition of their own in August sometime?'

'Yes, yes, but this is an opportunity to raise the profile of the local artists. Some of them are of a very high professional standard. One of the problems is that they don't have many opportunities to showcase their talent.'

'That's true,' I said. I didn't want Deborah's boss taking advantage of the captive audience at this reunion, not when I had been involved in organising it. This idea of siting the exhibition in the Pavilion might be a very bad one. 'When exactly are you going to be on Bute?' Already I knew the answer, but had a sneaking hope Sylvester might have had second thoughts, opted for a different weekend.

'Why at the same time as your reunion, of course,' Deborah butted in again before Sylvester could speak. 'It seemed too good an opportunity to miss. After all there are sure to be plenty of well heeled potential buyers among your old colleagues.'

I wished I could disabuse her of this idea about my 'rich' colleagues. Most of them had ended up, as I had, in jobs in the public sector. 'But surely if you sell these paintings you're bringing to the island, there will be nothing left for the exhibitions on the other islands?'

She shook her head vigorously. 'No, no, you don't understand. The idea is to use the big names to draw people in and then let them see what talent there is locally.'

Now it made sense, but there was no point in any further discussion about this exhibition. Before I knew it she would have me fronting a desk, selling the paintings, as if there wasn't enough to do trying to keep up with Betsie's requests.

As we spoke Sylvester's gaze was wandering round our lounge, but he would be lucky to spy anything here of any value. The nearest item we had to an antique, currently in use as an umbrella stand in the hallway, was a large Egyptian vase Simon's great uncle had brought back from his travels in the days before you were penalised for travelling with more than cabin only baggage. Even I could tell that it wasn't worth much, was something specially made for the tourist market.

An hour passed slowly as we sipped yet another cup of tea and I racked my brains for further topics of conversation. I knew nothing about antiques, even less about paintings and Deborah seemed so in awe of her employer that once she had told me the details of the Bute exhibition, she was uncharacteristically quiet, hanging on his every word. Searching feverishly for something to say to fill the silence, I ventured, 'Perhaps you know my friend Betsie? She's in antiques.'

A fraction of a pause, then he frowned as a shadow passed across his face. 'Betsie?'

'Yes, Betsie O'Connor,' I said. 'She's also in the antiques business, like you.'

He hesitated for longer this time, as though giving the matter serious thought, before replying. 'I may have come across her somewhere, but I can't be certain.' A wave of the hand, 'One meets so many people in this business.'

'Oh, mum,' interrupted Deborah, 'that's like asking someone from New York if they know a member of your family. The antiques world is big with lots of different levels of expertise and involvement. I doubt,' another sidelong look at her boss, 'if Betsie would be anywhere in the same league as Sylvester.'

Sylvester seemed to take this as no more than his due. 'I do know all the big names,' he replied, with a modesty that struck a completely false note.

Finally, as I thought the evening would never end and there was still no sign of Simon, Sylvester said, 'I think we had better be going, Deborah. People will be looking for us at the gallery.'

Deborah sprang to her feet and I caught a glimpse of her pleasure that Sylvester had included her in the form of 'we'.

'Of course,' she said. 'Sorry, mum, we should be getting along. We'll have to come back and meet dad another time.'

I couldn't raise the energy to press them to stay longer. 'If you must,' I said, trying to keep the relief out of my voice.

They put on their coats in the hall: Deborah kissed me on the cheek and Sylvester shook my hand firmly. 'A great pleasure to meet you,' he said and with that they disappeared down the path to where Sylvester's large red car was parked. He was obviously doing very well: the antiques business must be thriving. The recession didn't affect everyone.

As the car roared off round the corner and out of sight I closed the door and leaned against it with a sigh. Why didn't I feel better disposed towards Sylvester? He had been very polite, had responded to all my topics of conversation, limited as they were and had seemed very solicitous of Deborah. What was bothering me then? Was it because I'd never met anyone like him? This was not the world Simon and I moved in. In the end it all came down to concern about Deborah and I really had to try to be more level headed about this. 'Well,' I said to Motley as he came purring round my ankles, 'It's all my imagination. There's nothing wrong with Sylvester de Courtney and I guess we might be seeing a whole lot more of him.'

My tranquillity at their departure was short lived. The phone in the hall rang. Let it go to the answering machine, I thought. All I wanted at the moment was to sit down quietly, but the phone had no sooner stopped than it rang again. A second time I ignored it, all to no avail. This time my mobile rang and Betsie's name came up on the screen. For a split second I considered letting this also go to voicemail, but then with a sigh realised she would go on calling until there was an answer.

'Hello, Betsie, how are you?' Those were probably the last words I would say as Betsie, once in full flow, is impossible to stop.

'All going well? Are you going to Bute again?'

'No need. Everything is in hand. We'll catch up soon,' I said firmly after she had rambled on about arrangements made, arrangements not made, arrangements that might be made.

'That all sounds fine, Alison. I only wish I could do more, but I'm so busy going back and forward between France and Germany at the moment with this exhibition I can't afford the time to come over to Scotland,' she said. 'I won't be able to make it over before the reunion at this rate.'

'There's no need to worry about that,' I replied. 'Simon and I are going over to Bute a few days before the reunion starts. We can deal with any last minute glitches then.' There was a nagging worry that if she became involved at this late stage, she might want to make changes.

'That is a relief,' she said. 'I don't know what's wrong with me. I've not been feeling at all well this past couple of weeks.'

'Have you seen a doctor?'

'I've no time for that. Probably I've been working too hard, that's all.' Then she added. 'See you on Bute.'

Little did I know that the next time I would see her, it wouldn't be in the way I expected.

ELEVEN

The Bute reunion, Jessie's death, the Hereuse Nursing home, Deborah and her new job, not to mention a busy time at school with all the Christmas activities: no wonder it was difficult to switch off long enough for some quality sleep.

'I want nothing more than to put my feet up in front of the telly and watch some programme that requires no thought at all,' I said aloud. As I was alone in the house except for Motley there was no response, though he did stop and stare at me for a few moments, meowing loudly. 'Mmm, that's not sympathy,' I said to him, 'that's as appeal for food.'

Simon wasn't yet back from one of his golf matches, probably by now at the nineteenth hole if he had ever left there, considering the weather. Deborah was catching up with one of the many friends she seems to acquire everywhere she goes. Hopefully it was a sign she didn't want to spend all her time with Sylvester as I was becoming increasingly unhappy about him. I had only met him once after his visit to our house - by accident in town. It had been a strange encounter.

I was more convinced than ever he wasn't at all Deborah's type. For one thing, in the harsh light of morning, he looked a good deal older than she is, if anything closer to Simon's age than hers and secondly, I didn't take to his over smooth approach when Deborah spotted me. I mean, what man in this day and age actually kisses your hand, especially in a public place, with a 'How wonderful to see you, Mrs Cameron.'

Deborah seemed besotted, he could do no wrong in her eyes and I knew better than to interfere in my daughter's life.

The sound of the phone ringing startled me from thoughts of Sylvester. 'How did you get on about Jessie?' my mother asked. 'Did you collect her belongings? Was there anything that might tell us what really happened to her? What might have caused her death?'

'I haven't had time to look through everything yet,' I said, cross at this tirade of questions.

'I thought the idea was to have a short visit? Haven't you been back for several days?'

What was the use of going into a long explanation to someone who was so far away? Instead I said, 'I'll sort out Jessie's bits and pieces this evening and have them ready for when you return, don't worry.'

'You'll call me as soon as you know anything more? Or find anything in her belongings? Promise? Phone me tomorrow and let me know what's happened.'

'Don't expect too much,' I replied, 'there's very little left.'

'But remember she said she would leave me some of her jewellery. There might be some of that in the box.'

Fortunately the rest of the conversation was cut short as there was a loud hissing on the line and then the connection dropped.

'Unless, of course, you would like me to...' I realised I was talking to empty air.

I stood for a moment, frowning at the receiver before replacing it. She imagines I have lots of time on my hands. Then again, a part-time job in a school sounds fine, except there's often some crisis or other where you're asked if you could possibly 'fill in'. Tomorrow was one such day. My colleague was still off on long term sick leave and I'd been 'volunteered' to take on a more regular commitment of an extra day a week to help out. That meant spending most of the evening preparing and catching up on marking for other classes. As the colleague concerned had a track record in long term absences, no one had any expectation he would return but, bureaucracy being what it is, the school had to cover until he made a decision.

In the living room the television was tuned to some programme about ancient pyramids, which seemed to involve the presenter in making journeys back and forth across vast deserts in a very luxurious jeep. The number of times this was in full camera shot made me suspect it was all a bit of a tax fiddle and, having missed the beginning and with no idea what was going on, I switched off.

Back in the kitchen I fetched a glass of well chilled wine from the fridge, hoping this might be more restoring than a cup of tea.

In the hallway sat Jessie's box, abandoned on my arrival home, tempting me to open it as I gazed at it, sipping my glass of wine. Why not? The others wouldn't be back for ages yet and I didn't feel inclined to read or watch some mindless programme on television. It was unlikely there would be much of interest among an old lady's effects, but I'd be able to phone my mother, give her details and hopefully make a quick decision about whether the contents should be left until her return from holiday or taken straight to the charity shop.

I carried the box through to the living room, put it on the coffee table and stood looking at it for a moment or two before tugging at the thick brown parcel tape to open it up, but the sight that greeted me was disappointing. What few items remained seemed to have been thrown in together, piled up in a random fashion and although the box contained no more than bits and pieces, the way the nursing home had dealt with Jessie's last belongings seemed disrespectful.

Where should I begin? At first there didn't seem much point in unpacking everything but once started I couldn't stop. Under the top ornaments, there was the little wooden box that had sat so long on the table in Jessie's front room, together with old books, some of them decidedly musty, a few gaudy scarves, old theatre programmes, some antiques sale catalogues and a collection of very old photos. My mother might recognise some of the people here, so these went carefully to one side.

Poor Jessie - all her treasured possessions now crammed into one little box. But this was no time to be dwelling on thoughts of mortality. Though Deborah wasn't likely to be back till long after I was in bed, Simon would appear in an hour or so and I wanted to have a quick look through everything before his return.

A further rummage produced little else of any interest. There were a few more ornaments and several books with surprisingly racy titles so perhaps Jessie was not the quiet old lady we had imagined. What there most certainly was not was any jewellery. My mother would be disappointed though it wasn't too surprising as any valuables would be part of her estate. I made a mental note to ask for more details about the jewellery.

All these bits and pieces went on top of the coffee table and I felt about in the bottom of the box, pulling out the last odds and ends: a sewing kit, a miniature barometer, a collection of teaspoons obviously gathered from trips to a multitude of seaside resorts, many of them tagged with the 'A Present from...' label. It was difficult to tell if these had been acquired by Jessie or were what friends considered suitable presents for her. It was difficult to see what any one person could do with so many spoons. But there was nothing here to help me determine what had happened to Jessie, except the simple explanation she had died of old age. All I could do was put everything back in better order, tell my mother about the contents of the box and let her make the final decision about what to keep.

As I began to re-pack everything with some care, I glanced again at the books. Some of them were very old, though I didn't think there was much here of interest to a collector. Flicking through one of the slim volumes at the bottom of the pile I noticed that although it had the appearance of a novel on the outside, inside it was handwritten. My pulse quickened. Could it be a diary? I started scanning the pages rapidly for any clue but it wasn't what I first thought. It was a notebook rather than a diary, though some of the pages were dated and others covered with scrawls, crossings out and notes with lots of the words abbreviated. This was not something Jessie had written up with any regularity and the last entry seemed to be for a couple of weeks before she died. How had the Hereuse Nursing home missed this?

The remainder of my glass of wine lay untouched as I sat down to find out what Jessie might be able to tell us from beyond the grave.

TWELVE

The news item was one of those brief stories on the front page, tucked down in the corner well away from the main reports about the dire state of the economy and the latest cricket scandal, neither of which was of much interest to me. I can do nothing single handed to save the economy and haven't the slightest interest in cricket. After a quick glance at the headlines I turned over to something more interesting on the inside pages.

It was only later that morning that Simon said to me, 'Did you see that story about someone being found dead in their car?'

I shook my head. 'What happened?' I was only half listening, busy thinking about what I could pull out of the freezer for dinner. Perhaps we could go out to eat?

'You must have picked up the story. Someone was found dead in their car on the last Weymss Bay to Bute ferry.'

This was an interesting piece of news. I stared at him. 'No, I had no idea that's what it was about. The newspaper report didn't give details.'

'Mmm, I picked the story up on Radio Scotland.'

'What happened?' Now I was intrigued.

'No one is sure, heart attack or some such I expect. It must have given the CalMac employees a terrible fright.'

'Poor soul - not the way I would choose to go.'

'No name yet. I expect they're trying to trace relatives. All they're saying is it's a woman and she wasn't discovered until they started unloading the cars at Rothesay and her car didn't move.'

It was sad but I thought no more about it: I had plenty on my mind at the moment, including phoning Betsie again. There had been no reply to my e-mail to her summarising the recent arrangements agreed for the reunion so possibly she was travelling somewhere on business and hadn't had time to check? This wasn't like her. Quite the opposite because she kept in more regular contact than was necessary. I dialled her mobile number. It rang out and I tried again, checking to make sure it was the right number. Still it rang out. Leaving a message would be too complicated. I'd have to try again later.

The next call on my list would be difficult. Time to phone my mother. As anticipated, she was less than impressed by my efforts to find out what had happened to Jessie.

'She would be badly shaken by that problem with her hip,' I countered to her, trying to emphasis the death was probably natural, making every effort to soften the blow.

'She may have been a little depressed, Alison, but that was all. Last time I spoke to her she sounded fine. Plenty of people recover from an operation like that.'

'I'm sorry about Jessie, mum, but I'm sure the Hereuse did their best for her.'

'Well, it's too late now.'

Perhaps my mother was feeling more than a little guilty, given she hadn't visited Jessie since she had gone into the nursing home. But that wasn't my concern and I was about to change the subject when she said again, 'What happened to her money, Alison?'

This wasn't like my mother to be mercenary. 'We've talked about this. As far as I know she left everything to the nursing home.'

'You'll try to get a copy of her will?'

'What would that tell us?' This was something I didn't want to promise, knowing it wouldn't be as easy as my mother imagined.

'It would tell us if it was the right will. I was one of the witnesses.'

This put a different complexion on things. 'And were you due to inherit? Is that the problem?'

My mother sounded aggrieved. 'Jessie did insist on leaving me a couple of pieces of her jewellery I particularly admired, but the bulk of her estate was to go to various charities. So, Alison, if you could find out exactly what happened with her will, I would be happy. It's not about the jewellery,' she continued in case I had the wrong idea, 'but I would like to know that all had gone as Jessie wished.'

'What jewellery did she leave you?'

'There was a Victorian pendant - multidrop I think she called it. It had three stones: a blue sapphire, a pink gem of some kind and a white sapphire. Then there was a brooch that had belonged to her grandmother - a Scottish brooch with a bloodstone in the centre and a cornelian surround.'

'You seem to know a lot about them.'

'Of course I do. They were Jessie's favourite pieces and worth a bit of money. She particularly wanted me to have them.'

'There was nothing like that in her box.'

'I'm sure she wouldn't have forgotten me even if she did change her will. There's something odd about all of this.'

'I'll see what I can do,' I replied wearily. It was really none of my business, but sometimes it's easier to agree with what my mother wants than try to persuade her otherwise. Any available free time in the coming week would disappear if I attempted to do as she asked. I doubted I'd be able to gain access to this kind of information since I had no idea where to begin. Besides, it wasn't unusual for elderly people to change their mind about who should receive their money and their goods.

'At least go back to the nursing home next time you go over and find out what they know.'

'Okay,' I said, with no plans to be back on the island till the reunion. Still, it wasn't urgent, as nothing would now be of help to Jessie.

She seemed satisfied with this promise and we chatted for few minutes about family matters, though I didn't dare tell her about the developments in Deborah's new job.

I tried to phone Betsie again, but still there was no reply and by now my lazy morning was disappearing fast. Time for more coffee and a mid morning biscuit, but I had no sooner gone into the kitchen when Simon shouted from the living room.

'Alison, come and look at this.'

'I'll be there in a minute,' I said, switching on the kettle.

Simon's head appeared round the door. 'No, come now. It's important. I want you to see this right now.'

I put down the coffee cup and followed him through. The television was on, tuned to the local news channel. I gazed at the screen, scarcely able to believe what I was seeing and totally shocked, my legs buckling under me, I collapsed into the nearest chair.

The face of the woman who had been found dead on the CalMac ferry filled the screen. I didn't have to wait for the announcer to say who she was. It was Betsie.

THIRTEEN

The shock of Betsie's death put all other thoughts out of my mind. What was going on? Why had she been on the ferry to Bute? As soon the initial distress of seeing her on the television news wore off a little, I phoned the police. Thank goodness they didn't require me to identify the body, but I agreed to call in at the station and tell them all about the reunion and my relationship with Betsie.

The question I couldn't answer was why she was on her way to the island. I kept going over what she had said last time we had talked, how she had been adamant that the exhibition in March would take up all her time. What had suddenly made her decide to come over to Scotland and, even more puzzling, make the trip to Bute? Surely she would have been in touch with me to let me know. No matter what solution I came up with, none was satisfactory.

'There will be some reason she was going there. Perhaps she didn't have time to contact you,' said Simon. 'After all, as you've said so often, Betsie led the kind of lifestyle that made this sort of sudden death almost inevitable.'

'Yes, but I feel guilty I didn't insist on meeting her.'

'How would that have helped? And how could you have arranged to meet her if you didn't know she was coming?'

I had to admit my logic was more than slightly flawed, but his next question was more difficult to answer.

'What will happen now, Alison? About the reunion, I mean.'

I couldn't think of an immediate reply, still trying to make sense of why Betsie should be on the ferry to Bute when she had

65

most definitely said she couldn't leave Europe. 'To be honest I hadn't considered that.'

He continued, 'So will you take it on? Is there someone else who can do it? Or will you cancel it?'

'We're too far ahead with arrangements to cancel it, I think. A lot of people would be very disappointed … and we've booked all the venues and the hotels.'

He frowned. 'I'll do what I can to help you. I don't want to see you left to cope with this on your own.'

'What else can I do?' Difficult as it would be, it might be best to try to keep the reunion going, if that was what the majority of people wanted. I groaned at the thought of several evenings of e-mails and phone calls awaiting me.

Deborah's reaction was more than a little self centred as her first words were on hearing the news, 'Oh no! Surely this doesn't mean the reunion will be called off? Sylvester and I were depending on it to give a boost to our art sales. A lot of work has gone into setting this up.'

'Then it was most inconvenient of Betsie to die when she did,' I said, but the sarcasm was lost on her.

'Surely everyone will want to continue with the reunion. After all, look at all the preparation that has gone into it already.'

I was in two minds about this comment. Sorry as I was about what had happened to Betsie, Simon was right. I couldn't begin to imagine how much work there would be finalising the arrangements for the reunion on my own. On the other hand, those from more far flung places would probably have made their travel arrangements by now and it would be a disaster for a lot of people if it was called off. 'I suppose there will have to be an inquest because it was a sudden death?'

Simon frowned. 'That won't take long, will it? Heart attack was it?'

'I guess that was what happened. No surprise with Betsie's state of health. And she did say she'd been feeling ill.'

No more was said, but all evening the reunion hung in the air between us, leaving a frisson of unease. Whatever was decided, it would have to be soon.

And when it was over, Simon and I could head for somewhere warm and sunny, well away from Scotland, for a holiday. That thought kept me going as I rang or e-mailed the reunion delegates, one after another.

Little did I know that I'd soon be involved in not one suspicious death, but two.

FOURTEEN

Deeply disappointed, I put the notebook on the table and started to replace the rest of the items in the box. These momentoes could go to my mother, though there was certainly none of the jewellery she had suggested among these poor items.

Another hour of reading the notebook next day when I was again on my own had revealed nothing. It was more a collection of old notes, snippets of suggestions, brief accounts with the words so shortened there was no sense to them, prices unrelated to anything else in the notes, remarks on visitors to the home, comments on some of the programmes she had watched. Perhaps she had intended to write to the television company, but had never managed to do so.

I heard Simon's key in the lock and stood up stiffly, rubbing my right leg which had gone into a cramp. 'Hi, I'm in the living room.'

He came in and surveyed the scene of neat piles all over the floor. 'What's all this, then? Are you sorting all this out for a jumble sale? I thought you'd decided to leave this for your mother to take it to a charity shop?'

'I wanted to have one more look, in case there was something of interest, something I'd missed, but there's nothing. At least I don't think so.'

Why not pass everything straight over to your mother?'

'Mmm... she might decide a charity shop is the best place for it, though I suspect she'll put it in the attic with the rest of the stuff that's there.'

Simon made no further comment. Unfortunately, refusing to throw anything out is a characteristic my mother and I share.

'I'll put everything back and then we can have some supper,' I said.

Simon lifted several of the books, thumbing through them quickly as he said, 'I see there was more to Jessie than we thought: *The Lust of her Life* and *Two Men for One Woman*. Good gracious, are you going to pass these on to your mother?'

'Do you think I shouldn't?' This hadn't occurred to me.

Simon shrugged. 'Up to you, but it might be better to keep them.'

'So that you can read them?'

'Oops,' he said as he bent to pick up something that had dropped out of one of the books. He lifted and envelope and passed it to me. 'This is addressed to your mother.'

'What?' He was right; this long slim cream envelope had my mother's name on it.

'Are you going to open it?'

I turned it over, but it was firmly sealed. 'I don't think I should. I'll ask my mother when she phones, but I can always send it out to her. I shouldn't think it would take long to reach her in Canada and she won't be back for a while yet.'

Decision made, I put the books aside for the moment and closed the lid of the box on everything else, while the notebook went to one side to read again later. 'Can I put this box in the boot of your car?' I said. 'That way you might be able drop it off at my mother's on the way home from college, ready for her return? You do pass her house and it would save me time.'

'Fine,' said Simon, taking his car keys from his pocket and passing them to me.

I went out to his car with Jessie's box, now considerably lighter without the books and stood for a minute after closing the boot. If the notebook didn't provide information, I couldn't think of any way we could find out now what had really happened to Jessie, whether her death was suspicious or not. The episode was over, finished.

As I came back into the room, Simon said, 'I think you should hand the notebook over to your mother. After all, you've had a couple of attempts to make something of it without success. There's nothing in it.'

'I will do, but only when I'm absolutely sure there's nothing of interest in it.'

I had reservations about Simon's suggestion. When she returned from Canada, there would be lots for her to catch up on and I didn't want to upset her more than necessary about Jessie's death. 'I'll think about it,' I said. 'I'll take an hour again tomorrow and see what I can make of it all. If it's too difficult, or it seems of no importance we can pass it to her with everything else.'

There was no time for further discussion. We were hungry and Simon wanted to tell me about the latest crisis in the college: the main topic of conversation for most of his day. I put the novels with Jessie's notebook in the drawer of the cabinet and went through to the kitchen with Simon.

This time, the crisis, most unusually, was nothing to do with funding. 'He shouldn't have become involved with her,' Simon growled as he ended his tale about some member of staff who had been having an affair with one of the students in his department. 'Now there will have to be a full investigation and goodness knows what will happen then. The Principal is furious and of course the publicity will be really bad for our image.'

He might be completely wrong. The idea that the college might be a hotbed of lust might attract more students, not drive them away, but now was not the time to put this theory forward.

We ate supper quickly. I had marking to finish and Simon had phone calls to make. This college scandal was being milked for all it was worth, though in my opinion it was a storm about nothing, as it turned out the student in question was a divorced mother of a teenage son and the affair had started after she had finished her course. Still, it provided a useful distraction from the usual money worries that regularly beset the college.

In the room I use as a study (though it doubles as a guest bedroom and all my stuff is squashed onto a couple of shelves beside a table with the computer), I lifted my bag and headed for the dining room table where there was more space to spread everything out. I looked at the pile of exercise books, regretting bitterly my reluctance to make a start on them earlier in the day. Ah well, divine justice. The first of the third year essays didn't improve my mood, feeling an immediate sinking of the heart as I looked at the misspelled title. This did not bode well. If Ben couldn't copy the title correctly, what chance did he have of writing a decent essay?

Concentrating proved difficult with so many ideas buzzing around in my head. Perhaps it would be best to put these exercise books aside till the morning. I had an hour spare then. No, that was a stupid idea, yet another postponement. With a sigh I returned to my task, but my mind kept drifting to Jessie and the notebook she had written.

Ben seemed to have some problems with the timeline of the story he was telling me. It jumped about from month to month and then back again. I was about to write something in the margin but I stopped, pen poised in mid air. What if Jessie's notebook wasn't muddled as Simon suggested? What if the backwards and forwards scheme had been deliberate? She had been an intelligent woman and it wasn't beyond her to organise the inclusion of any information in that notebook in its proper sequence, if that was what she wanted.

I sat back and thought for a moment, but try as I might, no sensible suggestion as to why she might have done this came to mind. It was no good. I closed Ben's exercise book and put it back on top of the pile. I would have to hope that I could deal with it tomorrow because, at the moment, I simply had to re-read Jessie's notebook. If there was a mystery here, I wanted to solve it.

FIFTEEN

Well past midnight and it was impossible to make any sense of
Jessie's notes. There were no revelations about the Hereuse
Nursing home, nothing that might give a clue about evil deeds
there. It was all no more than chit chat and gossip and some
entries that obviously made sense only to Jessie. I tried reading
the scribblings all sorts of ways but they seemed to be no more
than the mundane ramblings of someone who had found a way to
vent her feelings through writing about them.

There were stories here of meals dismissed as awful which
struck me as strange given the services of the Independent
Caterers Limited, descriptions of carers of varying qualities,
anecdotes about excursions round the island - to Scalpsie, to
Kilchattan,to Mount Stuart and beyond to the shopping centre on
the mainland - some of which pleased her and some didn't. Those
which didn't were scathingly dismissed in a few words. There
were stories of visitors to the home, some dates underlined, some
in brackets. A few of them had a number beside them, but there
was nothing anyone could make sense of.

Here were all the trivial concerns of a closed community, the
minutiae of everyday life that means so much to the person
involved but nothing to people outside. The Independent Caterers
Limited cropped up several times and it was obvious she didn't
like them. Was she very fussy about her food? Or was she
suspicious she might be being poisoned or her food was being
doped? No, this was ridiculous. I was becoming as paranoid as
Jessie had been. Yet a feeling of guilt bothered me as I read these
descriptions. This was information, it would appear, written to

give voice to personal concerns, not something destined to be read by the wider world.

Going back to the beginning several times, reading every second word, reading only the first word of each line: nothing made her musings any clearer. There was probably no mystery at all. I had read too many thrillers where there is a code for the hero to crack. Why should Jessie hide information like this? She had disguised this notebook because her reflections were personal, a way of describing her feelings about the life she now had, not because there she wanted to conceal any great secret.

The pile of exercise books stared at me reproachfully. A whole evening wasted and now I'd have to try to make up time and correct all of these before going into class the next day. Too confused to give them the attention they deserved, I stood up and stretched, with the realisation that although tired, I wasn't at all sleepy.

In the dark of the bedroom Simon's bulk was taking over most of the bed. I gave him a nudge and he obligingly rolled over to the far side, muttering in his sleep as he did so. There was no way I wanted a lecture about staying up so late. I crawled under the duvet, but my head throbbed and sleep was no more likely than a few minutes before. I lay there, keeping as still as possible in the hope that sleep would eventually overtake me. Sounds came as though from a distance : a car door slamming, voices of late merry-makers as they passed the house, the gurgle of the pipes, the house settling down for the night.

Eventually I dozed, everything going round in my head until in that half state between waking and sleeping, I almost felt Jessie in the room with me. What if what Jessie had to say only made sense if it was taken together with something else in her possessions? What if those numbers, those underlined words were the key to something else? I lay for a while considering this possibility. The more I thought about it the wider awake I became. There had to be some solution.

There was no possibility of sleep now. Gently easing back the duvet and fumbling for my dressing gown and slippers, I slid out of bed. Simon flung his arm over and rolled onto his side to take up most of the bed again.

Unwilling to disturb him by putting on a light, I stumbled down in the dark, feeling my way by holding onto the wall and once back in the living room, took the notebook from the drawer, put it on the table and sat gazing at it for a few moments. Beside it, the pile of exercise books lay ready for the morning. I had a terrible feeling I'd be in no better frame of mind to mark them and would have to come up with some excuse. But that was tomorrow's problem. Meanwhile I'd a task to do and if I could make some sense of what Jessie had left perhaps I'd be able to sleep.

As luck would have it, I didn't have the opportunity to make much headway. I'd no sooner settled down with the notebook, together with pen and paper for notes, when there was the sound of a key in the lock and Deborah came in. Quickly placing Jessie's notebook under the pile of exercise books, I tried to look absorbed in marking.

I heard her foot on the first step as she obviously intended to go straight upstairs, but seeing the light on, she came through. She stopped abruptly as she spied me.

'Good gracious, mum, what are you doing up at this time of night?'

'I might ask you the same question,' I replied tartly, pen poised above the exercise book. 'Some of us have to be up late keeping up with work.'

She peered over my shoulder. 'You'd do it a lot quicker if you tried reading it the right way up.'

'I was about to make a start,' I said by way of covering up as she shook her head in disbelief.

She laughed. 'I'm young. I'm allowed to be out till all hours.' She threw herself into the chair opposite me. 'Anyway I told you I'd be late. There was another meeting about this exhibition on Bute and we went to dinner afterwards.'

'A bit late for dinner?' I raised an eyebrow.

She shrugged. 'You know what these artistic types are like. The evening doesn't begin until at least midnight. Sylvester was very keen that I go along. He sees a great future for me in this field.' What could I say? Obviously Sylvester de Courtney had cast a spell on her, made her feel confident. Even if I didn't like him, I couldn't fault him for that.

Suddenly she sat up and pointed to the book whose edge had slipped out from under the pile of exercise books. 'Not your usual reading matter, I guess. Is this some secret vice you've been hiding?'

My subterfuge of closing the notebook over and hiding it hadn't worked. Now I had some explaining to do. Best to tell her what was going on rather than become involved in another stream of lies.

'Very odd,' she said as I finished. 'Don't you think it might have been that Jessie suffered from some kind of memory loss in her later years? She was always rather absent minded according to gran's stories about her.'

'Possibly,' I replied cautiously. That was my concern also but I didn't want to discuss this with Deborah or with anyone, until I had some idea myself about what Jessie had been up to.

'Anyway, it's too late to discuss it all. I'm off to bed.' She gave a yawn as she stood up. 'You should go to bed too.'

'In a minute or two.'

She shrugged. 'Suit yourself, but you know you'll be grouchy if you don't get some sleep.'

I couldn't disagree with this. 'I won't be long,' I assured her but as soon as she left the room, I settled back to my task. The pages began to blur before my eyes and as the hall clock struck two and I found myself nodding off. Well, whatever Jessie had tried to conceal, she had made a good job of it. Perhaps Deborah was right and this was no more than that of a poor woman whose memory was failing. But my mother had been so sure Jessie was worried about what was happening at the Hereuse and even if Jessie was imagining things, my mother wasn't one to exaggerate. Besides, could memory loss come on really suddenly?

What had read I about this condition? It seemed to be a very gradual process, beginning with forgetting small things, putting keys in the refrigerator, forgetting names of loved ones. Perhaps it was something else to be checked out on the internet but the thought of adding to my already long list of things to do was not the least bit appealing. 'Oh, Motley, if only there was some easy answer to this puzzle,' I said as he jumped up on the table beside me and lay down, purring loudly.

I put Jessie's notebook back. In the morning, after a night's sleep, I might be better able to think about it all, but for the moment I was far too tired to concentrate. Any thoughts of tackling the marking were also gone.

It all seemed so strange. There was little of any consequence in any of her writings as far as I could make out from my attempts to decipher the notebook and if there was some kind of secret code, she had made it impossible to find. Somehow it didn't seem likely Jessie had been engaging in this kind of secretive behaviour.

This time I crawled back into bed and fell sound asleep, a restless sleep full of strange dreams. Sad to say, there was no sudden burst of inspiration, no sudden realisation in the half sleeping, half waking state in the middle hours of the night. Next morning no memories of my dreams remained, except that they were terrifying. The alarm clock startled me out of my slumbers and I groggily put my hand out to silence it. I had a dim memory of Simon leaving early, muttering something to do with a meeting but must have fallen asleep again when he left.

I jumped out of bed. It was after eight and I had to leave the house at half past, at the very latest, to have any hope of reaching school in time for my first class.

Downstairs the pile of exercise books sat where I had left them. All my good intentions about rising early and making a start on them had vanished. There wasn't even time for a cup of coffee. As I lifted the pile, the couple at the bottom fell open to the floor and I bent down to pick them up, clutching the others as I did so, catching sight of the title of the essay on the last one: *A story in pictures.*

I stopped. There was some idea lurking at the back of my mind. What was it? Was whatever Jessie wanted to say not in the notebook, but in pictures? Where had I seen something with pictures among Jessie's belongings? It would surely only take me a couple of minutes to check the notebook and then fetch the box and go through it again.

Then I remembered the box was in Simon's car and he had promised to drop it off at my mother's house. I'd have to think of an excuse to go round and retrieve it. Well, I could have another look at that notebook in the meantime.

I went to pick up Jessie's notebook, but stopped as I turned the door handle. There was no time now for further exploring or I'd be seriously late for school, something even less tolerated in the teachers than the pupils, but how I was going to contain myself during the day was difficult to imagine.

SIXTEEN

None of us had given much thought to poor Betsie's death. Overweight, diabetic, stressed by her job and a heavy smoker in spite of her protestations 'I have given up - several times' she had been a prime candidate for a sudden death.

Of course there had to be a post mortem, a mere formality, we assumed. There had been several attempts to trace her relatives and finally one niece in London had been found. That held proceedings up even further, so the guess was the funeral would take place the following week.

There was a message on the answering machine, a voice I didn't recognise, until she revealed herself as Nadine O'Connor, Betsie's niece, phoning from London. She sounded upset and the upshot of her long rambling message, after I replayed it several times, was that she wanted to come and see me. 'I've planned to be here for two weeks for the funeral before going to France to clear up Aunt Betsie's affairs there,' she said, 'but there have been complications and I absolutely have to speak to you, to someone who knew her well.'

Was it advisable to become further involved? Or was it easier to ignore the call? Finally conscience got the better of me and I tried to phone her back, only to hear the message 'the caller withheld their number.' With a bit of luck she wouldn't try to contact me again.

This would have been too easy a solution because shortly after ten o'clock the phone rang again and a voice said, 'Mrs Cameron? Thank goodness I've reached you. I would very much like to see you.' She sounded jumpy, more anxious than was likely considering, as far as I knew, she and her aunt hadn't been in touch for years.

'How about tomorrow morning? It's one of my non-teaching days, so any time will do.' Best to get this visit over with, though if I was being honest, I was more than a little intrigued. As I was about to ring off I added, 'Won't you even give me a clue as to what this is all about?' From the sound of it, it wasn't a social call.

There was a moment's hesitation. Then she said firmly, 'It would be much better to come and explain in person,' and in spite of my asking again, she refused to say more. 'Where can we meet?'

'I don't think this would be a suitable topic for a café or a restaurant, do you? Come over to the house.'

She accepted my directions without question. 'That sounds a good idea. I'll see you tomorrow.'

There was nothing useful I'd be able to tell her but perhaps it was a guilt trip for her years of neglect.

She arrived at ten o'clock sharp, so punctually my suspicion was she had been sitting outside in her car waiting for the appointed time.

'Let's get some coffee organised first,' I said, steering her into the kitchen. I had to look up to her as she was rangy, reminding me of a leggy colt. Her fall of ash blonde hair framed a face dominated by a generous mouth and wide blue eyes. Though Betsie had been dark haired, when I looked closely there was some resemblance in the pointed nose and the slightly jutting chin, features which made her a little less than beautiful. She wore tight jeans and a mock fur jacket, her long legs snugly encased in winter boots, the nod to fashion evident in the dangerously high heels.

She sat down on one of the chairs at the kitchen table. In deference to having a visitor, I had found a packet of real coffee at the back of the cupboard. We mostly drank instant coffee these days so I surreptiously sniffed it and judged it fresh enough, in spite of its time lurking in the dark. I waited for the water to boil and spooned the aromatic grains into the coffee pot, trying to make general conversation. Trite statements about the weather and the traffic limped along until we were settled with a steaming cup of coffee and a biscuit.

Nadine refused the biscuit, but having put them put on the plate what could I do but have one? This was why she was so slim, I thought, munching guiltily.

She pre-empted my question. 'I expect you are wondering why I wanted to see you?' She stirred her coffee as she paused.

I nodded, trying to swallow the last of my biscuit before speaking. 'I had an idea you might have wanted to talk over the funeral arrangements, as you don't really know anyone here?'

She swirled the remains of her coffee round in her cup. 'The funeral may have to be cancelled, at least for the moment.'

'Wasn't the post mortem a formality? Didn't she have a heart attack?' I tried to remember where that particular piece of information had come from.

She drank the last of her coffee and stared at me. 'That's what we all thought. But it seems it was more than that...'

'And... ' I prompted her.

'It's not so much that a heart attack killed Aunt Betsie. It's more what caused the heart attack.'

How could there be a problem about Betsie? Aloud I said, 'Everyone knew her health had been poor and she didn't take care of herself. Why, last time we spoke she told me she felt ill, but she refused to go to the doctor.'

Nadine made no reply but continued to stare into her empty coffee cup as I went on, 'And then she was diabetic and very overweight. And she smoked.'

She grimaced as she spoke. 'Yes, but there was some problem about her medication.'

I was still baffled and persisted. 'I don't understand this, Nadine. Surely when she was found on the CalMac ferry she had had a heart attack?'

She frowned and paused for a few moments as though considering exactly what she should say. 'I know it looked like that initially. But someone spotted there was a problem with her insulin: she hadn't been having the necessary insulin for some time.' Nadine looked at me, narrowing her eyes as though containing her anger.

'But Betsie had been diabetic for years, well used to injecting herself with insulin. Why would she make a mistake like that? Surely she would have noticed?'

'That's the problem. It doesn't look as if it was a mistake. It appears there was a deliberate substitution.'

I remembered Betsie saying how ill she felt during our last phone call. 'Why would someone deliberately go onto the CalMac ferry with the express intention of murdering Betsie?'

'I find it difficult to believe also. But they think it happened before she boarded the ferry. The insulin substitution happened before that last trip. '

'Someone was substituting her insulin,' I repeated, unable to believe it.

'That's what it looks like. The result is something called diabetic acidosis and it's fatal if not treated. That on top of her other problems…'

I seized on this. 'There you are then. It could have been an accident, pure and simple. She was so stressed by this exhibition she was organising she could have made a mistake, forgotten to take her insulin.' Was it likely that after years of dealing with her illness, Betsie would make this kind of error?

Nadine stared at me as though I had said something outrageous. 'No, it wasn't like that at all. She had been on insulin for a long time, knew all about it. She would never have neglected herself like that.'

'Who on earth would have done it? She was travelling over to Bute for goodness' sake.' And who would have had access to Betsie's medical supplies?

'Yes, but she wasn't alone on the ferry.'

'But she was found alone in her car, so who was travelling with her?'

'That's what they're trying to find out. Betsie was found alone in her car on the ferry but someone had moved her from the passenger to the driver's seat … there were two return tickets in the glove compartment of the car.'

SEVENTEEN

There was a moment of silence then Nadine said, 'The funeral has had to be postponed and now there will be a full police investigation. I don't know how long I'll be able to stay here. I do have to get back to work in London. I'll do what I can while I'm here but I wondered...'

I interrupted her. My mind was still on what had happened to Betsie. 'Even if there were two return tickets, that doesn't mean she was travelling with someone that day.' I cast about wildly. 'They could have been left over from some other time.'

She shook her head. 'Uh,uh. The Calmac ticket collector is sure he remembers that there was someone in the car with her, though he can't remember any details. And the receipts were dated.'

She took a long drink of her coffee and looked up at me through narrowed eyes. 'You knew Betsie well, didn't you?'

'I wouldn't say well,' I confessed. 'I knew her at college of course.'

'But recently - you had dealings with her recently?'

What an odd word to use I thought but said, 'She got in touch with me about the reunion, said she needed help tracking everyone down, making the arrangements.' I shrugged. 'For good or for bad, I agreed to help.'

Nadine stared at me. 'So you didn't know her professionally?'

'Good gracious, no.'

It was hard to tell if she believed me. 'I thought you knew her well, were in constant contact with her.'

Did she think I had something to so with Betsie's death? 'I had nothing to do with Betsie's business affairs, for goodness' sake.

I'm a teacher and that takes up enough of my time. All my recent dealings with Betsie were to do with the arrangements for the reunion on Bute to celebrate our thirtieth college anniversary.'

A look which could only have been relief crossed Nadine's features. 'I see. I thought you and Betsie were working together, that you were a business contact.'

The idea was so preposterous I almost laughed out loud but stopped myself in time as she frowned at me. 'So you've never had any dealings with Betsie's antiques business?'

Why did she keep asking me the same question? How many times had I to say no in order to convince her? 'Of course not. What would I know about antiques?' One glance round our very ordinary house would have told her that.

She stood up. 'I must be going. There's so much to do.'

Now it was my turn to ask questions. 'You hadn't seen your aunt in some time?' It wasn't intended as an insult but as soon as I spoke realised it might have sounded like one.

She shook her head. 'That's it, you see. That's part of the problem.'

This was a most unsatisfactory answer. Probably she felt as guilty about her lack of contact with Betsie as I did about the situation with Jessie. Best not to say any more.

There was a long pause and I had a good idea what she was going to ask next. 'I wondered,' she repeated, 'would you be willing to keep me up to date with anything you hear about Betsie?'

I tried to think of a reason to refuse, but none immediately came to mind. 'If I can,' I replied, 'but I don't expect I'll be able to help much. Until this reunion was planned, I hadn't seen her for over twenty years. We only managed to communicate by Christmas card.' At least Betsie had, a pang of guilt hitting me as I remembered dropping her from my list the year before as someone I wasn't likely to see again.

'I'll keep in touch with you,' said Nadine her face brightening, perhaps because she had managed to offload the problem on to me. She now seemed more vibrant, light-hearted but there was something strange about the way she was behaving.

I pulled my diary from my bag. 'You'd better give me a contact number.'

For a moment she hesitated. 'I think it's best if I call you,' she said. 'I am away a lot and very busy, so you might not be able to catch up with me.'

Why is it that people always assume they have so much more to do than you? 'I'm also busy,' I replied frostily. 'And often called in to school at short notice.'

There was a silence and it appeared she was going to tell me to forget all about it, that she would manage herself, but suddenly she seemed to come to a decision. 'I can give you a number to use in an absolute emergency, but honestly I would much rather you let me call you.'

She fished in her oversized black bag, too enormous to be called a handbag. 'Here's my business card and I'll write my address on the back.'

'And your phone number,' I prompted again.

She hesitated for a moment, her pen poised above the somewhat tatty card and then she scribbled something down and passed it over to me. Her address was Belsize Road, a place I knew well from my time in that area in the nineteen sixties. Once the haunt of students in large Victorian villas converted into a myriad of tiny pokey bedsits, it was now one of the smartest addresses in London.

She must have noticed my look of surprise, because she said, 'I don't own a property there, if that's what you're thinking. It belongs to a friend of mine and I rent a room.'

'I'll only use this if there is a real emergency,' I said firmly, tucking the card into the back pocket of my diary.

As she stood up she said, 'I'd be very grateful if when I phone you let me know exactly what is happening and if any other information has come to light.'

Did she think I would hide anything from her? 'Won't the police contact you directly?'

'Mmm,' she said non-committally, 'that's as maybe, but I do want the cause of poor Betsie's death confirmed. It's too awful to think about. You might be able to pick up local gossip in a way the police wouldn't, give me more information on what really happened.'

Now that she had enlisted my help she seemed eager to depart as quickly as possible, but as she reached the door she turned to me. 'I'd prefer to phone you, remember.'

'Yes, I understand,' I replied. You're not so interested you'd stay on to help, I thought, but I didn't say anything. Why should she concern herself with the death of this aunt, an aunt she scarcely knew, even though it was suspicious? I had the distinct impression, though Nadine didn't actually say so, that many years had elapsed since they had been in touch. If the police hadn't tracked her down she might never have known. A sudden flash of insight: this visit could only be to do with money. That was it, she was anxious to make sure she inherited Betsie's money, something that made me feel even less well disposed towards her.

She lifted her bag and shook my hand. 'Thank you so much. I can't tell you what a relief all of this is to me.'

'You can phone me at the end of the week,' I said.

'That would be fine,' she said. 'Remember, any information will be useful, no matter how trivial you think it is.'

I watched her as she walked down the path to her car. Why she should come to me only added to the puzzle and what could I find out that would be of interest to her?

Her car disappeared into the distance. I went back indoors, took the card from my diary and sat for a few moments staring at it. She seemed to be employed as some kind of manager for an organisation that dealt in importing goods from overseas, but there was little clue in the name of Wext Solutions Ltd. On the back of the card she had written her phone number. There was something odd about it but several minute of racking my brains for an answer produced no solution so I returned it to the pocket at the back of my diary. Whatever was nagging at me, I wasn't going to solve it now. With a bit of luck, Nadine would find the information she was after and forget all about me. I took the cups and the plate of almost untouched biscuits back through to the kitchen. No need to put them all back in the tin, I reasoned.

By now it was almost eleven thirty and there was a long list of jobs still to be tackled, including yet more marking. Somehow I didn't feel like doing any of them, but didn't want to waste the entire day. I decided to set out for the local shops and walk instead of taking the car in the hope it might help to blow the cobwebs away.

A surfeit of shopping later, I regretted the decision to leave the car at home. I had, as usual, bought much more than intended and strained under the weight of several large carrier bags, at least one of which looked as if it was about to give at any minute and spill its contents all over the pavement. It was with some relief I reached home and as I was struggling to find my key and open the door without putting my bags down, Deborah pulled it open.

'Hi mum,' she said, 'Can I give you a hand?'

With two of us working, it didn't take long to arrange the shopping in some semblance of order in the kitchen.

'Cup of tea?' Deborah lifted the kettle to fill it. 'Had a busy day then?'

'And how!' I hesitated for a moment, before deciding to tell her about Nadine's visit. '…and I ended up agreeing to help.'

Deborah's eyes grew wide. 'Oh, for goodness' sake, haven't you enough to do taking over the arrangements for this reunion?'

This was the problem. 'What else could I do?' I said. 'I'm sure I won't hear from her again. I'm not likely to find out any more about Betsie than the police do.'

Deborah shook her head. 'Dad will be worried. He'll say this is yet another scrape you've got yourself into.'

'Let's forget about it all. I'm sure I won't hear from her again once she realises how little help I can give her.'

'Why not ring her and tell her you've changed your mind?'

'I couldn't do that.' There was hesitation in my voice. Why not? I was under no obligation to Nadine and already doing enough to help poor Betsie by continuing the work of the reunion, bitterly regretting being so weak willed.

'I don't see why you shouldn't change your mind,' said Deborah, echoing my thoughts. 'She had a bit of a cheek asking you in the first place. From what you've said it's not as though you're even a close friend.'

In spite of Deborah's attempts to steel me, I shrank from phoning the formidable Nadine so soon and backing out of our agreement. 'Maybe.'

'Did she leave you a contact number?'

'She said only to use it in an emergency. She wants to contact me. She's very busy, apparently,' I ended lamely.

'Never mind that. Where is it?' Deborah held out her hand in a way that brooked no argument.

I ferreted in my bag, found my diary and handed her the card Nadine had left.

Deborah seized on it eagerly and then frowned. 'This is a business address.'

'Turn it over,' I said. 'The phone number is on the back. It's her London number, she lives in Belsize Road.'

'No, there's something wrong.' Deborah stared at the number, tapping the card with her thumb as though that would produce an answer.

'Give it to me.' As I took the offending card from her and looked at the number again, the realisation about what had been troubling me all along came to me in a flash. A good number of years ago, because of the pressure of the increasing number of phones on the London system, new codes had been introduced: one for outer London and one for inner London. And the code Nadine had written on the back of the card most certainly wasn't the right one for inner London. 'So what should I do? It must be some kind of mistake. She's made an error putting down the numbers.' There had to be a simple explanation.

'There's an easy way to find out,' said Deborah in her usual breezy fashion. 'Ring the number.'

'She won't be back yet,' I said, reluctant to take any action. 'She might not have been heading south today. She said something about staying in Scotland for the funeral.'

'I thought you said she lived in one of those large houses with several others? Maybe one of them can help? Anyway, if it's not the right number you'll hear one of those funny tones.' Deborah can be very persistent and there was no option but to dial the number.

As she suspected, the number wasn't a real one and instead of a ringing tone there was only that strange high pitched sound when the number is unobtainable. I put the phone down and tried again but was no more successful this time. 'Perhaps in her rush she made a mistake? That can happen.' How weak this excuse sounded.

'Well, you could try a different combination,' Deborah suggested. 'But if you're going to try all possible permutations you could be here all day. Have one more try.'

Deborah stood beside me as I re-dialled but I could see the expression on her face, looking very disapproving. Needless to say this new combination didn't work either. 'All right, I admit defeat,' I said.

'So the question is why would she give you a false number? And even stranger - why did she not give you a mobile number? If she's away on business as much as she says, that would be the simple solution.'

'I have no idea.' Deborah was right. A mobile number was what everyone used now. 'Perhaps she really doesn't want to be contacted. After all she did stress she would get in touch with me.'

'What's the point of that? I thought you said that she wanted you to pass on any information. What's this all about?'

I was as baffled as Deborah and had no answers. It was a bit too late to think of all the questions I should have asked Nadine but a bit of me wanted to defend my decision to help her.

I put the card back in my diary, suddenly thinking, 'What about this firm she works for? Perhaps it would be possible to contact her through them?'

Deborah looked doubtful. 'These days I don't think employers are willing to give out phone numbers of their employees.'

'No, I understand that. But they might be willing to pass on a message to her if I explained the circumstances.'

Deborah said, 'It's worth a try, I suppose,' but she sounded unconvinced.

This bright idea would have to wait until the morning as by now it was well after office hours, much to my relief and a way of postponing the problem. Besides, I had plenty to occupy me that evening, but in any spare moment my thoughts drifted back to Nadine. Why should she go to all the bother of contacting me, asking me to keep in touch if she then gave me useless details? None of it made sense. Besides, what did she think I'd be able to find out about Betsy's death that she wouldn't be able to?

Then I reasoned that Nadine would have been in touch with the Rothesay police and perhaps they would be able to shed some light on this episode. They wouldn't tell me much. After all, I wasn't a relative, but if I explained the circumstances they might be willing to provide some basic information.

I looked at my watch. It was late, but not too late to phone the police station. How best to frame the question? I still wanted to believe that, in her haste, Nadine had merely written down the wrong number. There was no way I'd be able to sleep if I didn't make some attempt to check and in the end decided to be absolutely honest. If the police weren't able to help, I'd phone her place of work in the morning. I dialled the Rothesay number before my courage failed me.

'Rothesay Police here. Can I help you?'

Of course rehearsing something to say and actually saying it are two quite different things, but after a couple of false starts I succeeded in explaining my reason for phoning.

There was a long pause at the other end of the phone. 'I'd like to assist you, Mrs Cameron, but I'm afraid I can't.'

'That's fine,' I said hastily, 'I realise such information may be private.'

'It's not that,' said the policeman. 'Betsie O'Connor's niece has been in today and I'm afraid her name isn't Nadine O'Connor.'

'Are you sure? Maybe she had two nieces?'

'Sorry, it's all been checked and there is only one. Whoever this Nadine is, she's not Betsie O'Connor's niece.'

EIGHTEEN

The next morning the decision was made to contact Nadine's employers and try to get to the bottom of this mystery. By the time a morning's teaching was over and I'd dismissed twenty sulky teenage girls, more interested in the latest TV programme than the novel we were reading, my first need was for a strong, very strong, cup of coffee.

It was almost eleven o'clock when I eventually found a quiet corner to use my mobile. The best place for privacy was the library, but noise there was still frowned upon by the librarian, Dougal, who fought a constant battle against the loudness of pupils and their apparent inability to do anything without munching non-stop. 'I know it's not possible to phone in the library, but could I use your office?'

His eyes behind his pebble spectacles told me he was consumed by curiosity about my need for so much privacy. Old fashioned in manners as well as dress, he was too polite to ask. 'Yes, go ahead, Mrs Cameron. I have to sort out these books.' He lifted a pile of books, one perched precariously on top of the other and started to carry them carefully over to the bookshelves on the other side of the room.

Poor Dougal - how much longer would he reign over the library in its present form? Already the IT staff were pressuring the Head at every opportunity to create space for yet more computers and he had no idea he was so close to being taken over by the machines. The last staff meeting had been particularly acrimonious, according to staffroom gossip, but Dougal wasn't the kind of person who could easily defend his corner.

His office was no more than a glass partitioned section in the corner of the large room serving as the library, an afterthought some time in the past few years. It wasn't large and his desk and chair took up most of the space, but at least it was quiet and secluded. Space is at a premium in our school, housed as it is in two old buildings and a series of prefabricated huts behind the main playground. Once upon a time we were promised a brand new school, but that seems to have dropped down the list and now with the economic state of the country it may be a very long time before we have anything new.

I dialled the number on the card and waited impatiently as a tinny voice went through a litany of options. The voice stopped. With no idea about which of the many options to choose I started again, this time selecting number one in the hope that whoever answered could put me on the right track.

'Good morning, Wext Solutions Ltd here. Can I help you?'

'I'm not sure this is the correct number,' I said hesitating, though this wasn't a good start. 'I'm trying to contact Nadine O'Connor.'

There was a pause. 'I'm sorry; she doesn't work in this department. But I'll put you through to someone who should be able to help.'

More tinny music while I hung on, hoping there was enough calling credit on my pay-as-you-go phone to last out the call.

The helper turned out to be the main switchboard and again I explained my problem.

'I'll check for you,' she said and the music started up again this time so loudly I had to hold the phone away from my ear.

A few moments later she came back on the line. 'Sorry, caller, no one of that name is listed here.'

'Are you certain? Have you tried checking just the initials?'

A hint of impatience in the voice at the other end of the telephone as she said, 'I'm very sorry; there is no one here with that name or anything like it.'

I thanked her and shut down the phone. I stood for a moment amid the clutter of Dougal's office, wondering what to do next.

At the far end of the room Dougal was speaking eagerly to two of the older school pupils, keen to encourage them to borrow books and to keep his numbers up in the fight against the IT department. All his persuasion seemed to be to no avail and he turned and came ambling over to his office. There was no way I wanted to be delayed by his tale of woe and I grabbed my handbag and was out of the office door before he reached it.

'Thank you, Dougal, that was most helpful.'

'Don't you want a cup of tea?' He looked so gloomy I hesitated for a moment, but only a moment.

'I've a class in ten minutes and I have to collect my materials.' I'd enough problems of my own without taking on Dougal's.

This at least seemed to satisfy him as an excuse. 'Perhaps later?'

'Perhaps.' I left him looking sadly after me.

There was no more time to think now about the problem of Nadine. There was only one class on my timetable before lunch, but it was a challenging one requiring all my stamina and concentration. Yet the questions about Nadine and what she was up to nagged away at the back of my mind all day. What was going on? The home phone number Nadine had given me was incorrect or, even worse, deliberately false and she certainly didn't work for Wext Solutions Ltd. If she wanted news from me about Betsie, how was I supposed to get in touch with her? If not, what was the point of it all? Who this person who had gone into the Rothesay Police station, claiming to be Betsie's niece? And if Nadine wasn't Betsie's niece, who on earth was she?

How I wished my friend Susie was still here in Scotland, teaching with me, to thrash out this problem over coffee and a doughnut in Gina's café across the road from the school. Her latest e-mail made it doubtful she would make it back for the reunion, so busy was she with her new life in America, which I suspected included a new boyfriend.

There were lots of questions, but no answers. What was worse I wasn't even sure there was anything to ask without seeming foolish. There was no option but to wait for Nadine to contact me, then ask her exactly what was going on, why she had told me so many lies.

NINETEEN

When I arrived home Deborah was waiting with news that completely distracted me from the problem of Nadine. However, if my mind hadn't been so focussed on the phone call to Wext Solutions Ltd I might have been more alert. No sooner was I in than she came rushing out of the kitchen saying, 'Like a cup of tea, mum? What kind of day have you had?'

'Sounds good,' I said going through to the living room to switch on the television and catch up on the news.

As soon as we were settled with the promised cup of tea she said, 'I think I'll be moving out, mum.'

'Oh, yes?' My first reaction was one of pleasure for Deborah: it was time she was independent again. 'Are you flat sharing with a friend?'

A guilty look crossed her face and she stared into her teacup, avoiding my gaze as she said, 'Actually I'm moving in with Sylvester.' She stopped and then rushed on defiantly, though I hadn't uttered a word, 'We get on really well together. He's not as odd as you think.'

Sipping the scalding hot liquid was a way of avoiding replying to this startling and most unexpected news. To my recollection there had been no discussion about how odd Sylvester was. Deborah was totally taken up with him, but I thought it was because she admired his success and his style.

She looked at me in silence, eager for my response, till I could bear it no longer. The words were out before I could stop myself. 'He's twice your age, Deborah (at least, I added silently)...and didn't you say he's married?'

'So?' was her reply. 'What does that matter? Nowadays it's not the same as when you were my age. Anyway,' with a dismissive flick of her wrist, 'his last wife has left him for someone else. It's not as though I'm breaking up a happy home.' She was so prickly, so defensive, there was no point in asking any more questions. She was right, of course, things were different now, but this was not what I wanted for my younger daughter.

I sighed. Here we go again, I thought. Deborah seemed to have a way of choosing the most unlikely partners. Least said and all that. Wrong again. Her next words were, 'I'm moving in at the weekend if that's okay.' Then with the ghost of a smile and an obvious attempt to forestall any objections she added, 'You and dad have put up with me for long enough. Time you had some space to yourselves.'

There was some truth in that, but I wasn't sure her parents should be used as an excuse. 'You hardly know him. You've only been working for him for a couple of months.'

The mutinous look on her face decided me there was no sense in Sylvester becoming the cause of a rift in the family. I went over and hugged her. 'It's your life, Deborah. You know we'll always be here if you need us.'

She laughed and gave me a kiss. 'Don't be silly, mum; I'm only moving into a flat in Glasgow, not disappearing to the ends of the earth.'

'I thought Sylvester lived in London?'

'Yes, but he has a flat in Glasgow as well. It gives him a base for all the travelling in Scotland.'

We drank the rest of our tea in an uneasy silence, half watching the news on television, though my mind was working overtime.

Deborah put her cup down with a clunk. 'Did you find out any more about that woman, what was her name? Nadine? Did you find out if she worked at that place?'

This change of subject was a relief, though I hadn't intended to tell Deborah about my phone call to Wext Solutions Ltd. No harm in asking her advice. I shook my head. 'I did phone them but they said no one of that name worked there.'

'How strange. Why on earth would she give you false information if she wanted you to phone her with any news?'

I corrected her. 'Uh, uh, actually she made it very clear that she would phone me and that the numbers she gave me were for an absolute emergency.'

'So she thought that such an emergency would never arise?'

'Looks like it.' I sighed. 'As if I don't have enough to do.'

'Then forget it. Sort out the reunion and once that's over, that's your duty done as far as Betsie is concerned.'

'I'm sure you're right, but I'm intrigued to find out exactly who Nadine is. Not that I can waste any time on it,' I added hastily, seeing her frown at me.

She stood up. 'Well, I had better go and start to pack,' she said.

She left the room, humming to herself. Obviously she thought moving in with Sylvester was the right thing to do and by telling me she had passed on the responsibility of informing Simon, a task I didn't relish. Stop it, I said to myself, she's grown up, not a child. There's only so much control you can have. As I pondered this the sound of the phone interrupted my thoughts. What now?

It was my mother. 'Alison, I've some news about Jessie. The letter you sent over has arrived.'

Still thinking about Deborah's news, I said absentmindedly, 'Good.' I couldn't understand why she was phoning me to tell me about the efficacy of the postal service between Britain and Canada.

My mother sounded cross. 'I have that letter from Jessie.'

'And what did she say?' I hoped that whatever Jessie had said it wouldn't be too long winded. Upstairs I could hear Deborah moving around, packing up and there were a few questions still to ask her, mostly to have an answer for Simon.

'Don't be so abrupt, Alison, this is one of my oldest friends we're talking about.'

I tried to concentrate on what my mother was saying. 'Sorry. What was Jessie's letter about?'

My mother still sounded huffy. 'I won't read it all out as you are so busy,' (with a strong stress on the busy) 'but mostly what she says is that she is being pressured to change her will in favour of the Hereuse Nursing home. If that isn't a reason for them murdering her, I don't know what is. I knew there was something odd going on. I was right and,' she continued before I could make any comment, 'she says that she wants me to make sure I get the jewellery she's left me - a Victorian pendant necklace and the Victorian Scottish brooch that belonged to her great grandmother.' There was a note of triumph in my mother's voice as she concluded. 'So, you see, I was right.'

I waited in silence for her next words, able to make a good guess at what she would suggest.

'I think you should go along to the nursing home, tackle them about all of this, tell them about the letter.'

There was only one excuse I could think of for not doing as she wanted. 'But you have the letter.'

'You can still speak to them. Much better than waiting till I come back.'

'I can't promise but,' thinking of a way out of this, 'when I'm over for the reunion I will go along to the Hereuse and talk to them.'

Fortunately at that moment Deborah came bursting into the room, carrying her laptop. 'Mum, come and see this. I had this great idea of searching for Nadine O'Connor on the internet. If she's anyone at all there would be some information about her.'

'I'll have to go,' I said. 'Promise to get back to you later,' ringing off before any more instructions could be issued.

Deborah opened her laptop. 'Sit down and we'll see what we can find out about her.'

We sat together on the sofa and I waited patiently as Deborah called up the name. There were several people with that name and we very carefully went thorough them one by one. Each had a photo but as we examined them in some detail we realised none of them bore the slightest resemblance to the Nadine O'Connor who had claimed to be Betsie's niece. Another dead end. Who was she and what did she really want?

TWENTY

After wrestling with the options for the reunion for several nights after Betsie's death and spending most of them awake, I had e-mailed everyone on the list. 'The others can make the decision,' I said to Simon. 'If they want to continue, I'll do what I can to see this through.'

The e-mails came back thick and fast. Few wanted to cancel and there were many offers of assistance, though how many would translate into action was difficult to predict. Now even the stragglers had replied and numbers were looking very healthy indeed. Simon had promised to help me as much as he could and anyway, I consoled myself, most of the arrangements were made.

'Let's book the Kames Castle lodge for the full week before the reunion as well as the week after,' Simon suggested. 'That way we can be on the spot to iron out any problems. Not that there will be any problems after all your work,' he added hastily.

It was good to have something to take up my energies. Deborah had gone, left for her new life with Sylvester. The afternoon after she went, I sat on her bed, thinking about this relationship with Sylvester. Her wardrobe door was ajar, the way she had left it, empty except for a few wire coat hangers; the room depleted of photos and her collection of shells, a left over from childhood she had never quite managed to give up. She wasn't a child anymore, she was a grown woman and entitled to do exactly as she wished, but like most mothers I was sure she was making a big mistake. This was all so sudden. One minute she was about to have an interview for the Regius Gallery, the next she was moving in with the owner. It was all too quick, too hasty and would end in grief.

Was it something about the youngest child? Maura, my older daughter, was so sensible, so settled with her long term partner Alan in London and Alastair was still the eternal student (in spite of his title of Senior Lecturer at a Canadian university). Deborah was so different. She was strong willed and determined, but not entirely sensible. Well, time would tell.

I thought about my mother's phone call and the request to go along to the Hereuse Nursing home but, remembering my last visit there, I felt my cheeks flush bright red. Jessie may have promised jewellery to my mother at one time, but if she had changed her mind - and her will - then there wasn't much we could do about it. These things happened.

I had to log on to the internet and try to sort out some of the last minute details for the reunion, now approaching fast. Several genuine offers of help had come in, but most of those would be useful during the weekend itself. 'I won't be doing this kind of thing again,' I said, when Simon asked me about progress, 'I've learned my lesson this time.'

He raised an eyebrow and went back to reading his paper, his gesture infuriating me much more than anything he could have said.

I returned to the e-mails on the computer. There were twenty new e-mails in my inbox but three of them were from firms offering goods for which I had absolutely no need and quickly deleted. I re-organised the remaining tasks, doubling up where appropriate to give the illusion of fewer than there actually were. Some of them were easy, like re-checking the number of people coming to the event, but others were more difficult including making sure the various permutations of food preferences were catered for.

That was enough for the moment. Time for a break. I re-read the list I had printed off as I waited for the kettle to boil. Where would all these tasks be fitted into my busy life? My inclination was to take my coffee through to the living room and sit down with the morning paper, still lying on the doormat in the porch.

I carried through the newspaper and my coffee knowing the pile of marking would be calling to me like some siren voice not to be resisted. Or if I did, I would bitterly regret it in the morning, facing my class of fourth years with their work uncorrected. Not for the first time, thoughts about my choice of a career as an English teacher surfaced. How much simpler would life have been had I chosen some other subject? Or even better, another job? It wasn't too late to change; you heard all the time about people who had completely altered their way of life, taken up a completely different career.

That wasn't a consideration at the moment while there were still all these essays to mark. I put my coffee on the table beside me, picked up the first exercise book and prepared myself for twenty essays on *Life in the Future*.

Almost immediately the front doorbell rang. I put my pen down and frowned, tempted to ignore it, thinking it would be some door to door salesman offering me goods to change my life.

'Are you expecting anyone?' I called to Simon. A lack of response meant he was in all likelihood upstairs listening to music through his headphones.

When the bell rang again, more insistently this time, there was no option but to answer it.

Mumbling in annoyance, I pulled the door open, about to say, 'I'm sorry I'm not at all interested,' but I stopped, totally taken aback.

There at the door stood Nadine. 'I suppose I owe you an explanation,' she said.

TWENTY ONE

Nadine smiled at me for a moment, no doubt registering my astonishment, but I could only stand and stare at her until she said gently, 'Would it be okay if I came in?'

I nodded, standing aside to let her pass and gesturing her towards the kitchen, eventually blurting out the only thing I could think of, 'Would you like some coffee?'

'That would be good.'

I busied myself taking a mug from the rack and pouring coffee as she sat watching me in silence. I was desperate to hear what she had to say, but determined to wait until we were settled and then she could do the explaining. There were too many questions, too many possibilities churning around in my brain at the moment.

She sipped the steaming cup of strong black coffee in front of her, declining milk and sugar, letting out a long sigh. 'I suppose you're looking for some explanation about what's been happening? Why I contacted you?

I sat looking at her, still silent, waiting for her to continue.

'Why I've been giving you a false story?'

'And a false phone number and address.'

She put the cup down on the table and leaned forward. 'I am involved with Betsie but not in the way I suggested.'

The silence hung between us until she spoke again. 'I scarcely know where to begin...'

'How about at the beginning?' I said. I gripped my mug of coffee tightly, beginning to feel annoyed at this theatrical display.

'It's a long story.' She hesitated, but there was no way I was going to prompt her, help her with an explanation.

100

'I'm in no rush,' I said, though in truth I had one eye on the clock, remembering that pile of exercise books waiting for me.

Nadine took a deep breath. 'Okay, here's the real story, what's been happening. I've been trying to trace my family for some time now. I was adopted at birth and only found out the truth when I applied for my first passport. My adoptive mother was a great person, but she became almost paranoid I would seek out my real mother and abandon her. You can imagine what a shock it all was.'

'I've heard that happens,' I said icily as she paused. If she thought I would jump in with expressions of sympathy she was wrong.

When there was no response from me, she went on, 'Well, I can understand why, but in my case there was no way I would have done anything like that. I appreciated all my adoptive parents had done for me and even if my mother had had a great reason, I wouldn't have left them.'

A flash of inspiration. 'Betsie was your mother?'

'Yes, that's it,' she said eagerly, 'she was my mother. I found out all I could about her without actually contacting her. There was no way I could do that until my adoptive parents were dead … and then of course you know what happened.'

'Do I?' I was becoming bewildered by this tale, if it was true. After all, she had lied once, what was to say she wasn't lying again?

She looked at me strangely. 'Well, of course you do. She was found dead on the ferry to Bute before I had any chance of contacting her, getting to know her.'

'How awful.' The words were said, but not heartfelt. I should feel sorry for Nadine, but why did I not trust her, not feel fully convinced by what she was saying? Was it the way she avoided my gaze as she spoke? But some response was needed so I said, 'So you didn't have a chance to meet up with Betsie.'

She shook her head. 'It was a dreadful shock and the problem was I had no way of finding out what really happened. My adoptive mother died - my adoptive dad died several years ago - and as I was about to contact Betsie, she was found dead on the ferry.'

'How did you find out about Betsie? Being your mother, I mean?'

She gave the ghost of a smile. 'It was all by chance, really. We were in the same business - antiques - and one day we ended up at the same conference, a big yearly event in Paris. Someone remarked on how similar we looked and that set me thinking, but I didn't want to approach her till I was sure and that took some time.'

'Why did you say you were her niece? What possible difference could it have made?'

'You know what Betsie did, don't you? What her job was?'

'Can't say that I knew the details. She travelled a lot, was something in antiques, but that's about it.' I tried to recollect anything else I might have gleaned over the years. The truth was I had been in touch with her so infrequently with little interest in what she was up to.

Then I remembered my conversation with the Rothesay police and frowned at Nadine, wondering best how to put the question without sounding insensitive. 'But I thought the relative who identified Betsie was someone else?'

Nadine stared into her now empty coffee cup. 'Yes, Anna, Anna Flint is her niece. All they needed was someone to identify the body.'

The look of amazement on my face made her hurry on. 'Don't worry; I have been to see them. That's all sorted out.'

This wasn't convincing. 'What on earth did you think I knew that demanded this secrecy? As far as I could tell, Betsie died from natural causes, brought on by her lifestyle. It wasn't till later it was discovered there was something odd about her death. Even then, how would I have any idea about what might have happened? And,' as the memory struck me, 'I suppose you've nothing to do with Wext Solutions Ltd?'

She fiddled with the top button of her jacket. 'No, I have to say it was a card I had in my bag from somewhere, but you were so insistent...' Her voice tailed off. The she looked up and said, 'I'm sorry about deceiving you. To be robbed of my mother before having the opportunity to meet her was bad enough, but to learn there was something suspicious about her death made me determined. Determined to find out what had happened. '

'Have you? If you have any ideas at all, you must go to back to the police.' This was something I didn't want involved in, not when there were still so many questions. 'Why all the cloak and dagger stuff? All that misinformation about where you lived and what you did?'

Nadine looked sheepish. 'I thought you knew more than you were telling me about Betsie's death. I was trying to find out what exactly you did know and when you denied all knowledge about a connection to her business it gave me time to find out a bit about you. That's why I thought I'd better come back and explain a little.'

'I can't imagine what you thought I would know about Betsie's antiques business? I did tell you why I was involved with her and this reunion.' Now I was angry, not only that she hadn't believed me, but that she had been spying on me, asking questions about me, suspecting me of knowing something about Betsie's death.

She appeared genuinely contrite as she held up her hands. 'I am really, really sorry, but she was my mother. I feel robbed of the opportunity to know her.'

'Now you're willing to leave it all to the police, I hope. I certainly won't be able to help you,' adding under my breath 'and even if I could, I won't.'

She stood up as though to leave, much to my relief. 'No, afraid not. You see, I feel I owe it to her to find out what happened.' She stared hard, daring me to challenge her. 'I have some ideas about what was going on in Betsie's life, what happened about the insulin, why her death wasn't an accident, but the trouble is I've no proof.'

TWENTY TWO

In the dead hours of the night strange dreams haunted me, where Mrs Bradshaw appeared, looming over me, threatening me. In the morning all that was left was the sense of unease nightmares produce. Nothing more sinister than worry about the reunion, now fast approaching. Or so I told myself.

Then there was the ongoing problem of Deborah. I had this nagging feeling moving in with Sylvester wasn't working out as planned but she wouldn't admit it. I balked from asking her, knowing she would tell me when she was ready, if indeed there was a problem. Our last conversation had been brief. 'Have you made all the arrangements for the exhibition?' I'd said brightly, trying to keep the conversation as light as possible.

'I have,' was her reply. I detected a note of bitterness in her voice.

'What does that mean?'

'Sylvester seems to have to spend a lot of time in London, which means I have to do most of the work for the exhibition on Bute.'

Aloud I said. 'He's probably involved with lots of different exhibitions. These jobs aren't easy nowadays and his clients may well be very demanding,' but this wasn't what I was thinking.

'Why are you defending him? I asked if I could go to London with him on one of these trips and he positively refused. "I need you here, Deborah," was all he said.'

'Perhaps after the exhibition on Bute is over, you'll be able to go then, be able to travel with him?' My attempts at soothing her ruffled feathers were having no effect. And why was I trying to excuse Sylvester's behaviour?

'Mmm,' was her non-committal reply before we moved on to talking about more mundane matters.

Given all these variables, it was with mixed feelings I packed for Bute. We had rented the lodge at Kames Castle for two weeks, well away from the others, an attractive option as the demands of some of the delegates became increasingly difficult.

'How should I know if the Montrose Hotel has a power shower system,' I wailed after the latest missive from Rodney, travelling from New York. 'As far as I remember he was brought up in a very poor district of Glasgow. He probably didn't see a shower till he moved to America.'

Simon grinned. 'Let's not exaggerate, Alison. Calm down and remember you're not responsible for everything. You've done a great job taking all this over.'

My husband was in good humour these days. At the moment the college had plenty of students and the right kind of students, including a number from overseas who brought in much needed extra finance. From time to time I hinted that given all seemed secure, I might consider leaving teaching, doing something different. He ignored any suggestions made about that, though I was thinking about it more and more. It wasn't that I didn't like the school or the staff or even the pupils and there were lots of things I would miss, but I was itching for a change, any change, before it was too late. That was all for another day and with a sigh I scrolled to Deborah's number. The call went to voicemail. I left a quick message.

Otherwise everything seemed to be going well. I'd phoned or e-mailed all the venues: Mount Stuart House had gone without a hitch. Used as they were to making arrangements for all kinds of events, the hosting of a reunion gala dinner presented no problem and a check at the Pavilion had re-assured me everything there was as we'd agreed.

What's more, my mother was home at last and I'd been able to leave decisions about the contents of Jessie's box to her, including the notebook, as Simon had suggested. In spite of the time spent trying to make sense of it I'd failed miserably. Now all I had to think about was the reunion. Yet I had this curious feeling it was all going too well, too smoothly.

'Thank goodness we arranged to go down some time beforehand,' said Simon as we set off. 'I couldn't cope with you fretting about it all and not being on the spot.'

We had decided to use Simon's car - a much more reliable beast than mine - and a surprisingly smooth journey down to the ferry terminal put both of us in a holiday mood.

There were few cars waiting and we went out on to the quay to watch the ferry MV Bute swing round as it came into Weymss Bay and berthed. 'Good, there won't be much of a queue in the café,' said Simon, rubbing his hands. 'I could do with a cup of coffee.'

I looked out over the water. With only a flurry of white tops to the waves, we were promised a gentle crossing. After all my hard work I felt my spirits lift and made up my mind to enjoy the weekend reunion, no matter what.

Even so, as we drove on to the ferry I shivered a little, remembering Betsie and her last ferry journey. No word as yet on what exactly had happened, nothing to tell those attending the reunion. If I had no news, that was possibly for the best.

A sudden death on the Calmac ferry was an almost unheard of event. Not surprisingly Betsie's death yet again dominated the front pages of The Buteman, the local newspaper that had served the island well for over one hundred years. I purchased a copy from the onboard café on the ferry as it headed out into the Firth of Clyde from the ferry terminal.

The attendant smiled as I handed over the money for my copy. He was a tall thin man, with a solemn expression. 'We've had to order a second batch of these this week,' he said. 'Everyone wants to read about it.'

I scanned the headlines and frowned. 'It was a heart attack as far as anyone knows?' In spite of Nadine's concerns there had been no further word about the cause of Betsie's death.

He paused in his task of frothing milk at the coffee machine and seemed to give the matter his utmost consideration. 'Mmm …most likely, though there are some who would like to read something more sinister into it.'

I glanced up sharply. 'Such as?'

He tapped his nose with his finger. 'That would be telling.' He went back to making coffee and dismissed me with a 'Next please?' There would be no further information from him.

What he had said intrigued me. How could what had happened to Betsie be anything but a simple heart attack, given her obesity and other health problems? Yet as I returned to my seat I couldn't help but wonder. Here was another, separate source of information suggesting there was something not quite right about Betsie's death. Was Nadine's story true after all?

'I'll take my coffee out on deck. Are you coming?' said Simon, breaking into my thoughts.

I elected to stay snug in the passenger lounge and sat down and stared out of the window, sipping my scalding hot drink. What on earth had the attendant meant? Was he making a wild guess? The people of Bute had a way of finding things out that baffled the rest of us and there was some gossip going about, that was for certain.

I turned to my copy of the local paper. If I expected to find some clue in The Buteman I was to be sadly disappointed. Apart from a report which was interesting enough, there was no indication there was suspicion of anything unusual. Was it all being kept secret until there was more information?

I closed the paper, put it on my lap and gazed out over the water. We were already passing the lighthouse at Toward and the ferry coming from Bute was in sight, speeding through the waters, an indication we were half way to our destination of Rothesay.

The reunion wasn't all I had to think about. My mother had phoned, reminding me about the jewellery Jessie was supposed to have left her and my promise to find out what I could. It looked as if there was no option but to go back again to the nursing home, not a task I was looking forward to, but one that had to be done.

With a start I realised we were about to arrive in Rothesay and hurried down to join Simon on the car deck, sliding into the passenger seat as he started up the engine and the front of the ferry began to move slowly down. As we drove off in a sedate line, my mind was troubled by thoughts about poor Betsie and that last journey she made. Was the Calmac attendant right and was there really something odd about her death? Or was she a warning about becoming overweight, about eating and drinking too much? But then Nadine had also voiced concerns, was convinced it hadn't been that simple, that there would be evidence found that her death wasn't natural.

Once on Bute, we made straight for Kames Castle: out through Rothesay, along the Shore Road through Ardbeg to Port Bannatyne. The castle, the oldest inhabited castle in Scotland, is now a holiday complex, composed of a Keep, the Lodge house and several holiday cottages. The single storey stone lodge, immediately inside the huge wrought iron gates, overlooks Kames Bay, a peaceful, calming scene, exactly what was needed at present.

'This will do nicely,' I said as we dumped out cases in the little hallway and went into the snug living room. The furniture was basic but comfortable and the table and chairs at the window gave a view out over the curve of Kames Bay towards the village of Port Bannatyne.

'Yes, a great place for a holiday and the golf course is no more than five minutes up the road,' Simon replied, examining the logs beside the fireplace. He turned to me, 'Do you think we need a fire?'

'Good idea,' I said, stretching out on the sofa. I was happy to agree to anything at the moment. As I rooted in my handbag for a pen, there was a message winking on my mobile. 'I'll have to go outside to check this,' I said to Simon, who was on his knees blowing into the fire he had set to make it spark into life. We were well out of practice with lighting a fire and at this time in April it was still chilly indoors.

He looked up, his face spotted with little smuts of soot. 'Can't you leave it until later?'

'It might be important, it might be Deborah.' I went outside and walked through the gates and across the road to the grassy slope overlooking the bay. In the distance a couple of yachts were making the most of the Spring weather as they sailed sedately down the Kyles of Bute. The boatyard at the end of the village was a hum of activity, even at this time of day, with sailors busy painting their boats after the long winter sleep, ready for better days.

I checked the message. It was from Deborah, thank goodness. I had had to deal with too many problems from the reunion delegates while all I wanted was a quiet few days before the event itself.

I checked the voicemail, then wished I hadn't. She sounded upset but the message itself was terse, saying no more than she would try to contact me later. Whatever was the matter, there was no way of finding out what was troubling her at the moment though that wouldn't stop me fretting. I sighed and scrolled to her number, but the call went to voicemail. There was nothing more to do, but as we settled down for the evening, all kinds of possibilities disturbed me. I agreed eagerly when Simon said, 'Why don't we go along to the pub in the village for a drink. It's a fine evening.'

From the window we could see the still waters reflecting a glow of fiery red and purple as the sun set and the moon rose high behind the hills of the Cowal shore. We put on our coats for the short walk along to the Port Inn. 'We can have a drink here and then one in the Anchor,' Simon suggested.

That is what we did, walking back to the lodge feeling mellow and at peace with the world under a sky bright with stars and a full moon hanging low above the Port Bannatyne quay, after a pleasant evening spent in the company of other visitors to Bute and a few of the locals who dropped in for a pint and a chat.

Little did I know what awaited me in the week ahead.

TWENTY THREE

I decided to go over to the Hereuse and try to sort out the business of Jessie for once and for all. There was absolutely no evidence her death had been other than natural and she had been perfectly entitled to change her will at any time, in spite of what she'd said in that letter to my mother. It was only a couple of pieces of jewellery, after all, valuable to Jessie no doubt, but of little commercial worth.

Simon was happy to squeeze in a game of golf. 'It is a holiday,' I urged him, anxious to go on my own to the nursing home. He agreed without any demur, as I knew he would.

For a moment I toyed with the idea of not going, of pretending that I had visited, but I'm not a good liar, especially not to my mother. And I was curious because there was this nagging doubt that what was in Jessie's notebook might be important after all.

The parking spaces in front of the home were almost full. This must be visiting time. Apart from several cars, much of the space was taken up by the Independent Caterers Ltd van and a bright yellow minibus. There were several people clustered round the van, but it was too far off to make out exactly what they were doing. To my surprise Jason came out of the front door, carefully balancing a large metal box. He must have spotted me standing there, but when I waved in recognition, he completely ignored me. Feeling very foolish indeed, I let my hand drop and turned back. Was I so invisible? Perhaps his temporary job at the Pavilion had ended and he was now working for Independent Caterers Limited and was a little ashamed of the change in his circumstances.

The minibus was parked immediately outside the front door and several of the residents were carefully negotiating the steps into it, while a few very infirm residents were being wheeled up the ramp at the back. I looked round but there was no sign of any of the staff, certainly not anyone I recognised: the stout man and his equally rotund companion who were helping them on board were most likely to be employees of the bus company.

I suddenly had a bright idea, if only it was possible to put it into practice without any of the Hereuse staff spotting me. Some of these residents would have known Jessie and a few minutes with them might be a way of gleaning some information without going anywhere near the dreaded Mrs Bradshaw.

I parked the car round the side of the building, ignoring the notice which said No Parking Allowed in this Area in bright red letters, edging it as near to the line of bushes as possible in the hope it wouldn't be immediately visible.

Having locked up, I strode purposefully towards the minibus, now fully laden with the elderly passengers and ready to set off.

'Excuse me,' I said to the stout man who was climbing with some difficulty into the driver's seat, 'could I have a quick word with the group?'

He paused in his attempt to wriggle himself into a comfortable driving position and eyed me suspiciously. 'Who are you?'

Fishing in my bag for something which would identify me, but not too clearly, I came up with my sports club pass, pristine through so little use and flashed it in front of him, hoping that he wouldn't examine it too closely. 'I'm making a final check on the numbers and want to make sure everyone is comfortable. It's a health and safety issue.' It was the first time my sports club pass had been of any use in many months.

'We've never had any trouble with health and safety before.' He shifted in his seat as his fellow worker came alongside.

'Trouble, Norm?'

Norm shook his head. 'Dunno, this woman says she's from Health and Safety. Do you know anything about that, Sandy?'

Sandy looked puzzled. 'Naw, never heard such a thing. Maybe someone in the home will know what's going on.' He made a move towards the front door.

I blustered and held out my hand in front of him. If they decided to consult with Mrs Bradshaw I was in big trouble.

'No problem, this will only take a few minutes. I need to make sure all the residents are happy with the arrangements for their trip. It's new health and safety regulations: we're required to do a spot check every now and then.'

There was a muttered conversation during which time I took the opportunity to climb on board. 'Promise this won't take long,' I said gaily.

Of course it wasn't as good an idea as I had thought, what with those who were hard of hearing 'Speak up a bit, dear,' and those who were uncertain about what was happening, I could see the task was going to be much more difficult than imagined.

Norm had joined his fellow worker at the side of the bus and they were moving restlessly, again pointing in the direction of the front door.

This was useless: there was no way I was going to get anything out of these elderly residents. It had been a really stupid idea.

'Thank you all,' I said in a voice loud enough for Norm and Sandy to hear. 'I'm glad everything is in order and I hope you'll have a wonderful outing.'

'We're only going as far as Rothesay, dear,' said a little white haired lady. 'We'll be back within the hour. Hardly an outing. A lot of fuss for a short trip.'

'Still, better safe than sorry,' I said.

The little white haired lady peered at me over her spectacles. 'Don't I know you?'

'I don't think so,' I replied. 'I'm very new to this job, in fact it's a completely new job,' I said as Norm came lumbering up the steps.

The little lady wagged her finger at me. 'I never forget a face. I do know you: you came to see Jessie.'

I put my fingers to my lips. 'Not so loud. Yes, I did come to see Jessie. Did you know her?' Perhaps I would learn something here after all. I looked at her closely. Of course, she had been in the resident's lounge the first time I had visited the nursing home and had spoken to me briefly.

She chuckled, an extraordinary loud chuckle for such a small person.

I went up right beside her so that she would hear even if I whispered. 'You knew Jessie well? I'm trying to find out what happened to her.'

She drew back and looked surprised. 'Why, she died of course. Didn't they tell you? It was some time ago and the funeral is well over with. How remiss of them not to let you know...'

'No, no,' I said, 'I know she died, I'm trying to find out why.'

'She was old, you know. Not as old as I am but then I come from a family of long livers. My own mother was ninety six and my uncle was....'

I tried to stop her in full flow. I didn't think there was any more information about Jessie to be gathered from her this way and now others on the bus were leaning forward, trying to listen to our conversation.

'What are you saying, dear,' said a podgy man at the back of the bus, while 'Is there a problem, Celia?' a tall bespectled man beside him asked as the murmur of voices rose.

In desperation I said, 'Could I come and visit you?' If I could speak to Celia on her own I might find out more information. Besides, out of the corner of my eye I could see Norm climbing back into the bus and the expression on his face was far from happy.

'Why that would be lovely, dear. I don't get any visitors, not since my dear sister passed on. She wasn't as healthy as the rest of us...'

I made one last effort. 'I don't know your full name.'

'Celia, Celia McInrie,' she said with a smile.

I stood back and turned as the driver and his companion came alongside me. 'Well, that all seems to be in order. I'll be on my way,' I said loudly.

For a moment of panic I thought Norm wasn't going to let me pass and then I realised it was only because he took up so much space in the narrow aisle.

As I left the bus and hurried round to my car, they both stood and watched me. Once inside I sat still for a few minutes, waiting for my heart to stop pounding. I hoped they wouldn't say anything to Mrs Bradshaw about my visit, would be too keen to take the residents in to Rothesay and back and would forget all about my intrusion. If they didn't, I might be in more trouble.

I hadn't learned much more about Jessie's death from my visit today, but Celia might prove a good contact and I would certainly visit her soon. With so much else going on, I had to wrap up this problem about Jessie.

Of course none of this helped solve the problem of Jessie's missing jewellery.

TWENTY FOUR

The opportunity to visit Celia again arose much sooner than expected. Simon and I were in the Discovery Centre, trying to sort out accommodation for some of those who had decided at the last minute to come along to the reunion.

It was good news though: at the last count over sixty people were coming to Bute for the event. Not quite the whole year group plus partners and friends, but enough to make the event viable and make me feel better. I'd had sleepless nights about the decision to continue the reunion after Betsie's death in case, when it came to it, some of them would change their minds. But no sooner had I breathed a sigh of relief, thinking all was done and dusted, when there were a couple of frantic last minute e-mails from people who had left it late.

'Was it a good decision to let people bring their partners and friends?' said Simon.

'Betsie's idea, not mine,' I replied, then felt guilty at the abruptness of my tone. Poor Betsie - this had been her dream, this idea of bringing us all together after so many years had been her ambition and extending the invitations had guaranteed a sizeable group. It was a pity she wouldn't be here to enjoy her success.

Simon patted me on the arm. 'Don't worry, it will all be fine,' he said before ambling off to look at the display boards of times past when Bute was the main holiday destination for Glaswegians and coming 'doon the watter' was an honoured tradition. In those days visitors were happy to cram into the many houses offering 'rooms' as holiday accommodation and in some, chalk marks were made on the floor to delineate the space to be occupied by different families. I didn't somehow think those coming over for

115

the reunion would be happy with such basic living quarters and we were sure the Discovery Centre could help us with accommodation, even though it was last minute.

The young man behind the counter was on the phone to one of the small hotels in Rothesay and I crossed my fingers behind my back. The Aldover would be the last hope. He'd tried everywhere else we weren't already using.

He put the phone down and turned to me, smiling. 'I'm glad to say that's the rest of your visitors accommodated. A last minute cancellation of a coach party means the Aldover has four rooms spare.'

I could have hugged him. I said, 'I'm very grateful for all the effort you've made.'

'That's my job.' He smiled again and handed me a slip of paper.

I went over to join Simon, clutching the details. 'That's it all sorted,' I said triumphantly. 'Unless we have a huge influx at the last minute everyone has somewhere decent to stay.'

'Thank goodness for that. I was beginning to worry we might have to try to squeeze them in beside us at the lodge.'

We left in silence, having resolved the last of the problems. 'Where now?' he asked as we reached the pier. Are we going back to the lodge?'

'It would be better if we checked out this hotel,' I said. 'I'm sure it's fine, but it's not one I know,' I went on hastily, 'so let's make sure.'

'If it will stop you worrying, then let's do it.'

We walked along to collect the car from the Albert Pier and headed out towards Port Bannatyne and the Aldover hotel.

The hotel was in Ardmory, a little before the Port, up a winding road at the back of the village. We came upon it suddenly as we crested the hill.

'Look, there it is.' The sign Aldover Hotel in large illuminated letters made it difficult to miss.

'I hope the people who are staying here are fit,' muttered Simon as we took in the long steep driveway leading to a large redbrick Victorian house.

'It'll be fine. We can arrange some transport.'

116

We parked alongside the main entrance. The house itself was even larger close up: a basic Victorian structure with many additions. Not all of them were successful, particularly the decidedly shaky looking wooden balcony running the length of one side of the house and facing on to the steepest part of the hill overlooking over the bay.

'I don't think I'd be sitting out here,' said Simon, peering at the precipitous drop.

'I'm sure it will be more than suitable inside…and it is only for a weekend.'

We rang the gigantic bell, well in keeping with the size of the rest of the house and heard it echoing down a corridor. It was only a minute of two before the door was opened but it seemed much longer as we stood there trying to shelter from the wind blowing across the water.

The man who eventually answered was tall and thin, very thin. 'Can I help you?' He kept the door only slightly ajar and peered round it. Not very welcoming, I thought.

I explained why we were here and he looked puzzled.

'I don't know anything about this,' he said. His grizzled hair was stretched tight across his skull and he was wearing an old, much darned grey pullover on top of shorts and carpet slippers that had seen better days.

'You must know about us,' I said, a note of panic creeping into my voice. 'We've only just come from the Discovery Centre and they assured us you could book some of our party in.' I tried to stay calm. Had we come to the wrong place?

'You must be mistaken. We have no such accommodation here. We don't take in strays.' He moved to close the door.

I waved the form we had brought from the Discovery Centre in front of him. 'But….'

Before I could finish a young woman came bustling out, wiping her hands on her apron. She took the man gently by the arm. 'Dad, you know what I've said to you about answering the door.'

With a firm hand she guided him away from us and into one of the rooms leading off the hallway, where she sat him down in an armchair and we heard the sound of the television being turned up to maximum volume.

She opened the door wide. 'Come in, please.' Her voice dropped to a whisper. 'My father doesn't always remember,' she said. 'He's been at the Hereuse Nursing home for a week to give us some respite but I think he's more wandered than ever.'

Her expression was so sad I reached out and touched her arm. 'Perhaps it would be better if we came back a bit later?'

She shook her head. 'No, no, not at all. Come through to the kitchen. My father will be fine for a while,' seeing the look of enquiry on my face. 'The television is on in there and that keeps him occupied.'

We followed her through to a large airy kitchen, the dresser stacked with old fashioned china, the warmth of a cream AGA making the place cosy. She motioned us to sit at the chairs around the scrubbed pine table. 'Tea?' She smiled. 'I am pleased we could help you out.'

'As am I,' I replied honestly.

'No, thanks,' said Simon as I said, 'Yes, please.'

She laughed as she lifted three mugs from the huge dresser which filled a complete wall. 'It's ready anyway.'

The tea was strong and hot and she produced some home made cake which I ate greedily as we chatted about the arrangements for the reunion delegates.

'That all seems very satisfactory,' I said, looking round. It seemed very welcoming and great value for money. A quick inspection of the rooms available, including the lounge and the dining room, confirmed my first impressions.

'I'm sorry about your father,' I said as she showed us out.

She shrugged. 'It's good that at least he has the Hereuse Nursing home to go to for some care. He really likes it and they have said they will take him in if he becomes much worse. He has good friends there and Celia McInrie is especially helpful. She looks after him as if she were half his age.'

'Oh, I've met her,' I said, without thinking. Then my heart quickened. Was this an opportunity to ask for more information? 'She does seem worried that there are some problems at the nursing home.'

She frowned. 'I can't think why. I've always found them excellent.'

Something in her tone made me stop, prevented me from saying any more. I had lots of questions but could see Simon trying to catch my attention, signalling me to cease this line of enquiry.

'Mena Bradshaw is a very good friend of mine,' she went on. 'I don't know what we would have done if she hadn't been willing to take dad in. It's not easy running a place like this at the moment.'

I left it at that. She wouldn't be of any help in finding out what was going on at the Hereuse and there was no way I could tell her about Jessie. I was more determined than ever to go and speak to Celia. I was certain she knew something, something which might lead me to the truth about what had happened to Jessie.

TWENTY FIVE

My visit was less useful than I had hoped. I expected too much from what Celia might be able to tell me about Jessie, my belief she might reveal terrible things were going on in the Hereuse. What's more, Simon was surely becoming suspicious about my eagerness to urge him on to the golf course at every opportunity.

He'd brought his laptop with him 'to keep in touch with college,' but the lure of the outdoors had proved too strong and it sat in the corner where he'd set it up on our arrival. 'Are you certain I can't do anything to help?' he asked as he checked his golf bag.

'Absolutely... I'll need lots of help once the reunion is underway.'

'Well, as long as you're sure...?'

'Go and enjoy yourself.' I waved him off to a sunny morning on the golf course at Port Bannatyne. I stood and watched him as he walked up the hill and disappeared into the pathway opposite known locally as the Loop before collecting the car keys from the hall table and setting off.

I was in luck. When I reached the nursing home the person on duty was someone I didn't recognise: there was no sign of Sharon nor of Mrs Bradshaw, so no need to come up with some story about why I was back yet again.

'Celia's in the residents' lounge,' said this carer, an older woman whose calmness put me at ease.

I put my head round the door and had another bit of luck: Celia was there in the corner, the newspaper drifting off her lap, her head back as she snoozed. There were only a couple of men at the far end of the room, absorbed in a game of chess.

'Hello, Celia, sorry to disturb you.'

She woke with a start. 'I wasn't sleeping you know.' She seemed to have only the vaguest recollection of meeting me on the minibus and seemed even less interested in talking about Jessie.

'And what did you say your name was, dear?' she asked me several times.

I had gone to the home, laden with the biggest bunch of flowers I could find in the shop in Montague Street in Rothesay and had armed myself with a tale about Celia being a long lost relative in case the dreaded Mrs Bradshaw would be there. I was becoming a very proficient liar, I mused. Problem was, I would have to remember what it was I had said.

In other ways it had all had gone well. Celia had been delighted with the flowers until one of the chess players, a tiny, wizened, bald headed old man had said, 'I don't think I've seen so many flowers since the last funeral we had here.' That kind of chilled the atmosphere, but I hastened improve things. 'Let's go and find a vase for these flowers,' I said and we made our way slowly to her room.

It would have been heartless to rush away because this visit was turning out to be less than informative but after half an hour exhausting all the topics I could think of, I made ready to leave. Suddenly she said, 'I've lost all my valuables, you know.'

I stopped. 'Sorry, what do you mean, Celia?' What valuables?

'I had them when I came in here, the few precious items I had left. And now I can't find them.'

She must be mistaken. Whatever else was going on here at the nursing home, if anything was, I didn't see them stealing goods from the residents. I could understand the pushy Mrs Bradshaw encouraging people to change their will, to make the Hereuse the beneficiary of whatever remaining money they might possess, but not actually stealing. That seemed too far fetched even for my vivid imagination.

'I'm not making it up,' she said regarding me as though she had read my mind.

Best to humour her, not upset her. 'What do you think is missing? Jewellery?'

'No, no, not jewellery. I had a pair of antique Chinese ceramic pots and a large Chinese vase. They were very valuable you know. My great grandfather brought them back when he worked out in the East for a time.'

'Perhaps they are in safe storage somewhere?'

'Don't be ridiculous. I loved to look at those ceramic pots with their lovely blue and white pictures of birds and flowers. I wouldn't have asked for them to be shut in a cupboard somewhere.'

In an attempt to soothe her, I muttered something about 'I hope they'll turn up.' There was nothing more to be learned here and Celia seemed to have retreated into a world of her own, her eyes fixed on some distant memory.

'I'll come back and see you soon, Celia.' Now that I had made her acquaintance, I couldn't abandon her.

As I reached the door, suddenly she said, 'I'm not making this up, you know. They disappeared not long after that woman was here, snooping around us all.'

I paused, my hand on the door handle. 'What woman?' Was this another figment of Celia's imagination? I moved back to where she was sitting.

She grabbed my sleeve. 'Do you know her? She's been here several times.'

'Who was she, Celia?'

'I'm trying to remember her name,' said Celia crossly, furrowing her brow. 'I can't recall names these days.'

She tightened her hold on my arm and her face lit up. 'I do remember what she looked like. Dark haired woman... hair dyed of course. And about the same age as you.' She peered at me closely. 'No, it definitely wasn't you... she had dark hair.'

Celia sighed and wagged her finger at me. 'She was the one who spotted them when she came snooping round all our rooms. Tried to tell me they were worthless, then when I wouldn't sell them the next thing I knew they had disappeared. Everyone tried to convince me I had made a mistake, had forgotten what I'd done with them.' She stopped for a moment as though lost in thought. 'But I'm not losing my memory entirely, however they try to convince me.'

'Are you sure? Are you certain that they were taken?' I didn't want to upset Celia any further, but memory can decline with age. Chances were she'd asked for them to be put into safe keeping after this woman had gone.

She let go my arm. 'Of course I am. I know she's the one responsible,' she said scornfully.

'Sorry, I can't help. But I will mention it to Mrs Bradshaw.' Though I had no intention of doing any such thing, becoming involved in more problems. All I wanted to do now was leave the nursing home as quickly as possible.

Celia peered at me. 'Don't you think I haven't told Mrs Bradshaw? She was no help at all. Tried to tell me I must have sold them or passed them on. Tried to convince me my memory was failing me. All nonsense.'

What should I do now? Was there any truth in this story about Celia's missing valuables? Who was this woman she claimed had visited the Hereuse?

And yet, and yet. It seemed strange that Jessie's jewellery and now Celia's possessions had gone missing. It might be no more than coincidence... or something more sinister. If it was, was it anything to do with Jessie's death?

TWENTY SIX

Tomorrow the first of the delegates would be arriving. A number of them, especially those from some distance away, had decided to make a proper holiday of it. It would be a hectic schedule as I tried to keep up with all the events and make sure everyone was well taken care of, aided at last by several volunteers.

We'd double checked the accommodation, visited the library to discuss the seating arrangements for the various talks, been out to the Ettrick Bay tearoom which was hosting a Scottish Entertainment on the Friday night to welcome everyone to the island, checked all the details for the arrival and the ceidlih with the Pavilion and made what seemed like a million phone calls.

In spite of being so busy, I had to contact Celia. I hadn't paid enough attention last time I'd visited her and had assumed her story about the antique ceramic pots and the Chinese vase going missing was the product of an ageing mind. I should have known better, because otherwise she struck me as being very sharp. Would she be willing to talk to me again? Even more of a problem - how would I get back into the Hereuse Nursing home?

Added to all this there was still no word from Deborah and I wondered if she would she turn up at the art exhibition as planned. If it was cancelled who would tell the local artists the show they had worked so hard for had been called off at short notice? I'd more than enough to occupy me, without further complications. All I could think about was getting through the weekend.

Thursday morning dawned bright and clear with the promise of a fine day ahead and at breakfast Simon said, 'Do you need any help today? If not I thought I might fit in a last round of golf before the reunion starts.'

I couldn't believe my luck. I had been working up to saying to him that I had several things to do on my own. This included a trip to the Hereuse Nursing home, but I didn't intend to specify this. It wasn't actually a lie, more an omission, convinced there was no need for a lengthy explanation about why I was going back to the home.

Trying hard to conceal my relief at his suggestion I said, 'I'll manage fine on my own.'

He looked a bit sheepish. 'If you need help, say so.'

Oops, I thought, this might backfire. 'No, no, I'm sure I'll be fine. There are plenty of people around now to help ...and the exercise will do you good.'

'It certainly will,' he grinned, 'the course at Port Bannatyne is one of the hilliest I've ever played.'

'Think about the great views of the bay. And the fresh air will set you up for what promises to be a weekend inside for most of the time.'

All the main events had been arranged indoors, a decision which looked as if it would be a mistake, given the weather forecast. There were breaks in the schedule for delegates to have time outdoors if they so wanted, free time for exploring the island. The fittest could even try the West Island Way, the first way marked long distance path on a Scottish island. It's a fairly easy walk including seashore, moorland, farmland and forest and with two almost circular linked routes at the north and south end of Bute, delegates would be able to do as much or as little as they pleased.

Simon grabbed his jacket from the hallstand as though suddenly worried I might change my mind. 'Will you drop me off and then I'll make my way back later? At least on the way back it's all downhill.'

I drove with Simon to the entrance of the Port Bannatyne golf club and looking back saw him setting off with another two golfers. Perhaps this round wasn't as spontaneous as he had led me to believe. No matter, it suited my purposes well.

The village was quiet as I drove through, dozing in the early sunshine. Soon the window boxes on the buildings would be full of summer blooms, giving the place an almost continental air, but at the moment they hosted the last of the Spring daffodils. The only place with any sign of life was the post office and general store where all the tables in the café section were full. At this time of day, it was the village meeting place, the centre of information for those who lived in the Port.

Once through Ardbeg I encountered the tour bus, sedately making its way round the island. This was one of the attractions we had booked for our group, though it was too early yet for the first tour of the day and the commentary was silent.

I stopped off in Rothesay at the little Co-op to stock up on basic supplies for while we would be eating with the delegates over the weekend, I had the feeling we might like to escape now and again.

It was almost eleven o'clock by the time I reached the Hereuse Nursing home and I sat outside the main entrance thinking about how best to approach the problem. I had no idea how much Celia knew, if indeed she knew anything. She was very old and the little she had said might be no more than a figment of her imagination. Who was to say she hadn't sold off her precious antiques herself? Or been persuaded to? Then there was the problem of Mrs Bradshaw. How involved was she in what was happening?

I finally hit on the idea of saying that Celia was a long-time friend of Jessie, something I only realised when I met her last time at the home. And I was doing my Good Samaritan bit, visiting an old lady who had few if any relatives and friends left. I could say that I had some memento of Jessie's to give her. It all sounded feeble, even to my ears, but it was the best I could come up with in the circumstances.

As with most plans, this one didn't go as intended. As I locked up the car, the front door opened and Sharon came out with someone. For a moment I thought I must be making a mistake because the person with her was Nadine. I shrank behind the bushes, crouching down, hoping they might not notice me. Fortunately they were too busy talking and I was too far away to hear any of what they were saying, but Nadine turned suddenly and shook Sharon's hand before walking down the drive towards the entrance. I stayed perfectly still while Sharon lingered on the doorstep, trying to ignore the cramp developing in my legs from the uncomfortable position I had adopted.

'Can I help you?' a voice beside me boomed and I straightened up to see Mrs Bradshaw beside me. For such a large woman she had approached very quietly or possibly I had been too engrossed in the sight of Sharon with Nadine to hear her.

I was about to bluster, make some excuse and then I thought, why shouldn't I be honest, tell her what was on my mind. 'I would like to speak to you, Mrs Bradshaw.'

She didn't look the least put out by my request, nor by my strange behaviour. 'Then we had better go into my office, rather than conduct our business out here, don't you think?'

I followed meekly behind her as she marched up to the front door, past Sharon who glared at me as I nodded to her. Did she know I had seen her with Nadine?

We walked down the long corridor in the old building, passing one of the staff, a very fresh faced young girl. She was pushing a trolley with a gigantic tea urn and a tempting array of cakes and biscuits, a confirmation of how well the residents were cared for: these cakes looked home made. And anyone less sinister than Sally with her sensible uniform and neat appearance would be hard to imagine. I was becoming less and less certain of my belief that something awful had happened to Jessie.

Mrs Bradshaw ushered me into her room and sat down behind a large mahogany desk in the most spacious and lavishly furnished office I had ever seen. There had been no attempt to divide this room and it retained the elegant proportions the architect had originally designed. It might even have been the original drawing room of the house. Walls were papered in a traditional print of full blown peony roses rampaging over a border of ivy and the furniture, if not antique, was a very good reproduction. Several vases, crammed with flowers, sat on the small tables dotted around the room, so many their perfume made the room smell cloying.

A quick glance at one of the paintings on the wall and I was sure it was by someone famous, if only I could remember the name. I tried to commit the details to memory to ask Deborah later.

Mrs Bradshaw's eyes followed mine round the room. 'Yes, they are very good reproductions,' she said as though anticipating a question. 'The quality of prints is exceptional nowadays.'

I nodded in agreement.

'Please sit down.' She motioned me to a chair.

I eased myself into the large leather chair opposite her desk. This one was a good deal lower than the one she occupied. She knew a bit about psychology, then?

Not a woman to waste words, she came straight to the point. 'I'm glad you came over because I wanted to speak with you, Mrs Cameron.' She paused and narrowed her eyes. 'I know this is difficult, but you have to understand that many elderly people become confused, especially as they recover from a serious accident like Jessie had.'

In silence I waited to hear her next words. I hadn't asked any questions, yet here she was making what sounded very like excuses. This awkward pause continued until she said abruptly, 'Whatever you heard about her or from her, you should take with a pinch of salt.'

'Indeed,' I muttered. I had no intention of repeating to Mrs Bradshaw what Jessie had said in her letter, though no doubt she was trying to find out exactly what I knew.

Anxious to make sure I understood, she added, 'Residents here receive the very best of care. We're all one big family.'

'So much so that they change their wills in favour of the Hereuse?' It was out before I could stop myself.

This silenced her, but not for long. 'We don't try to persuade them, if that's what you mean.'

'That's not what Jessie said … and then there's the matter of her jewellery.'

Mrs Bradshaw raised her eyebrows. 'What about her jewellery?'

'My mother had a letter from Jessie,' I plunged on recklessly, 'and she made it clear that she was under pressure to change her

128

will in favour of the home. What's more, she was most insistent that my mother would receive her jewellery...and that hasn't happened.'

Mrs Bradshaw was dismissive. 'Mrs Cameron, this is a very respectable nursing home but good quality care doesn't come cheap. Jessie actually asked me to have her jewellery valued as a means of raising money.'

'What happened then?'

'We did as she asked, brought in an expert, but the jewellery turned out to be worth very little indeed. She sold it, but it wasn't worth anything like she expected.'

She stood up. 'I can see you don't believe me,' she said. 'Well, give me a minute.' She went over to a large filing cabinet which stood in the corner of the room and opened the top drawer, taking a few minutes to rummage through it. Finally she pulled out a file, saying, 'Yes, here it is.'

She handed it over to me and I opened it, not knowing what to expect. Sure enough it was a receipt for 'Jewellery, the property of Jessie McAdam' and the items were all scrupulously listed with the total at the bottom. But that wasn't what I was interested in. The name of the valuer was at the top of the page and it was Betsie O' Connor.

TWENTY SEVEN

Nothing made sense any more. Mrs Bradshaw had been so convincing, at least until I saw that invoice with Betsie's name on it. Betsie must have been the woman Celia had been talking about when she told me of her disappearing antiques. Were these items really worthless? Somehow I couldn't see Betsie making a living out of conning elderly people out of their valuables. If she did, was Mrs Bradshaw an accomplice?

And why was Nadine at the Hereuse Nursing home talking to Sharon? I had so many questions and no means of finding out the answers. Mrs Bradshaw had dismissed me with a curt, 'I think you should mind your own business, Mrs Cameron,' stressing the foolishness of my ideas. If I was right, if there was something odd going on at the nursing home, I could think of no plausible excuse for returning there and passed the rest of the day discarding one theory after another. Perhaps I would never know the truth of the matter. After a night of tossing and turning, I crept out of bed shortly after five o'clock and sat staring out over the bay, trying to read my book and not succeeding.

This was the first day of the reunion and I fretted so much about re-checking the Pavilion arrangements we arrived there before the manager to find the doors still locked.

'I told you it would take no time to get here,' said Simon as we drew up in the deserted front car park.

'I'll have a look at the back entrance,' I said. 'That might be open.'

Before he could reply I hurried round the corner of the building. To my surprise the Independent Caterers Limited van was parked there, hard up beside the open doors. That was odd.

We hadn't ordered anything from them. Suddenly there was a noise and Sylvester came out, closely followed by Jason, who locked the doors behind him. I ducked down behind the wall as they went into the van and manoeuvred it out on to the main road.

As soon as they disappeared from sight, I ran round to rejoin Simon.

'Any luck?' he said.

I shook my head, still trying to make sense of what I'd seen.

'No point in waiting here then: let's walk along to that café in town. I could do with some breakfast.'

'Good idea,' I said, remembering guiltily my last words as we left the lodge, 'We have to go now, there's no time to eat.'

We were the only customers in the small café on the edge of Rothesay. It was tiny, only big enough to squeeze in five small tables and ten chairs, but that didn't matter so early in the day.

'You're up with the lark,' the waitress said as she placed steaming mugs of coffee and well buttered fresh rolls before us. 'Here on holiday?'

'Mmm,' replied Simon through a mouthful of roll.

'We're part of the team organising the reunion at the Pavilion,' I said with a smile. 'We thought it best to be there promptly.'

She laughed. 'There's time and then there's Bute time. But that explains it. I've seen you around town. You've been here before, haven't you?'

'Yes,' I replied. 'I know the island well.'

'I've heard about this reunion - old college friends, isn't it? Annie, my friend who's a cleaner at the Pavilion told me all about it. But what terrible news about Betsie. You must have known her well? What a thing to happen.' She shook her head.

I nodded, not quite sure of an appropriate response.

She went on as she laid the cutlery and the paper napkins on our table, 'This is such a quiet place, nothing like that ever happens. No one can believe it.'

'It is dreadful,' I agreed, making a start on my breakfast, unwilling to be further involved in this discussion.

'And on the last ferry to Bute.'

I didn't see what difference that made to anything. Maybe it had some significance for her or having a chat was a way of passing the time at this quiet hour of the morning.

Simon had opened up his paper and was studying it intently. He appeared to be reading the same article several times as a way of avoiding this conversation.

But then, as she turned away she said something which made me choke on my coffee and he leapt to his feet, patting me on the back. 'Are you all right?'

'Fine,' I spluttered, though I was far from fine.

The waitress looked very concerned. 'Can I get you a drink of water?'

I gestured her away and swallowed some more coffee. 'Sorry, but I didn't quite catch what you said?'

She looked puzzled for a moment, and then realisation dawned. 'Oh, you mean about Betsie? Yes, I knew her very well, went to school with her. We were good friends for a while. Of course she left the island to work in her father's antique business. Her mother was from here. They divorced, I recall and that's why Betsie was brought up on Bute. I remember...'

I could see this conversation was drifting away from the original point. 'Yes, but what was it you said about her, about some threats?'

For a moment she looked worried as though regretting having said anything about Betsie, out of some sense of loyalty perhaps.

'So you said....' I prompted her.

She gave a long deep sigh. 'I shouldn't have mentioned it, it sort of slipped out.'

I couldn't let her comment pass. 'I'm sure it won't do any harm to tell me. I am involved. Because of Betsie's death, I was left with all the work of organising the reunion.' I added hastily, 'Not that I mind, considering what a terrible thing it was that happened to her.'

She screwed up her face as though trying to come to a decision about what she should say next.

'What harm can it do her now? Most people on the island know anyway, though it doesn't seem to have helped the police move any further forward.'

She glanced over her shoulder to the main part of the shop where another assistant was busy setting up the display of freshly baked goods and then sat down abruptly, close beside me. Out of the corner of my eye I could see that Simon, in spite of his earlier disinterest, was now very intrigued indeed.

'It was the threats, you know. They'd been coming for some time, but she refused to take them seriously.'

The astonishment must have showed on my face because she put her finger to her lips in case I spoke too loudly.

Recovered I said, 'Who on earth would want to make death threats against Betsie?' This was Bute, for goodness sake, not some Mafia run domain.

She shook her head. 'That was the whole point. It all seemed so strange and she wouldn't say why she was being targeted, at least not in so many words. When she told me about it I tried to insist she go to the police. She wouldn't. The last thing she said to me, last time I saw her, was 'I'm sure I've sorted it all out - those threats. I told them what I would do if they didn't stop.' But I have no way of knowing if that was the reason she was killed.'

'Did she give you any indication for the reason behind these threats?'

She shrugged. 'Not really, though I'm sure it was something to do with her antiques business, someone she was involved with.'

She stood up abruptly. 'I need to go. I've said more than I should. If you knew Betsie well, you might be able as an outsider to find out more about what really happened to her.'

I opened my mouth to ask her another question, but she disappeared into the room at the back of the cafe.

I looked over at Simon who was regarding me carefully through narrowed eyes. I knew that look well. It meant 'Don't get involved, Alison.' But how could I not? I was already. Suddenly several bits of information came together. Betsie was in the antiques market, Jessie's jewellery was nowhere to be found and Celia was convinced her precious goods were missing. And she had told me about the 'strange woman' who had visited the Hereuse. What had Betsie been up to? And what did any of this have to do with the reunion?

TWENTY EIGHT

The Pavilion was a hive of activity. The two young women we had recruited locally to look after the front desk were busy checking everyone in, but could hardly cope with the throng of people around the table.

The chatter rose to a deafening level as long lost acquaintances greeted each other. Some shook hands in time honoured tradition; others attempted a more modern approach, kissing on the cheek. However, in that Scottish way, many didn't get it quite right and ended up either missing altogether or getting the number of kisses wrong. I deftly avoided the queue, if it could be called that and made my way upstairs to have a look at the re-organised café. This was where we would have our coffee and our lunch and I was looking forward to seeing the reactions as the delegates came in and saw the view from the window. Soon everyone would be checked in, issued with the correct name badge and a pack detailing all the activities and the weekend would at last be under way.

I had been in the main hall for most of the early morning, checking that everything was set up for the first speaker. We now had a sizeable number of delegates, enough to make the hall the right choice. 'The sound level isn't quite right,' I called to Dave, our sound engineer, who was perched high above the stage in what looked like a very precarious box. Though I had been assured that it was perfectly safe, I hoped there would be no nasty accidents.

Dave stuck his head out. 'Nearly there, Alison. .'

The Pavilion was looking at its best. The Art Deco furnishings were sparkling, massive pots of exotic ferns were arranged in the foyer and on the stairways, the wooden floor of the main room was polished and gleaming, the chairs for the welcome event set out in perfectly symmetrical rows.

'That better, Alison?' Dave poked his head out again as the strains of some soothing music floated across the room.

I gave him the thumbs up. 'That's fine if you can keep it at that level,' I called. I glanced at my watch. Half an hour before we began. Time enough to grab a cup of coffee, though I doubted that the butterflies in my stomach would let me drink much of it.

I had spotted Sylvester earlier, setting up the exhibition in the entrance and the main foyer, but there was no sign of Deborah. I nodded to him, unwilling to engage him in conversation, preferring to wait to talk with my daughter, find out from her what was going on.

In the small downstairs room where delegates were collecting their packs of information, the level of noise was deafening as people competed to catch up on the years. As I stood helping identify the name badges, a tall woman, elegantly slender, grabbed me by the arm. 'Alison, how good to see you.'

I smiled at her, desperately trying to place her as I did so, but she laughed. 'Don't you remember me?'

I was about to lie, 'Of course I do,' but as I took in her bright red hair piled high, secured with a chiffon animal print scarf and her carefully made up face, I realised that would be stupid. I had no idea at all who she was. I had already made several mistakes and in spite of running through the list of delegates in my head her name didn't spring to mind. 'Sorry,' I said. 'There are so many people here today. You know how it is with colleagues you haven't seen in a long time.' My garbled reply didn't appear to disturb her in the least.

She didn't take offence, but merely said, 'I'm Hilary, Hilary Roupton.'

We went back out into the foyer and I dredged my memory again. The only Hilary I could remember had been very large and had long bleached blonde hair, the class hippy, long after most hippies had vanished from the scene. She had delighted in wearing the most outlandish collection of tops and leggings, overdressed in long flowing skirts and always poking her nose into everyone else's business. Perhaps the dress style she had affected then had made her look enormous. Or did I have the wrong person? She looked much younger than the rest of us.

She could stand my discomfort no longer. 'I'm not surprised you don't remember me. I looked a lot different back then, when we first knew each other.'

So I was right. It was her, but my goodness how she had changed. 'Of course I remember.'

The bell sounded for the delegates to take their seats and I breathed a sigh of relief, hastily turned into a cough, worried about offending her. 'Sorry, Hilary, I have to dash. I'll catch up with you later.'

She grabbed my arm and tried to stop me as we started to walk upstairs. 'Alison, there's something I have to talk to you about. It's really important and I don't know what to do.'

'Hello, Mrs Cameron.' Sylvester was right behind me, wrestling with a large painting. 'Is the conference going well?' He nodded politely to Hilary but she turned away, ignoring him. There was no sign of Deborah and I thought it better not to ask.

'We haven't started yet,' I replied rather frostily and moved off.

Hilary wasn't so easily shaken off. She grabbed my arm again. 'I absolutely must see you alone, Alison. It's about Betsie…and other things,' she added.

'Shh, not so loud,' I said, looking round, but the other delegates were moving upstairs, chatting and laughing, and Sylvester was busy admiring his montage of paintings.

'We can catch up later, once we've had dinner perhaps?'

'Good idea. Maybe over a drink? It really is very important.'

As I walked upstairs to the main hall, I dredged my memory furiously for what I remembered about Hilary. Not a lot, apart from her appearance, now so changed it was no wonder I hadn't recognised her and I didn't relish the prospect of a drink with her. There's nothing more difficult than an evening spent with someone you can scarcely remember, trying to recollect anything from the past we might have in common.

Dinner was scheduled for seven and then we were heading to the Ettrick Bay tearoom for the Scottish Entertainment so by the time all that was over with I could plead a headache and go to bed, avoiding those who would be happy to sit up chatting and drinking until the early hours of the morning.

I couldn't imagine what it was Hilary wanted to talk about that was so important, but that was a problem for later. I was in no mood to reminisce about Betsie. At the moment my concern was our first speaker, hoping his talk would go well and ensure the weekend was off to a good start.

My fears were groundless. Alfie was first-rate, making the theme of his talk 'Memories and how we deal with them' hugely entertaining. He had lots of stories and anecdotes from his time as an adviser of studies at a university in England and the audience was in a very good mood, laughing uproariously at his jokes.

All seemed to be going well. Dave had managed to get the pitch exactly right and Alfie could be heard perfectly at the back of the hall where I was standing, far too nervous to sit down.

'Happy, Alison?' Dave had come up beside me.

'Relieved more like,' I replied. 'Thanks for all your help.'

It was an excellent beginning to the day: old acquaintances renewed, new people met and the prospect of an action packed weekend away from the hustle and bustle of everyday life was enough to make most of the delegates happy. Now I had to admit Betsie had been right to choose Bute as the venue for this event. In spite of all my earlier misgivings I felt relaxed; convinced the weekend would go well. Already I could see from the window the local van from the Electric Bakery drawing up with the mid session goodies, fresh from the oven, as the aroma of freshly brewed coffee wafted into the hall. Thank goodness the manager had persuaded me the regular coffee machine would be most unsuitable for such a large number of people.

Alfie had finished his talk and was taking questions from the audience. A couple of people had been primed to start and avoid the possibility of an awful silence when the request for 'any questions' went out. I needn't have worried: they came thick and fast, so much so it looked as if we were going to over run and miss coffee.

But Jackie, one of the volunteers, who was skilfully chairing the first session, said, 'Thanks, everyone, I'm sure we're all ready for a break.' After an enthusiastic thank you, the audience filed out, chatting amiably and headed towards the café.

While the next speaker started her talk, I took the opportunity to slip out and phone my contact at Mount Stuart. The gala dinner was to be held there on Saturday evening, starting with cocktails in the magnificent marble hall. Though I had checked everything a number of times there was no harm in making absolutely sure. I was beginning to look forward to these events at last. Surely the fact that this first one had gone so well was a good omen?

The voice on the other end of the phone sounded more than a little amused. 'We have had a lot of experience of this kind of event,' he said. 'I can assure you everything is in order and we look forward to seeing you all.'

'Need any help, Alison?' I turned to find Simon at my elbow.

'I thought you were going over to look at St Blane's?' I said.

He grinned. 'Thought I'd stay for a while in case you might need some moral support.'

'Everything is going very well, thank goodness, although I might call on you later,' I said but he made no reply, merely kissed me on the top of my head. There was a surge of applause from upstairs. 'I'll need to go, that's the last speaker finished.'

'I'm off to have a look at St Blane's now,' he said. 'I'll come back in a couple of hours, in case there's anything you need me to do.'

'I'm sure everything will be fine,' I replied, then thought better of it. 'Though if you do have time, it would be good if you were here for any emergencies.'

He laughed. 'Of course, I'll see you later.'

The lunch was more than successful: people mingled, chatted and said how good the food was as they lingered over a buffet meal of produce from the island: homemade soup, sandwiches and locally made pastries. It was all going a bit too well, I thought. And I was right.

TWENTY NINE

Hilary cornered me again at the end of the afternoon. 'Don't forget I wanted to have a chat with you later.' It wasn't so much a request as a command.

'Of course, of course,' I said glibly, 'but I am rather busy at the moment.'

'But you'll be around later,' she said firmly. 'This is important, Alison.'

This was the Hilary I remembered. All the cosmetic surgery in the world, and she'd certainly had some, couldn't disguise her bossy nature. I couldn't possibly imagine what would be so important that she would have to talk to me urgently. She was as nosey as ever no doubt, wanting to find out what I could tell her about Betsie, unaware that the answer was very little and there had been no more news about Betsie's death. I put it to the back of my mind. I'd have to find some time for her but not now, at the start of the weekend, when all my efforts had to be concentrated on making sure this good start continued.

We had reached the final session of the afternoon. 'The panel of speakers is assembling in the hall for the question and answer forum,' I said to her, moving to shepherd the stragglers upstairs. 'We'll have plenty of time to chat later.'

Johnnie Slater, poised on the last step, turned to look at me. 'You'd never guess you'd spent so many years as a teacher, Alison. You have that air, but then you always did have.'

'That's as maybe,' I said. Strange to think Johnnie, who had been the class pin up we had all swooned over, was now paunchy, his grey hair grown long in a futile attempt to disguise the fact he was going bald. Trouble was, he didn't realise his lothario days were behind him and still behaved as if he was the gorgeous hunk of many years ago.

He winked at me and touched me lightly on the arm, ignoring the fact that I shrank back as he moved closer. 'Still the same old Alison. Maybe we could have a drink together later, for old times' sake?' He grinned, displaying a wealth of gold fillings.

'I don't think so,' I replied, then remembering my role as hostess for this event I added, 'I still have a lot of bits and pieces to check and I don't think there will be much time to relax and socialise just yet.'

'Still as disorganised as ever, then,' he said and hurried up to the main hall, leaving me staring furiously after him before I could think of a suitably cutting reply.

Apart from that the day had gone well and I allowed myself a quiet glow of satisfaction as several people came up at the end and thanked me for my efforts. Unfortunately, Hilary appeared yet again. 'Remember we have to talk, Alison,' she said. 'I'm not sure it will wait till later.' There was a peremptory tone in her voice that irked me and made me more determined than ever to ignore her for as long as possible.

I disguised this, smiling in what hopefully was an encouraging way. 'I'm so sorry but I'm afraid it will have to keep for a bit longer.' I still had the evening's entertainment at Ettrick Bay to look forward to but when that was over my aim was to return to the lodge and fall into bed, unlikely as that was to happen: the delegates were out to make the most of this weekend and enjoy every minute. The prospect of sitting up till the early hours talking to Hilary held no appeal.

And now I realised with a shock that it was all about one upmanship really. These were people I hadn't seen for many years, hadn't missed in all that time. Why should I suddenly be so interested in what they had done and what they were doing? Some of them I had as little interest in now as I'd had when we were all at college together. No doubt they felt the same way about me. Think positively, I told myself. I had made a commitment to this weekend and was going to do my best to enjoy it. A voice at my elbow broke in on my thoughts. 'Not having a cup of tea, Alison?'

140

I turned to find Johnnie beside me, waving a large cream cake. 'These are absolutely delicious. You should try one.' He chuckled. 'I will say the catering has been first class. I'm glad it's only a weekend. Any longer and I'd be losing my svelte figure.'

I smiled weakly. 'I'll wait till later' and edged away.

He wandered off to speak to the little crowd gathered at the door, but as he went past the table I saw him sneak a second cake. Well, at least something was meeting with his approval.

But enough standing around because there was still work to do, including making sure everyone knew exactly what the arrangements were for the evening. As soon as all the delegates were back in the hall I went up on to the platform. I had to bang hard on the table before the noise subsided, but at least teaching gives you plenty of practice in projecting your voice well. 'Any queries, please ask immediately, before you leave.'

I waited after finishing my instructions, but although there were a few mutterings, there were no questions. Everyone began to move very slowly out of the hall, the volume of noise rising again as they did so.

As I made my way out of the Pavilion, chatting idly to some of the group, I caught sight of Sylvester in the shadows of the far corner, half hidden by the greenery and arguing fiercely with someone who was obscured by the shadows. I tried to make out who it was, thinking it might be Deborah.

'I'll join you in a minute,' I said and detached myself from the group. I went back inside and lingered in the foyer, appearing to scrutinise the paintings now adorning the walls, but all the while edging as close as possible without being seen. The voices were low, but the anger in them wasn't difficult to pick up.

The person in the shadows moved forward a little and I flattened myself against the wall, but not before I had a glimpse of his face. It wasn't Deborah there, talking to Sylvester. It was Jason … and he was very angry indeed.

THIRTY

The weekend was disappearing in a whirl of activity and before I knew it, it was time for the gala dinner.

My intention was to arrive at Mount Stuart well before the rest of the group so I hurried back from the last talk at the library to change into something suitable. I had packed several outfits, but this had been a mistake because now there was the decision about which one to wear.

'Put on any one of them,' Simon said as I changed for the umpteenth time. 'They're all fine.'

'You don't understand,' I replied struggling into my blue chiffon suit again.

'No, you're quite right. I most certainly don't,' he said.

'Trouble is I hadn't realised the style would be quite so glamorous: even for the daytime events most of the women are wearing stunning outfits. I can't turn up in jeans and a jumper.'

Simon looked puzzled. 'I don't see what difference it makes.'

'At any event I've been to lately everyone dresses very casually,' I replied. 'I suppose it's a generational thing.'

I was in a good mood. The entertainment at the Ettrick Bay café the previous night had been a great success, mostly provided by local singers and fiddle players as well as a 'reciter of verses' who had us laughing loudly. The talks at the library were well attended in spite of the many other attractions of Bute on what was turning out to be the hottest weekend of the year so far.

Eventually I settled on a long dark green dress which was the most glamorous of my outfits, bought years before for a New Year's dinner dance. Trouble was I hadn't tried it on since and it was somewhat neat. I convinced myself it would be fine if I held my breath and didn't eat too much. Anyway, it was too late to change my mind again now.

Simon was standing at the door, tapping his foot. 'Come on, Alison, I thought you wanted to be there well ahead of the others?'

One last look round the disarray in the bedroom and we were off. Any tidying up would have to wait till later.

With a clear road we passed through the village and along the main road through Rothesay. We headed out past Craigmore and up the Mount Stuart Road past the toy town village of Kerrycroy, snugly set round the little bay, arriving at the main entrance to the Mount Stuart estate by six o' clock, well before the rest of our group. We drove slowly up through the extensive grounds, resplendent with ancient conifer trees, palm trees and crowds of rhododendrons, a riot of purple and pink thanks to the exceptionally mild climate of Bute, all the while carefully avoiding the many squirrels that scampered into our path and finally catching a glimpse of the waters through the trees as we reached the front of the house.

We crunched to a stop on the gravel drive at the magnificent portico that was the entrance to this red sandstone mansion built in grand Gothic style, a replacement constructed by the third Marquess of Bute when the original house burned down.

This is a more than fitting setting for a gala dinner, I thought as we went up the steps into the house and through to the marble hall where the pre-dinner drinks were to be served. In the hall I stood for a moment, gazing up at the stunning vaulted ceiling adorned with themes from astrology and astronomy, resplendent with the all the stars of the night sky. The evening sun streamed in through the zodiac stained glass windows and beyond the hall, through the open entrance to the white marble chapel, we could see the sunset turning the marble rose red.

'What a brilliant choice of venue,' whispered Madge, coming up close beside me. As one of the volunteer helpers, she took her duties seriously.

'Betsie's choice, not mine,' I had to admit.

Everything was in order, the drinks set out on the large table at the end of the room, the Mount Stuart staff hovering discreetly in the background, leaving me plenty of time to check my appearance again before the rest of our group arrived.

Simon wasn't happy when I suggested 'popping out for a few minutes.' 'For goodness' sake, you look absolutely fine. I hope you won't leave me to greet these people.'

But I was back at his side well before the first arrivals, headed up by Johnnie who was now sporting a purple velvet suit which would have looked stylish sometime back when we were at college. Now it looked not only out of place, but far too tight. Of course he though it looked fine and greeted me with a flourish, obviously having forgotten about our spat earlier. Or perhaps he was so impressed by the surroundings that he didn't dare make a comment that might upset me.

The hour before dinner passed so quickly there was no time to talk to more than a few people in a couple of the groups. Several cocktails later and everyone was in fine humour, the sound of laughter echoing round the marble hall. Buses had been arranged for the end of the night, so there were no worries about drinking and driving, though a few of the more sedate members of our group had elected to come by car.

As we began to wander down towards the room where the dinner would be held, Johnnie grabbed me by the arm. 'Have you seen Hilary? I don't think she's arrived yet.'

'Bother. Was she not on one of the buses?'

'No, she decided to drive.' He sniffed. 'Perhaps it was beneath her to journey with us all on a bus.'

I detected a whiff of envy for Hilary's very ostentatious and much talked about (by her) new car. 'This is so like Hilary to want to make a grand entrance.'

'Well, we can't hold up dinner for her.' The groups were now splitting up and being shepherded in ones and twos out of the marble hall and along through the ante room to the dining room. I shrugged. 'I daresay she'll be along soon.'

The chatter died away as we looked about us at this room where squirrels and birds nestled in the foliage of the elaborately carved panelling, the sheen reflected in the light from the chandeliers and the candelabra. A large fireplace took up space at either end of the room, blazing brightly against the evening chill.

'If you would like to be seated,' one of the staff said and as though the spell was broken, we all made for our named places, chattering again.

I was more than a bit cross about Hilary's late appearance. When you have a group like this, it only takes one out of step to make life difficult for everyone. Well, she had missed cocktails and if she didn't make an appearance soon, she would miss most of dinner.

As the minutes ticked by and there was still no sign of her, I became more than a little restless. 'Excuse me,' I hissed to Simon who was sitting beside me. 'I'll have to phone Hilary's hotel. Perhaps she's ill.'

He was about to query my decision but seeing the look on my face, 'Don't worry, I'll hold the fort,' he replied and turned gamely to talk to the slightly deaf woman sitting on his other side.

I went out as quietly as possible, lifting the chair into place so that I wouldn't draw attention to my departure from the room. I particularly didn't want Johnnie to notice in case he rushed over with an offer of help.

Outside I went round to the side of the building to avoid the attentions of any of the diners who might be sneaking out for a sly cigarette, though the excellent starter of langoustines from the bay they were currently enjoying would keep all but the most determined smokers in the dining room. I walked to the far end of the car park and switched on my mobile phone, scrolling down to find the number of Hilary's hotel.

'Firthside Hotel here. Can I help?'

I explained the reason for my call. The voice at the other end sounded puzzled. 'Ms Roupton left here about five thirty,' he said.

'Are you sure?' It took no time to go from the hotel at Ascog to Mount Stuart. Why would Hilary leave so early?

'Absolutely. I even made a comment about how nice she looked, all dressed in her finery for the gala dinner.'

'Perhaps she was intending to call in somewhere on her way to the dinner?'

The hotel manager paused before replying. 'No, she didn't mention going anywhere else. She said it was one of the good things about Bute, that everything here was so close, it took so little time to get from one place to another.'

Even if she had driven really slowly, even if there had been a farm tractor on the road in front of her to delay her progress, or she had decided to take a detour (though I couldn't think why she should) it was no more than fifteen minutes from Hilary's hotel to Mount Stuart. I hung up, more concerned than ever, thinking about what she had said to me, the urgency of wanting to talk to me and the ease with which I had dismissed her request. I shivered. Where was Hilary? What on earth had happened to her?

Suddenly I had a very bad feeling.

THIRTY ONE

There was a choice, but not much of a choice: either stay at the dinner and worry about Hilary or go over to her hotel and try to find out what had happened to her.

'Surely there must be some mistake? Or has Hilary decided she didn't want to attend the dinner?' I asked Simon on arriving back, breathless and perplexed in the dining room where the main course of Bute lamb was meeting with wholehearted approval.

He shrugged as if to say, 'How should I know?'

'What if she's ill or has had an accident on the way to Mount Stuart?' Unlikely as that seemed, I had to check it out. A sudden change of heart about coming to the dinner didn't seem a likely reason, given the way she had been chatting to so many of the others over the past couple of days.

I ate my dessert slowly, scarcely tasting the almond cheesecake, usually one of my favourites and only giving the barest responses to Sylvia who was sitting on my other side. Fortunately she was sitting next to Johnnie and they seemed to be getting on famously.

We had an after dinner speaker, one of our former classmates who had made a good career as a comedian on the club circuit, in spite of, or perhaps because of, his decision to abandon teaching as a career. 'I don't think I can sit through this, responding in all the right places, while my mind is still on Hilary,' I muttered to Simon.

He was busy scraping the last of the chocolate mousse from his plate and appeared not to hear me. I nudged him.

'Can you cover for me once I've introduced Henry?'

'Why, where are you going now?'

'I have to get out of here for a while,' I said. 'You haven't been listening to me.'

Now he looked alarmed. 'Are you feeling ill?'

'Nothing like that. There's something I have to do: to check up on Hilary. I'm really worried.' I saw the look of alarm on his face. 'I promise it won't take long.'

'If you must,' he muttered, but I could tell he was unhappy at my temporary abandonment of him yet again. 'What will I say if anyone asks?'

'You'll think of something,' I said, not waiting for his reply.

I steeled myself. As soon as I had introduced Henry to thunderous applause, partly because of his reputation, partly because of the large quantity of wine the diners had consumed on top of several cocktails, I slipped out.

I had an hour. Henry was booked to speak for forty five minutes but once he started he was difficult to stop. At least that's what I was hoping.

He stood up as I crept out of the room, 'Never thought I'd be speaking to so many old folk,' was his opening remark. Mmm, perhaps he wasn't going to go down as well as anticipated. However as I scurried down towards the front door the sound of loud laughter followed me. Thank goodness: he had them entertained after all.

As I reached the car park I saw to my dismay my car was well and truly wedged in by a large Land Rover on one side and a minibus on the other. What to do? I couldn't go back into the building to find the owners. I walked round, trying to size up the space and eventually decided to take a risk by executing a hundred point turn, managing, more by luck than judgment, to squeeze out without a bump. At least I hoped it was without a bump. There was a slight grinding noise at the very last manoeuvre. No point in investigating - there was no time.

I reached Hilary's hotel in twenty minutes, delayed by my desire to keep a watchful eye out for anything that looked like an accident but there was no sign of trouble on the road. There were no other cars on the way down to the Firthview Hotel, so deserted was the area at this time of night.

I drove up the steep incline leading to the front door of the hotel and manoeuvred into one of the parking bays: there were only another two cars, but even so, given my recent experience at Mount Stuart, it seemed best to park well away from both of them.

The person on the desk wasn't the one I had spoken to on the phone and I had to explain about Hilary all over again.

'I'm sure she left,' she kept saying as I tried to convince her there was a problem. 'Her key is on the rack.' She turned to the board and pulled down a large brass key, waving it in front of me to make sure I understood.

I had a sudden brainwave. 'Do you know the registration number of her car?'

'I'm not sure we're allowed to give out that information,' she said.

'Oh, for goodness sake.' Now I was beginning to lose patience. There was no time for all this bureaucracy. I had to find out what had happened to Hilary and return to the dinner before Henry finished entertaining the party.

At that moment, greatly to my relief, the manager appeared. 'Are you the lady I spoke to earlier?' he said. 'Concerned about Hilary Roupton?'

'Yes, yes,' I responded eagerly. 'If you could just let me know the registration of her car.' To add emphasis to my request I said, 'I'm very concerned something might have happened to her.'

'I think in the circumstances that would be in order,' he replied, dragging out the register from under the counter and scanning through it. He wrote the number on a piece of paper. 'Let us know if there is anything else we can do.'

I left my mobile number with him with strict instructions that if he heard anything or if Hilary appeared back at the hotel he had to give me a call.

As I expected, a quick check of the vehicles outside the hotel showed neither number plate matched Hilary's so she had most certainly left the hotel. But where had she gone after that?

I drove as fast as I could back to the dinner, hoping no one would catch up with me for breaking the speed limit and screeched to a halt in the car park at Mount Stuart to begin my

149

task of examining all the cars. At best guess there were no more than ten minutes left before I'd have to rejoin the others and there were an awful lot of cars. Apart from our party there were several other groups of people here, including a full house at the separate restaurant at the Visitor's Centre. How on earth would I manage to check them all in the time?

Luck was on my side. As I reached the second line of cars, there was Hilary's car, sandwiched at the end between a large Volvo and an even larger Audi, so well hidden by the much larger cars I all but missed it. A double check of the number: there was no doubt it was her car.

I peered inside but there was no sign of anyone. Strangely, the car was unlocked and a close inspection of the inside came up with nothing, not even keys in the ignition. I went round to the boot and very gingerly opened it, not sure what to expect, wishing Simon was with me. But the boot was as empty as the rest of the car, apart from a first aid kit and a few magazines. So Hilary had come to Mount Stuart, intending to be with us at the gala dinner. What had happened to make her change her mind? Why had she not joined us?

I remembered how anxious she had been to speak with me and how dismissive of her request I'd been. Had I made a terrible mistake by not listening to her? Was she upset... or cross?

Or was something more sinister going on? With a feeling of horror I wondered if someone had made sure she wouldn't be able to tell me whatever it was she was so anxious about?

THIRTY TWO

As usual the person I turned to for advice was Simon. Not that he was in any mood to help as I started to tell him what had happened, sliding in beside him at the table.

'Where on earth have you been?' he hissed. 'Henry finished ten minutes ago and everyone wondered where you were.'

'But Henry always talks for longer than he's asked to. The problem is getting him to stop.' I was astonished to have so misjudged him.

'Well, not on this occasion, Alison. What's more, I suspect he had downed more than a few glasses of wine before he stood up to speak.'

As he saw the look of horror on my face he added in an effort to make me feel better, 'Fortunately everyone else has also had a few glasses so it wasn't as noticeable as it might have been. And no, don't worry; Johnnie did the vote of thanks.'

That was a relief, but I wished it had been anyone other than Johnnie who had filled in for me. That would give him something else to crow about when we next talked. But that was for later. For the moment there was still the problem of Hilary and why she hadn't turned up. 'Has Hilary made an appearance?' I scanned the room, earnestly hoping I would see her familiar face, perhaps at the end of one of the tables where she had sidled in late.

'Nooo,' said Simon, also looking round as if she might suddenly materialise, though the likelihood of his recognising her was small as he'd only met her once.

'Then we have a problem, a real problem.' I tried keeping my voice as low as possible so that no one else would hear. Not that I need have worried: the noise level in the room drowned out

151

everything else. Simon was having great deal of difficulty making sense of my story. I looked at my watch. Almost midnight. We had to wind up the evening and dispatch everyone to their respective hotels, though I guessed some of them would decide to go into Rothesay to prolong the festivities.

Sylvia came bustling over to our table saying, 'We're supposed to be out of here by midnight, Alison. Do you think we should start to think about breaking up the party and continuing it elsewhere?'

'How should I know?' I said sharply, though those had been exactly my thoughts. Then I added, 'Sorry, Sylvia, I'm a bit fraught,' as I saw the startled look on her face. It was evident few people had missed Hilary.

Sylvia was right. It was time to move everyone out of here. We had another long day ahead of us: after a free morning, there was an afternoon on the tour bus and a ceidlih in the evening. The problem of Hilary would have to wait till I could discuss it properly with Simon and decide what to do next. I spotted Johnnie advancing towards me and started to call out, 'This way everyone: the buses are waiting.' Not that I'd checked, but was sure they would be on time.

I dodged round the back of one group as Johnnie neared me but too late as he said, 'Alison, where on earth did you get to?'

I pretended not to hear him and continued with my role of shepherding everyone out of the room and towards the main entrance.

Clearing the room took a long time. Everyone was in a very merry mood and no one was inclined to rush, preferring to dally with friends, to delay the end of an enjoyable evening. The coach drivers waved people on as the throng slowly, very slowly made its way to the various boarding points but at last they were all safely off to their destinations round the island: the few more robust revellers would be dropped off in Rothesay to continue the festivities.

'I'm exhausted,' I said to Simon as the tail lights of the last bus disappeared into the inky blackness. 'Thank goodness that's us finished with this group for the night.'

He put his arm round my shoulder. 'Let's get you back to the lodge. It's another early start tomorrow.'

'Don't remind me,' I yawned, 'I'm so tired I could fall asleep on my feet,' adding, 'Do you think everyone will be fit for tomorrow? We've a guest speaker at nine o'clock. I should have realised and made it even later.'

Simon took my elbow and steered me towards the car. 'That's tomorrow's problem. Tonight you need to have some rest.'

Thank goodness he was driving. I couldn't summon up another ounce of energy. The thought of collapsing into bed was very attractive and meanwhile I put my head back to doze for a few moments until we reached the lodge.

Simon started up the engine and I suddenly jerked up. 'Stop,' I called to him, grabbing the steering wheel.

'What's wrong?'

'Hilary's car - it's here in the car park. What are we going to do about it?' How on earth could I have forgotten about this?

'Can't we leave it till the morning?' His tone was hopeful. 'I'm certain you're worrying about nothing. There will be some perfectly simple explanation, I'm sure.'

I shook my head. 'Where is she? If her car is here she must have driven up earlier for the dinner. If she suddenly decided not to attend surely she would have taken her car?'

Even Simon couldn't dispute the logic of this. He gripped the steering wheel tightly, possibly in case I would try to pull it from him again. 'What do you intend to do?'

'Call in at the police station and report it.' At least then the problem would be someone else's.

There was a moment's pause while he considered this. 'I suppose so. Anyway there's no way you will rest until you have made some kind of effort to find out where she is.'

He started up the car again and we drove into Rothesay and up the High Street to the police station. The policeman on duty appeared promptly in the foyer when we rang the bell, then asked us numerous questions about Hilary, many of which I couldn't answer.

'I'm ashamed to say I don't know much about her,' I said. 'It's thirty years since I had any contact with her and we only met up

153

again at this reunion. But as her car is at Mount Stuart and she didn't show up for dinner, I felt I had to report it.'

'Quite right. Better safe than sorry, though she'll probably turn up,' he said. 'If there's no word tomorrow, we'll initiate a search.'

We left, promising to contact the station first thing in the morning, either to say Hilary was safe or to let them know she was still missing.

As we drove back towards Port Bannatyne underneath a starry sky my mind was in turmoil. How I wished I hadn't put her off when she said there was something she had to tell me. It might have been nothing at all, might have been Hilary trying to make herself out to be important, but still it nagged at me.

And if there was something she wanted to tell me, was there any connection between whatever it was and her disappearance?

THIRTY THREE

Tired out by all that had happened, my mind was racing so much sleep would be impossible. I tried everything - counting sheep, deep breathing, but the harder I tried to doze off the less likely it became. When I did finally nod off somewhere towards dawn, as the morning chorus was beginning, it was to a troubled, nightmare-filled sleep. My thoughts kept returning to Hilary and what could possibly have happened to her. Why should her car be at Mount Stuart? Why had she not come along to the dinner? And what was it that she was so eager to tell me? As soon as possible I'd have to try her hotel again, in the hope she was safe, her absence easily explained. But what would we do if the news wasn't good?

Finally about six o'clock I gave up any hope of further sleep, crawled out of bed to make some coffee in the little kitchen and took it through to the table at the window overlooking Kames Bay. The sun had begun to rise in a mist across the water, promising another fine day. A lone seagull walked jerkily along the edge of the shore and in the distance at Ardmeleish an early riser was walking his dog around the grass verge.

For a moment I was tempted to pull on my jeans and wellingtons and head out, but better sense prevailed and I contented myself with gazing at the view from the table at the window, sipping my coffee and going carefully through the list of items for the day. Thank goodness the weather would continue fair, especially as the afternoon schedule included the open-top bus tour of the island.

The oyster catchers were now gathering at the edge of the shore, shrieking as they jostled for the best position for food, bobbing frantically along the sand. The seagull eyed them disdainfully and then flew off towards the Kyles seeking more congenial company.

I couldn't focus on my list of tasks. Perhaps more coffee would help? My mind kept drifting to only one thought: where on earth was Hilary? If I found out today that she had merely decided to skip the dinner and was snugly tucked up in her hotel I would be more than cross, but that would be too simple an explanation. I heard Simon stirring in the bedroom and looked at the clock. It was almost seven thirty and there was still so much to check before we started today's activities. I called through, 'Would you like some coffee?' and took the returning grunt as a 'yes.'

As the coffee percolated I went outside to get reception on my mobile. There were no messages, no missed calls. No news is good news, I thought, though I did have a niggling doubt about what was happening with Deborah and Sylvester.

The smell of coffee reached me, tempting enough to entice me to yet another caffeine boost. It might be my last one this morning. The schedule for today was straightforward: talks at the library this morning and after lunch we would head down to Guildford Square to board the open topped bus for the tour round the island. A few had elected to take off to walk the West Island Way rather than join the others on the bus, but one way or another, everyone was catered for. But first I had to go along to Hilary's hotel and check the situation, find out if she had returned there last night and if there was still no sign of her, my next stop would be the police station.

Simon joined me a few moments later, still rumpled with sleep. 'Coffee ready yet?' he yawned.

'Good heavens.' I rushed through to the kitchen where the pot was bubbling merrily on the stove, sending little cascades of overdone coffee onto the hob.

I put some milk into the microwave in the hope that a very milky coffee would disguise the overdone taste but didn't wait for Simon's verdict on my culinary efforts. 'I really must go over to the hotel to find out if there has been any word about Hilary.'

Simon nodded, stirring his coffee. He was in no mood to chat and I made good my escape. 'I'll be back to change well before the next event,' I said, grabbing the car keys from the hall table.

I heard Simon say something about '... leave it to the police,' but I didn't stop to answer him. I knew they were the best people to handle this, but I had a responsibility to Hilary, to find out why she hadn't turned up at Mount Stuart.

I sped through the village, gaining momentum as I did so, only slowing down for the traffic lights at the ferry port in Rothesay. I reached the hotel at Ascog, trembling from head to foot: either worry about Hilary or too much coffee, but it was difficult to tell which. I parked close to the hotel door and took a deep breath, crossing my fingers that all would be well, that there would be some rational explanation for Hilary's non-appearance at the gala dinner last night. In the reception area a very worried looking manager greeted me.

'Mrs Cameron, am I glad to see you. Your friend hasn't made an appearance yet. We did try her room this morning, but the bed hasn't been slept in.' He looked at me as if I might be able to solve this problem of Hilary's disappearance.

'Are you sure? No phone call? Nothing? We found her car in the Mount Stuart car park last night.'

'Nothing,' he repeated firmly. 'She most certainly hasn't been back here.'

'Are you sure she didn't say anything to any of the staff before she set out last night?' I said, sitting down on the chair beside the desk.

'But you've told me her car was at Mount Stuart,' he replied, not unreasonably. 'Surely that shows she did intend to join you all for the dinner?'

I had no answer, but there was no point in lingering here. Time was going on and now I'd have to go over to the police station in Rothesay to tell them what had happened, phone Mount Stuart about the car and prepare for the afternoon tour while trying hard not to alarm the others. I stood up. 'I'll be in touch as soon as I know anything.'

'What about her room?'

'Sorry?' Surely he wasn't thinking about letting it out again? 'Hilary might turn up,' I said frostily.

'No, no,' he responded hastily. 'I mean should I lock it up?'

'Oh, yes, of course.' If anything had happened to Hilary, it would be best to leave everything untouched.

I left hurriedly. Of all the scenarios I had thought of when Betsie had persuaded me to help with the reunion, I could never have imagined this. All I could do was grit my teeth and try to get through till Monday afternoon, when it would finally be over.

At the police station I spoke to the constable on duty. He was one of the older policemen and tried to calm my fears. 'It's likely there's some perfectly sensible explanation for what has happened, but if she hasn't turned up by the end of the morning we'll start the search.'

I felt perfectly re-assured as I spoke to him, but once back out on the street all my doubts returned. And I still had to go back to Mount Stuart. I scrabbled in my bag for my mobile, switched it on and saw the ominous 'low battery' sign. Damn! I had forgotten to charge it up last night.

I gazed round, looking for the familiar sight of a red telephone box. But there was no sign of any. I'd have to stop off in the town or go back to the lodge and use Simon's phone. I looked at my watch. Time was running out: going back to the lodge was the only option. I jumped into the car and screeched off, hoping to have a clear run back to the Port, narrowly missing a tractor lumbering up towards one of the farms outside town.

Simon was sitting by the window, idly gazing at the view when I drove through the gates of the lodge.

'Quick, can I borrow your phone?' I said, running in.

He looked up. 'What's the panic now, Alison?'

'I need to make a phone call and my battery is dead.'

He shook his head, but said nothing as he handed me his phone. I went out to the patch of grass outside the lodge and dialled the Mount Stuart number, trying all the while to still the frantic beating of my heart.

A cool voice, quite at odds with the way I was feeling, greeted me. 'Mount Stuart House. Can I help you?'

As briefly as I could I explained the reason for my call. 'There will be a car number HAR 4444 in the car park.'

'Just a moment and I'll check for you.'

I listened impatiently to the click of heels on the marble floor, but she returned a few moments later.

'Mrs Cameron? I'm sorry, I think you must have made a mistake. There are no cars in the visitor car park.'

'Are you absolutely sure? Hilary Roupton's car was left there last night. It was still there when I left and I was last off the premises.'

'I'll double check.' Another click of heels down the marble hallway and then, 'I've checked with Kieron. He does the rounds first thing every morning. I can assure you there are no cars there apart from the usual staff cars.'

I could scarcely say, 'Thank you' as I shut the phone down. Had Hilary come back for her car after we had all gone? If so how had she got there? And if it wasn't Hilary who had retrieved her car who had ... and why?

THIRTY FOUR

We had arranged to meet in Guildford Square in the centre of Rothesay. The square is small, space taken up by trees and benches and the road beside it now a paying car park. There was no possibility anyone would be missed or left behind. When I arrived at two o'clock, in good time for the two thirty departure, the bright red West Coast bus was already there, awaiting its passengers.

I had been looking forward to this part of the weekend. In spite of numerous trips to Bute this was as much a new experience for me as for the delegates, most of whom had opted for this rather than the walk. I'd made sure of one of the upstairs seats right at the front with the best view by taking up Johnnie's offer to help me by being the designated person in charge on the downstairs deck. I suspected he had an ulterior motive, having noticed he was walking with a slightly stiff gait, a sure sign of knee problems. He would never in a million years admit it but, never mind, it suited my purposes very well.

The earlier mist had completely cleared, drifting off towards the mainland, leaving a day of cloudless skies and bright sunlight and we chatted in little groups as we walked to the bus, everyone now well used to the relaxed way of life on the island, or perhaps some of them were suffering from the after effects of the evening before.

As though he had read my thoughts, Johnnie appeared beside me. 'Any news of Hilary yet?' he whispered, delighting in his role as self appointed supervisor.

'Nothing. She seems to have vanished into thin air. I can't understand it. Still,' with a forced brightness, 'I'm sure it will all work out. There's probably some good reason she didn't come to the dinner last night.'

Johnnie didn't look convinced. 'I hope you're right. We wouldn't want any more problems this weekend,' he said, almost as if he thought Hilary's non-appearance at the gala dinner was somehow my fault.

I ignore this pointed remark saying, 'I think we should start asking people to board this bus.'

'Good idea.' And with that, he began to shepherd everyone aboard with indecent haste.

The driver regarded me with some curiosity as I climbed on. 'Don't I know you from somewhere?'

'They say everyone has a double,' I responded weakly, unwilling to talk about my previous trips to the island.

'Mmm,' he replied, but I could see him mentally trying to place me.

I scrambled up to the top deck. 'Here, Alison,' called Sylvia as she patted the empty front seat beside her. 'You've no idea how difficult it was to keep this seat free,' she sighed. 'I claimed organiser's privilege for you.'

The excited chatter almost drowned out the sound of the engine as the driver started up and we set off on the first part of our journey. I know the island well, have visited most of the favourite spots from Port Bannatyne to Kilchattan Bay, from Scalpsie Bay to Ettrick Bay, but sitting so high up on this bus gave me a completely different view of the beauty of the landscape.

The bus driver was an excellent guide. A native of Bute, a Brandane by birth, he switched off the recorded commentary most of the time and gave us his own insight into life on the island. So although the colourful history of the island was of interest - tales about the Stuarts that didn't make it into the history books - his own personal stories were much more exciting.

We had chartered the bus for the afternoon. With some relief we piled off for a welcome cup of tea at the Ettrick Bay tearoom and, except for the most determined dieters (and they were few), a slice of home made cake.

I sat at the table in the far corner with Sylvia and a couple of the others, at the window overlooking the beach, watching a small group of people walking along the water's edge, a family where dad seemed to be accepting gracefully the attempts of two little boys to bury him in the sand and even a couple of intrepid bathers making their way slowly out from the shore. Soon it would be high summer and the beach would be crowded but at the moment the early visitors were making the most of having all this space to themselves.

Conscious we had to keep to some kind of timetable, I stood up and tried to persuade everyone to make their way back on the bus, but it was hard to be heard above the babble of conversation. 'Sorry folks, we need to finish up and resume our journey,' I repeated several times to the last of the stragglers reluctant to leave the tearoom.

There was a frisson of disappointment, especially from the driver, who was engrossed in conversation with Carla, a widow for more than ten years, who looked much younger than she was. Johnnie came to my aid and I was grateful again for his help, in spite of my reservations about his motives. 'Alison's right. We want to see as much as we can and we do have the evening scheduled in.' Perhaps I had misjudged him.

'Thanks,' I said as the last of the group began to move, finishing up cups of coffee or cake.

It took a few moments to settle us all again, especially as I had to prompt Carla, still chatting animatedly to the bus driver, 'I think it would be a good idea if we all took our seats now.'

The next part of our journey took us towards Scalpsie Bay, where the plan was to stop at the new viewing platform and marvel at the sweep of bay stretched far below, though it might be too early yet to see the grey seals basking on the rocks. On either side of the road out to Scalpsie the countryside was green with all the promise of summer to come. Occasionally the cows in the fields beside the farms would look up as we passed and then go back to contentedly cropping the sweetening grass. We passed another farm where a cloud of pink clematis tumbled carelessly over ancient walls and in the field beyond the white-washed farmhouse a grey horse raised its head, pausing for a moment from munching a bale of hay. Everyone was in such a good mood, so happy, that for a moment I could almost convince myself that Hilary's disappearance had an easy explanation, that she would turn up apologising for the trouble she had caused.

The driver was talking again, telling everyone about the latest archaeological dig at Scalpsie Bay. 'You can see the trench where they found the remains of the Bronze Age beaker,' he was saying. 'There's a lot of work going on there at the moment.'

I looked down and sure enough several archaeologists were busy at the site beside the new car park. As we drew nearer they paused and looked up, waving to us, before resuming their quest for evidence of early settlements on the island. There wasn't much shelter out here in this stark landscape and I hoped the white tent they had positioned at the side of the dig would be enough to keep them dry should the weather change.

Near the entrance to the car park another team was busily engaged in repairing the old stone wall, carefully placing stones one on top of another, without using any form of mortar or cement. This skill of 'dry stane dyking' might be dying out in many places, but not here on Bute.

We crested the hill and pulled in at the picnic area immediately opposite the new wooden viewing platform, from where you could see over the field of rampant vegetation down to the broad sweep of the bay at Scalpsie.

'There's one! There's a seal,' shouted Sylvia excitedly as we left the bus, pointing to a large rock far below on the water's edge as everyone craned forward to see.

But it wasn't the seal that caught my attention. There was something down in the undergrowth at the foot of the hill, a bulky object of some kind, pieces of some gauzy material fluttering in the light breeze. I felt my heart begin to pound. Whatever it was, it certainly didn't belong here.

I ran back over to the bus. The driver was standing outside, contentedly smoking a cigarette. 'Is there a path down from here to the beach?' I asked.

He took the cigarette from his mouth and ground it underfoot, evidently surprised by my question. 'Well, there is, but I'm not sure you should use it at this time of year. The ground's very treacherous.'

I ignored his warning. 'How do I get down?'

He pointed towards the viewing platform. 'There's a gate just at the side that takes you onto the hill and down to the beach. I wouldn't advise it....'

His remaining words were lost as I ran across the road and tugged open the gate. He was right: not many people ventured this way among the thick bracken on the hillside. I picked my way down carefully, crunching the vegetation under foot, trying to keep to the overgrown path. I pushed small branches aside, twigs snapping underfoot as I stumbled towards the bundle I'd seen. Once or twice I almost fell, but managed to grab on to one of the bigger tree branches.

By now most of the bus party had crowded on to the viewing platform and their comments came drifting towards me.

'What on earth is she up to?'

'Surely if she wants to have a look at the beach she should go in by the gate at the car park.'

As fragments of sentences reached me, it was obvious they thought me mad to be attempting this climb down towards the beach and while I could only agree with them, some force impelled me on, desperate to find out what this object might be.

As I came nearer it was what I most feared: it was a person lying here, the bulk of a body lying at a strange angle in the undergrowth. I edged closer, wary of what was lying there, but how could I mistake that mane of red hair? As I came up closer I knew without a doubt my suspicion had been right. It was Hilary, lying here on the hill above Scalpsie.

What on earth had led her here? Had she been brought against her will? Whatever the reason, she was most certainly dead.

THIRTY FIVE

A stunned silence, followed by a babble of excited voices as I scrambled up the hill to arrive breathless and agitated back at the viewing platform. There was plenty of advice about what to do, but I ignored it all. 'There's no option. I have to phone the police.'

'Are you sure it's a body and not a bundle of rags?' Sylvia asked in a high pitched voice, biting her fingernails as she spoke.

'Of course I'm sure, it's ...' I started to say, and then decided it would be better to keep my thoughts to myself. But it was too late and most people had realised who it was.

'She must have tripped and hurt herself. Poor Hilary, lying out here with no one to help, what a way to go,' Megan shuddered.

I didn't ask her why she thought Hilary might have decided to go for a walk on the hills above Scalpsie when she was supposed to be at the gala dinner at Mount Stuart several miles away.

None of it made any sense. Why would her car be left in the car park? She must surely have arrived at Mount Stuart and then what had happened after that? Why had no one seen her there? I gazed around. Where was her car? The only vehicle here was the tour bus. There was no way that any of this could be explained but as we waited for the police to arrive, speculation was rife. Johnnie barged forward. 'I think I should go down in case you might be mistaken, Alison.'

I managed to move quickly to plant myself firmly in front of him, my determination evident even to someone as insensitive as he was. 'That isn't a good idea, especially for those,' deliberately looking at his knee, 'with mobility problems. We don't want to have to rescue you. I've already disturbed the scene more than I should and more people tramping over it, destroying any evidence isn't a good idea, is it?' This last addressed to the general crowd, most of whom shrank back at this explosion on my part.

'You mean you don't think it was an accident?' Carla looked horrified as did some of the others, but I was in no mood to offer words of comfort. Something had happened to Hilary out here, something truly awful and there was no sense in making the job of the police any more difficult.

Madge came up to me and stood close beside me. 'What do you think happened, Alison? Do you think whatever happened to Hilary was deliberate?'

'I have no idea what happened.' I had my suspicions, but wasn't going to voice them to anyone here. 'It might be best if everyone goes back onto the bus,' I said firmly.

'We're not going to continue the bus tour and leave poor Hilary lying here, are we?' said Madge, pointing down to the body.

'No, of course not.' I could hardly contain my impatience at this ridiculous suggestion.

'Don't be cross with us, Alison. It's hardly our fault that Hilary has had an accident here. We've nothing to do with it.' Sylvia sniffed and flounced off across the road to the picnic tables where I could see her muttering to Carla and occasionally looking my way.

Johnnie was obviously disgruntled I'd stopped him from going down to the scene to see for himself. 'I think you're taking too much on yourself, Alison. I know you're in charge of the reunion, but it doesn't mean you're in charge of everything. We're all concerned in this. We all knew Hilary.'

I stared at him. That was the question, wasn't it? Was it possible that a member of our group had in fact had something to do with Hilary's death? But as quickly as the thought came into my mind, I dismissed it. No one here could possibly have a motive for killing Hilary.

In the distance we heard the welcome sound of a police car as it made its way towards us. Whatever had happened, this was now out of my hands. The police would take over, sort out the evidence, unravel the story.

It sounds very heartless to say our schedule was well disrupted, given poor Hilary was dead, but in a selfish way all I could think about was keeping this reunion together, getting through the rest of the weekend and saying goodbye to them all.

'What's to happen now?' said Madge, her face white with fear.

'I'm not sure. The police will want to interview us all but apart from that, who knows.' I was struggling to keep calm, but not succeeding very well. There wasn't much any of us could tell the police. 'We'll have to wait till the C.I.D. come over from the mainland. They'll want to interview everyone on this reunion, everyone who knew Hilary.'

This was not good news. We watched in silence as another car drew up and one of the doctors from the island who acted as police casualty surgeons picked his way carefully down through the thick vegetation on the slope towards the spot where the body lay. The blue and white tape was unrolled to seal off the area where poor Hilary was lying. This was the end of our involvement for the present.

The bus driver was taking a long time with the police officers. I wasn't sure if it was because they thought he might know something or because being an islander he might know them socially and though I edged closer it was impossible to hear anything.

We were interviewed one by one 'we'll have to speak to everyone again later' then finally we were allowed back onto the bus and set off for Rothesay, the remainder of our trip abandoned. There was little conversation as we drove back towards the town. Occasionally there was a murmur of voices, subdued tones, but as quickly as the noise rose it fell again. No one was in a mood for idle chit chat, everyone wanted to talk about the incident at Scalpsie but no one wanted to be the first to broach the subject. Anyone who tried to speak to me about it was quickly dismissed. I had too much on my mind including trying desperately to recall exactly what Hilary had said to me on that last occasion. It was all something to do with Betsie, wasn't it? How I wished I'd paid more attention, had made time to listen to her. It was too late now and, try as I might, I couldn't remember anything she had said that might help.

Once back in Guildford Square I summoned my strength to address them all as they left the bus. 'We can vote on this if you like. We have a choice - we can carry on with the reunion as planned or we can end it here and let you make your own plans for the rest of the weekend.'

There was no way of knowing how they would react. It was one thing that Betsie had died before the final arrangements had been completed. Some of the delegates hardly remembered her. But Hilary was different. After all, she was one of us, one of our party. Whatever the group agreed was fine by me as long as it wasn't my decision.

There was a buzz of conversation. 'Take your time,' I said. 'If you want to wait till later then that's fine. I appreciate that Hilary's death must have come as a shock to you.'

Still the talk continued, as people split into groups, then other groups, as they discussed the options.

'What about the others?' said Sylvia. 'I mean those who decided to go on the West Island Way walk?'

In all the excitement I had completely forgotten about them, but I wanted a decision as soon as possible. 'There aren't many of them,' I said, 'so let's make a decision here and then we can consult them to see if they agree.'

There was a nod of heads and a general murmur of assent to this suggestion and Johnnie came forward, clearing his throat, evidently in preparation for an important speech. In spite of the terrible situation, I had the feeling he was enjoying his role as spokesman.

'We've had a lot of discussion about this, Alison and as you can imagine there is a real division of opinion.'

Oh no, I hoped they didn't want me to have the casting vote.

I needn't have worried because Johnnie now stepped in front of me, completely blocking my view. He cleared his throat again and then, raising his voice, he addressed the solemn group in front of him.

'I know we are all upset by what happened today. I know some of you want to leave and go home and you are of course perfectly entitled to do so. But some of us have come a long way for this reunion and even if the events are cancelled we'll have to stay on the island until Monday. So I'm going to ask for a show of hands. If you don't vote, I'll assume you want to go along with the majority. Does that seem satisfactory?'

There was a general murmur of approval. He took a deep breath. 'Then let's put it to the vote, everyone. All those who want to abandon the rest of the reunion?'

There was a forest of hands and I tried to count them quickly. Just under half of the total number. Already I could see what lay before me, including explaining to the various venues about what had happened, trying to have money refunded.

'And all those who want to continue?'

Again a number of hands raised: about the same number as wanted to leave.

Johnnie sighed. 'We have several abstainers. Can we do it again? Please try to make a decision this time. Remember we won't be having another of these reunions for a very long time, if ever,' he added darkly.

I certainly won't have anything to do with another reunion, I muttered.

Johnnie's words seemed to have the desired effect. On the second count there was a slow show of hands, the numbers little by little increasing until there was a clear majority for continuing.

Johnnie looked well satisfied with the result. 'Great! That's it all settled. We go on and those of you who don't want to continue have another think about your decision. We'll get final numbers tonight.'

Well, Johnnie had done a good job, I had to admit. Some of them, like the timid Sylvia, wouldn't want to wait, but hopefully the remainder would stay on till the end of the weekend.

Of course that was before we knew for definite that Hilary had indeed been murdered.

THIRTY SIX

The message on my mobile from Deborah was brief but clear. There was some problem about Sylvester and it wasn't anything to do with his business.

'Don't you think it's time you invested in a new phone?' said Simon as I played the message again.

'Nonsense. There's nothing wrong with this one,' I replied, going back to listening to the message one more time, trying to ignore the varying levels of sound my phone liked to provide.

Deborah sounded upset but she gave no details. It wasn't possible to tell exactly what was happening except that there was some difficulty she wanted to discuss.

I would call her back later. At the moment I had to decide how to deal with the evening ceidlih. It seemed heartless to be going on with this event, yet I couldn't think what else we could do. The Pavilion hall was organised and set up, the band booked, the catering of a traditional Scottish meal of haggis, neeps and mash followed by a dessert of raspberry cranachan ordered well in advance. 'Do you think there's any alternative? Should I take the unilateral decision to cancel it?'

Simon looked up from his book. 'I don't think so, not when the agreement was that it all goes ahead, though I suppose you could have the meal and then go. It will mean paying for the band and everything else.'

'I know, I know, but I can't face an evening of jollity with poor Hilary dead.'

'I thought the decision of the group was to continue as normal, or as normal as can be in the circumstances? Don't worry about it. They've made the decision. There are only a couple of events

170

left and that will be this weekend over with. Besides,' he added, not unreasonably, 'what is everyone going to do for the rest of the evening if you do cancel?'

'I suppose so.' I went back to my list only half convinced by his argument. There was always the option of finishing early if the evening didn't go well and after the river cruise tomorrow, following a 'free morning' to allow people to explore the island at their leisure, the reunion would be at an end. And I had to admit that Hilary hadn't been the most popular member of our reunion: too bossy and too nosey for most.

Now the decision about what to wear for the ceidlih faced me. Simon, in common with most of the other men, would elect for a kilt, but I wanted something glamorous for this last event. With so much to arrange I'd had no time to go shopping before leaving Glasgow, bitterly regretting my lack of foresight now. Reluctantly I went into the bedroom to examine the contents of the suitcase of clothes I'd brought.

'Are you ready yet, Alison?' came Simon's impatient voice from the front room.

'Nearly,' I called struggling out of my third choice for that evening. There was nothing else for it; I'd have to make do with the pale blue mid length skirt and matching top I'd bought once in a sale in the vague hope we might go somewhere smart enough for me to wear it. As I surveyed my image in the mirror my first thought was that I looked overdressed for a ceidlih but it was too late now and I consoled myself this was an opportunity to wear something that had languished at the back of the wardrobe for ages.

Simon was pacing restlessly up and down the room when I joined him, looking very smart in his dress kilt of Cameron tartan. How lucky men were I thought; either a suit or highland dress solved the problem of what to wear for most occasions.

'Is this all right?' doing a twirl as I spoke.

'You look great, Alison,' he said, kissing me on the cheek. 'Now let's get a move on.'

We set off at speed from the lodge towards the Pavilion. In spite of Johnnie's efforts, I had no idea how many people might have decided to opt out of this evening's event.

My concerns were short lived. As we drew up at the front entrance little groups of people were already arriving and though there was a subdued air as they made their way in, the general mood seemed to be one of making the best of the evening in spite of the experiences of the afternoon. Perhaps it would go well after all.

'Most people seem to have decided that it would be better to carry on usual or at least put a brave face on it,' said Simon, squeezing my arm to re-assure me.

Madge joined us as we went through the doors. She smiled encouragingly. 'Don't worry, Alison, we thought it would be foolish to give up the reunion at this stage, especially after all the hard work you've put in to making it a success. After all, it's not your fault that Hilary somehow ended up at Scalpsie Bay.' She patted my arm. 'Let's have a good time tonight and forget all that business.'

She scurried ahead of us to meet up with a small group waiting for her at the top of the stairs.

I stopped suddenly and turned to Simon. 'Have you seen Deborah?'

Simon shook his head and sniffed. 'She may well be inside already with Mr Sylvester de Courtney.'

'Probably.' I remembered with a jolt of guilt that in all the excitement I hadn't phoned her back.

We went into the Pavilion to join the chattering, bustling throng with high hopes that this evening would turn out better than expected. That wasn't quite what happened.

THIRTY SEVEN

The ceidlih was in full swing. The dancers whirled and skirled on the floor, laughing and breathless as they tried to keep up with a spirited rendition of the music for the Dashing White Sergeant. We had opted out to sit at one of the tables with some of the more sedate members of the group. A double set of Strip the Willow had been more than enough for me.

Maria, unable to take part because of a recent broken ankle, leaned across to shout to me over the noise of the music. 'Don't you think it would be a better idea if they alternated the dances? We could do with a St Bernard's Waltz to give everyone the chance to recover from all that frantic activity.'

Much as I agreed with her, there was no way I was going to tackle the leader of the An Cala highland dance music band. Six foot six at least, with a mane of dark hair and a long beard, he was someone who looked as if he might be most upset if his judgement was questioned. No, we'd have to do what we could to keep the dancing going.

There was still no sign of Deborah. As far as I could remember she and Sylvester had been planning to attend this evening's event, hoping to chat to potential customers. Had something happened to delay them? 'I'm going out for a breath of fresh air,' I announced to those sitting at the table. With the level of noise, I had to repeat myself.

'You're going to phone Deborah, aren't you?' muttered Simon.

'I might give her a call while I'm out,' I replied, deliberately casual.

'I think you should leave her alone,' he said. 'She'll be in touch in her own good time. Stop interfering.'

I wasn't sure if he really meant it wouldn't be a good idea to phone Deborah or whether he didn't want to be left alone with Maria and several of the other non-dancers, at least two of whom were more than slightly deaf. 'I won't be long,' I replied firmly and made good my escape before he could volunteer to join me.

Downstairs in the hallway and in the foyer the pictures from the art exhibition were still on display, many of those by local artists with red stickers to show they had been sold. Thankfully this part of the weekend had been very successful.

Outside the Pavilion building the air was cool and refreshing after the stuffy, sweaty atmosphere of the hall and I perched on the little wall overlooking the main road and breathed deeply, gazing at the streetlamps round the bay. At the pier the ferries were berthed for the night, their lights still shining out, their reflections shimmering in the water. We had been so fortunate with the weather on this reunion even if it didn't compensate for everything else. Wet and windy Atlantic weather would have been a disaster for everyone. I shivered a little but it was hard to tell if it was from cold or from the remembrance of what had happened in the past few weeks. I couldn't sit here for long and after a quick call to Deborah I'd have to re-join the others.

I flipped open my phone and called up her number, but there was no reply. I waited for a few moments and tried again, finally leaving a brief message on her voicemail service, trying to sound cheerful rather than worried.

Time to go back to the revellers inside and I hurried through the doors and up into the main hall where the band seemed to have taken pity on the dancers as a very sedate Canadian Barn dance was taking place. The pace of this seemed to have encouraged even the most reluctant dancers and Simon was sitting alone at the table where I had left him.

'Have the others gone?'

He shrugged and gestured towards the dance floor where there was little space to be had. 'It would appear that even Maria can manage this one.'

'Good.' I sat down in the chair opposite him.

'Anyway,' frowning at me, 'what did Deborah say?'

'That's the trouble. There was no answer.'

'Are you certain she said she'd be here tonight?'

'Absolutely positive. She said Sylvester was very much looking forward to it. He's never been to a ceidlih and the whole idea seemed to intrigue him enormously.'

Now Simon appeared to share my concerns. 'Have you tried the hotel?'

I shook my head. 'I suppose I could, but do you think she would be lingering there if she said she would come along to the dance?'

'Well, it's worth a try. Do you want me to call her?' He got to his feet, anxious no doubt to escape in case I tried to lure him back on to the dance floor.

'No, no, I'll do it.' I sidled past him, phone at the ready and hurried out into the upstairs hallway.

There was no reply from her room at the hotel either, though when I thought about it, why would she not answer her mobile? Like most young people, Deborah has her phone welded to her hand.

I was at a loss. Perhaps it was all worry about nothing. There would surely be some explanation. Perhaps Sylvester had taken cold feet at the last moment at the thought of being thrust into the demonic dancers. Or perhaps I had misunderstood? Possibly they planned to have a meal and join us for the last part of the evening?

I sighed. There was really nothing else to do at the moment. The events of the past few days were clouding my judgement, making me see danger everywhere.

Back in the hall the frantic pace of dancing had resumed with an astonishingly fast Gay Gordons. This was one I would sit out, in the good company of many of the party. Simon was nowhere to be seen, unless he was among the whirling mass on the dance floor. He would be very unhappy with me if he was now in the clutches of one of these determined ladies.

No sooner had I sat down than Maria came over and prodded me in the ribs. 'Is that not your daughter just arrived?'

I turned round, smiling in relief, but the smile froze on my face when I saw her gazing wildly round, her anguish evident and as I beckoned her over, I felt very concerned. What on earth had gone wrong now?

Deborah came dashing up, waving to me. 'I need to talk to you,' she said and up close I could see the tears in her eyes.

'The Pavilion hall isn't the place to discuss anything,' I said, ushering her out and downstairs into a quiet corner of the foyer. I turned her round to face me and before she could speak, I said, 'Is it Sylvester?'

'I can't believe it,' Deborah gulped. 'He's married. He divorced his first wife, but he married again and he's still with her. It was only a temporary separation, a very temporary separation. I only found out because someone in the Glasgow gallery let it slip. That was why he didn't want to take me to London with him: she lives there, that's where his main house is.'

'Oh, dear,' I replied. Anything I said was certain to be the wrong response so I contented myself with soothing murmurs.

She lifted her head from the wad of tear soaked tissues she held in her hand. Her makeup was streaked, the run of her black mascara giving her the look of a very soulful panda. It took her a few minutes to calm down and then she said, hiccupping, 'He led me to believe he was on his own, that his marriage had ended years ago.'

It wasn't the first time I had heard this kind of story and I daresay it wouldn't be the last, but it was entirely different when it was my own daughter. What was it about her? She seemed doomed to be unlucky in love.

As though she read my thoughts she sobbed, 'Why does it always happen to me like this? Why do I always choose the wrong kind of person?'

Because I couldn't think of anything else to say, I asked, 'What happens to the exhibition now?'

She grimaced. 'Stuff his exhibition! I expect it will continue for the rest of the week but I most certainly won't be having anything to do with it.' She wiped her tearstained face.

This was going to be very awkward indeed. 'What are your plans now?' I didn't know whether to be more upset about the loss of her lover or the possible loss of her job.

'I don't have any,' she said sadly. 'But,' with a sudden spark of anger, 'I'm not working for that man again.'

'You'll give up your job?' The sudden realisation struck me that this news could have consequences and not only for Deborah.

She shrugged. 'What else can I do?' she said, using the tissue to wipe her eyes but she only succeeded in smearing the mascara all over her face even more. It was hard not to laugh without hurting her feelings.

'I suppose so.' Now wasn't the time to lecture her about sticking with a job, even if she had landed herself in difficulties by having an affair with the boss.

'To make matters worse, he tried to blame me,' she said suddenly. 'Claimed I knew all along that he was still married, that he and his wife were only having temporary difficulties.'

'Did you?' As soon as I spoke I realised this might not be the right approach.

'Of course not.' She was scornful of my suggestion. 'He never said anything about her all the time we were together.'

Should I believe her? Sometimes Deborah can ignore what doesn't suit her. 'I'll help you pack if you want to return to the mainland tomorrow. It's too late for tonight as the last ferry has gone.'

She had other plans in mind. 'I don't think I'll let him spoil it all,' she said. 'I might join your party for the last day.'

She looked so woeful what could I do but agree, though I didn't think she would be the best of company judging by the state she was in. 'Where are you going to stay?'

'I thought I could stay with you in the lodge house. Isn't there a put-u-up in the living room?'

'Yes, I suppose that would be fine,' trying to guess what Simon's reaction would be to this sudden change of plan.

And I wasn't sure what I would say to Mr de Courtney when we next met. It would be uncomfortable to say the least.

177

THIRTY EIGHT

Distracted by all that was happening, perhaps I wasn't paying enough attention. My mind was a jumble of thoughts and questions. Even so, having been brought up in a city, I was always careful when crossing the road, even on Bute. For whatever reason, I scarcely registered the silver car parked outside the Discovery Centre as I headed from the ferry terminal towards the main street in Rothesay.

The car door opened so suddenly that there was no time for me to jump out of the way, even if I hadn't been so deep in thought. There was no time to take any action at all, though the whole event seemed to take place in a curious kind of slow motion.

It seemed as if this was something happening to someone else, someone outside my body. All I could think of was, I'm falling and I'm going to be hurt. What on earth am I going to do about the arrangements for the river cruise today?

My body hit the ground with an enormous thump but in those first few moments I felt no pain at all. Gosh, I'm fine, was my first reaction. Then I tried to stand up and the pain consumed my whole body, coming in searing waves.

I realised I was in the road, half concealed by the parked cars. If I didn't move there was every likelihood I would be run over by another car coming along the road. I tried again to struggle to my feet, expecting the driver of the car to rush over and help me but instead there was the roar of an engine revving up and the car sped off out of Rothesay towards the Mount Stuart road. Luckily others were more helpful and a couple of pedestrians come rushing over to my aid.

'What happened?' asked the first, a sturdy man with the ruddy complexion of someone who worked outdoors for a living. Just as well, as he had to try to help me to my feet.

The other pedestrian, an elderly lady fussed about. 'I don't think we should move her, in case she's been seriously injured,' she said.

'I'm fine,' I said shakily, though I felt far from fine. I tried to move, then felt myself carefully. 'No bones broken as far as I can tell.' There might be no bones broken, but I was sure to be very badly bruised.

'You've had a bit of a fright,' said the elderly lady. 'You need to go to hospital to be checked over.'

I shook my head. 'I'm sure I'll be okay. A strong cup of tea and I'll be right as rain.'

The man looked doubtful, but said, 'I'll call a taxi to take you back.'

'Thanks.' All I wanted to do was return to the lodge and check out my injuries. I said, 'Did either of you see what happened?'

Both shook their heads. 'Afraid not,' said the man. 'All I saw was you lying in the road.'

The taxi was there within a couple of minutes and I again thanked my rescuers profusely, deterring the old lady from coming back with me to make sure I was safe. 'My husband will be there,' I said firmly and this seemed to re-assure her. I wasn't too certain Simon would be there at the lodge, but I wanted to be on my own.

I eased myself into the taxi, gingerly moving to secure the seat belt and prepared myself for the short but possibly bumpy journey back to the lodge. In the event it was almost bearable, though I felt every tiny jolt in the road and once or twice had to stop myself crying out in pain. Was I all right? What if I had damaged myself in some way? As usual I hadn't been very sensible but I was too much in shock, convinced the 'accident' had been no such thing. The opening of that car door had been deliberate. Or else why would the driver have gone off like that? Why would anyone want to harm me? Was it a warning of some kind? I sat back, trying to control the waves of pain. So much for my free morning enjoying myself on Bute.

Simon wasn't at the lodge and he hadn't left a note which meant he was probably out again on the golf course, enjoying one of the last opportunities for some exercise and fresh air before we had to return to the polluted air of the city.

I dropped my clothes on the floor and crawled under the duvet, trying to find a comfortable position, but with every turn another part of my body throbbed. As I began to fall off to sleep sounds drifted in as though from a distance: voices of walkers taking the Tramway road up to Ettrick Bay, the sound of a car door slamming, the gurgle of the pipes in the kitchen.

When I awoke Simon was standing over me. 'Are you all right, Alison?'

Cautiously, I tried to ease myself into a sitting position but every bone in my body jarred. 'Not really,' I said, bursting into tears.

'Whatever's happened now?' He sat down on the bed beside me as I tried to recount the car incident. Trouble was, my memory of events was somewhat hazy.

He lifted my arms, prodding gently. 'Are you sure you haven't broken anything.'

'Sure,' I hiccupped, 'but it was very painful.'

'You can't have been paying attention as you crossed the road,' he said. 'Surely you don't think anyone on the island would do such a thing deliberately?'

'Why speed away like that? Why didn't whoever it was come over and check I hadn't been hurt.'

'Mmm, quite possibly whoever it was didn't see you.'

'It was an almighty thump,' I replied crossly. 'I don't really see how the driver could have failed to notice what had happened.'

But Simon wasn't convinced. 'I think you're imagining things, Alison. The other possibility was that the driver didn't want it to be known he was driving the car. Uninsured, maybe? Or underage? There could be all kinds of explanation.'

I said no more but lay down again. 'I think I'll sleep for a while.'

'Are you certain you don't need to go to the hospital, to be checked over in case you have concussion?' said Simon, standing up.

'Stop fussing,' I replied, 'I've done enough first aid in my time to recognise concussion.'

As he went out of the room he turned. 'I do wish you would be more careful, Alison. You seem to attract trouble.'

I knew his words were only because he was genuinely concerned about me. A bit of me had to admit he was right, this wasn't the first time I'd had this happen to me, but all the same I resented the implication that I went about looking for disaster. It was better to stay cosy under the duvet for a while, avoiding any more awkward questions. But in my groggy state I drifted off to sleep again and as I did so a picture of the car flashed in front of my eyes. The car had been silver and part of the number plate had read HAR. But how could that possibly be? Hilary was dead. There was no way it could have been her car. But then the car had disappeared from the car park at Mount Stuart. I'd have to contact the police. Then I thought, what if it was my imagination playing tricks? I drifted into sleep, still thinking about my narrow escape. Someone had been driving Hilary's car and what had happened to me had definitely been no accident.

THIRTY NINE

My recovery was thankfully rapid and by the afternoon I was feeling much better, though still decidedly stiff and sore.

I struggled to dress but consoled myself with the thought that this was the final day of the reunion. Once the afternoon cruise was over all that remained was a farewell afternoon tea in the Pavilion before most of the party headed for home. Any others who had elected to stay on for longer could fend for themselves.

Thank goodness for Simon's foresight in booking the lodge for an extra few days. Deborah had decided to head back to Glasgow: one uncomfortable night on a put-u-up had decided her she was better off at home. She seemed much calmer, more resigned; volatile by nature, her ups and downs were equally brief.

'I'll be fine, mum,' she replied to my concerns about her. 'I'm able to take care of myself. I can't believe how much I was taken in by that man.'

No doubt she was at this very minute taking her belongings from Sylvester's flat and bringing them back to her room in our house. Better not to think about that.

I examined myself carefully in the mirror but fortunately most of the damage had been to the parts that no one could see although there were a number of beautiful bruises on the right side of my face.

Should I try to chase up the driver of the car - if it was who I thought it was? It was too complicated to think about at the moment. If only I could put all these bits together I was convinced there was some link between everything that had happened.

The boat trip was difficult: getting on and off and up and down the stairs meant I elected to stay down in the passenger lounge for most of the time. A pity really, because it was a day of clear blue skies with only a few wisps of cotton wool clouds and as the boat made its way down, the Kyles of Bute were looking at their sparkling best. Everyone else seemed to be enjoying the sight of the gannets diving for fish and the seals out basking on the rocks, their mournful cries echoing across the still waters. There were plenty of photo opportunities for the camera enthusiasts.

'You're missing the best of the day,' said Madge as she sat down heavily beside me. 'Any word yet on who was responsible for your accident?'

How soon word gets round, I thought, shaking my head. 'Nothing. I guess it was no more than that, an accident. No real harm done.' I winced and shifted my position.

I didn't want to talk about the 'accident': I had other things to think about. Ideas were swarming about in my head, ideas that linked a number of the events and the people connected with this reunion. All I needed was something, some final piece of information that would tell me I was on the right track.

Madge gave up. Obviously I wasn't going to be the source of any interesting gossip and others upon deck might be more entertaining.

By now the boat was heading towards the Maids of Bute, those painted rocks that have stood guard over the Kyles for over one hundred years.

'This is fascinating,' said Madge. 'What are they?'

Johnnie sprang forward eagerly at this question, clutching a guide book. 'The most common story about the Maids of Bute is that two fishermen went out in a boat one night to fish and never returned. The fishermen's wives waited so long they eventually turned to stone.'

Even from below, in spite of the hum of the engines, I could hear the click of cameras, the shouts of excitement as we sailed past these vividly expressive rocks. Now, with everyone else otherwise engaged, I had time to think about what I knew so far. It had all started with Betsie's death and Hilary's death was connected to Betsie's in some way. If only I had taken the time to

183

listen to Hilary I might have saved myself a whole lot of problems. Too late now.

Where did Sylvester fit into all this? He was also involved in the antiques business and he knew Betsie, of that I was sure. Did he also know Hilary? She was nothing to do with the antiques business because, if my memory served me right, she worked in a university somewhere in England. She did know Betsie, of course, from our college days but as far as I understood they hadn't had contact for many years.

Then there was the Hereuse Nursing home. What was going on? There was some link, of that I was sure, even if it was only that Betsie had visited the place. Did she know Mrs Bradshaw? Were the deaths of Jessie and other residents as simple as they seemed?

And what about Nadine? I hadn't heard from her since our last meeting. Did she know more than she told me? She had also visited the Hereuse and she appeared to know Sharon. And was she really in the antiques business? It all seemed too much of a co-incidence.

I couldn't see where all these threads would lead me. There was some vital part missing, something I hadn't picked up. Was there any way to find it? Confirm my suspicions about who had arranged my 'accident'? Whoever it was had meant it as a warning, not to kill me. That didn't make me feel any better, but someone thought I knew much more than I did and that made me nervous, very nervous. My thoughts were interrupted by Simon's appearance at the top of the stairs. 'Don't you think you would be better with some fresh air, instead of being cooped up down here?'

I was about to say, 'I'm fine as I am' but realised how churlish that sounded. I was still feeling stiff and sore, but no doubt being on deck and having some of my cares blown away would help. 'Good idea,' I said, making an effort to sound cheerful.

He came down to the bottom of the steps. 'Let me help you,' he said, taking my arm carefully.

I rose slowly, holding on to the side of the bench that ran round one side of the salon, positioning myself carefully to cause minimum pain.

Once up on deck I did feel better. A little breeze had sprung up, not enough to be troublesome or to white cap the waves, but enough to make me feel much happier. This was almost the last event for the reunion and after the farewell meeting in the Pavilion it would all be over. We'd reported to the police station, left our details for further interviews. And, I vowed silently, I would never again be involved in organising something like this.

I moved to the far end of the deck where there was a little shelter and the possibility of a seat.

Madge came over again. 'I must say you did a brilliant job in taking over from Betsie,' she said. 'We've all had a great time. It's been so good to catch up with people you haven't seen in years.' Then she seemed to recollect herself and her face took on a sad look. 'It was a terrible thing that happened to Hilary, but that wasn't your fault.'

'Thanks, Madge. That does make me feel a bit better.'

'How on earth did you manage to take over, though? Betsie was so far on in the arrangements there must have been loads of documentation and lists to trawl through.'

I smiled. 'It was a bit difficult in the beginning but thank goodness for the internet and for e-mail. She had done a lot of the business by e-mail.'

'And I guess she was the kind of person who was used to organising. She dabbled in lots of things, specialist publishing for one. We picked up one of her catalogues at a country fair. All publicity for her antiques business, but still, really well done.'

Yes, Betsie had many interests, but which one had led to her death?

Madge drifted away to talk to some of the others, leaving me gazing out across the waters. Catalogues? That was something to think about. Then it came to me in a flash. There were catalogues in Jessie's belongings, now with my mother. Had she found time to look through Jessie's belongings? Or had she been too busy since her return from Canada?

I took out my phone, hoping the signal would be strong enough to let me phone her, ask her to check through those catalogues for anything that resembled the missing jewellery.

With a mounting sense of excitement I had the feeling that at last I was on to solving the puzzle about Betsie's death and the other mysterious events that had happened on Bute.

FORTY

I could hardly wait for the last meeting in the Pavilion to finish. A few delegates were staying on the island for extra days but for most of them this was the finale to the reunion. I was more convinced than ever that the answer to everything lay somewhere in Jessie's box. My mother had promised to do as I asked, examine the notebook, scour the catalogues and then call me.

There were lots of votes of thanks, promises of other events (count me out, I thought), calls for exchanges of addresses. Someone even suggested we have a newsletter to keep us all in touch but no one volunteered to take that on. Then Madge stood up and made a highly complimentary speech about all my efforts to make the reunion such a success and presented me with the most enormous bouquet of flowers of roses and gypsophila. I almost felt all the effort had been worth it, but not quite.

'We are grateful for everything you've done, Alison. It's been so good to catch up with old friends and make the acquaintance of new ones. This is one year none of us will forget.'

Nor will I, though perhaps not for the same reasons as you, was my reaction to this.

There was an enormous cheer from the audience. I was genuinely touched by this but not enough to suggest we meet again. If they wanted another reunion, someone else could organise it.

Johnnie rose slowly to his feet, a tear in his eye as he said, 'I'd like you all to stand for a chorus of Auld Lang Syne.'

It seemed as if the roof of the Pavilion would come off with the noise, as everyone sang lustily.

187

People began to drift away, with many promises of 'keeping in touch,' though most of them wouldn't. A Christmas card for a few years followed by guilt that they hadn't yet met up and then the usual concerns of life would overtake them.

I made no such promises. It had been good to see them -for the most part- but it was odd that no further mention had been made of Hilary. She hadn't been the most popular member of the group, as nosey when she turned up at the reunion as she had been when we were all at college, but still I did think some mention might have been made of her. Perhaps people felt it was easier to ignore it all, pretend it hadn't happened. Now that the reunion was over it had all assumed an air of distance, of happening to someone else. Whatever was going on, the police were now in charge, or so I tried to convince myself. But the more I tried to dismiss everything that had happened, the more it all occupied my thoughts. I couldn't let it rest.

Simon came up so quietly behind me that I didn't hear him until he said, 'Ready to go, Alison? You can be pleased at how it all went. Now it's time for a bit of a holiday.'

I was looking forward to the next couple of days at the lodge with nothing more strenuous than a walk along the Tramway route to Ettrick Bay for lunch at the tearoom. Even better, the weather looked settled for the next few days, though with Atlantic weather it's hard to be sure.

But when we came back to the lodge, after the last of the farewells and thanking the staff at the Pavilion for all their help, I was more restless than ever. I had to phone my mother and ask her if she'd read the notebook.

'It's all very strange,' she said. 'I don't know why Jessie would have sold these items.'

'Have you checked the notebook? Look at the numbers beside the Scottish brooch and the Victorian pendant. I think she put them down by their initials.'

There was a moment's silence. 'Yes, I've got them. But the amounts Jessie has written down aren't the same as the ones in those catalogues. What's going on, Alison?'

How could I test this out? Then I thought about Simon's laptop, still sitting unused in the corner. Of course. The

188

catalogues would be on line. 'Give me the details of those items and the names of the auction sites,' I said.

'Make sure you let me know what you find out,' she insisted as she said goodbye.

Simon came into the room as I switched on the computer. 'What on earth are you up to now? Put your feet up and I'll make something to eat.'

'I will in a minute,' I said stubbornly. 'This might be what I've been looking for all along. There's something in here, some clue.'

He sighed deeply and flicked on the television, scanning through the channels till he found a football match which took his interest.

I put the laptop on the table, together with the notes I'd made from my phone call to my mother and after a bit of trawling I found all three catalogues. Thank goodness for internet search engines. The information from Jessie's notebook was clear. TSB could only be the Scottish brooch and VP the Victorian pendant. These were the very items promised to my mother. What was of greater interest were the amounts Jessie had written beside them in her notebook and I clicked on one of the sale catalogues, scanning quickly to the pages corresponding with the numbers of the jewellery items. There they were, displayed in full colour. Far from being worthless the brooch was described as a 'special piece, the work of a master jeweller' and the necklace as 'a rare item, very seldom available.'

The price beside each item took my breath away. I went back to the information from the notebook to double check the other figures, figures that could only be the prices Jessie had been quoted or even sold them for. And they were nothing like those in the sale catalogue.

I sat back, too astounded to take this in and then decided to go through some of the other items. Some I didn't recognise, no doubt items belonging to other residents, but in one of the other catalogues I did recognise Celia's ceramic pots from the way she had described them, though there was no sign of the Chinese vase she'd told me about. Now I was angry, angry on behalf of Jessie, angry on behalf of my mother - not because she had been cheated

189

out of the jewellery Jessie had promised her, but because of what had happened to her friend.

So this was what was going on at the Hereuse: the residents were being conned out of their valuables, being offered a low price, persuaded to part with them and then they were put up for auction to realise their true worth. Or even worse, the items were just 'disappearing.' Jessie must somehow have obtained the catalogues - sent for them perhaps - and realised what was happening. Problem was she couldn't do anything about it. But I could. This was a matter for the police. I started to close down the auction site and suddenly a name on one of the catalogues sprang out at me. Sylvester de Courtney. It was no surprise that Betsie would know him. After all, they were in the same business. But it must more than that. They were in league to cheat the residents at the Hereuse Nursing home.

What should I do? This was all very vague, all speculation. There was nothing else for it. I'd have to find Sylvester and confront him. In spite of telling myself to leave well alone, there was no way I could rest until I'd talked to him.

FORTY ONE

I could scarcely believe that this was the link, the clue I'd been looking for. It explained why Jessie thought she was being murdered, what Celia was so concerned about.

Was Sylvester still on the island? He and Deborah had been booked into the Old Forge Hotel and according to Deborah they had intended to stay a few days longer because he had some business on Bute. Now I had an idea what that business might be. How could I have been so blind? If I was right, Sylvester's 'business' involved the Hereuse Nursing home and its elderly residents. All I had to do was think of an excuse to leave Simon and go over to the hotel to speak to Sylvester. There were others to check out as well: there was no doubt that whatever was going on Mrs Bradshaw was involved in some way.

This was no easy task. Now I believed Nadine, or at least believed some of her story, though there were some parts that seemed very strange. Betsie's death had been no accident. She had been murdered for some reason connected to this whole sorry affair. Was it possible she had been trying to get out of the whole nasty business? And that someone didn't want her blabbing what she knew? I remembered how Mrs Bradshaw had been determined I wouldn't pursue what had happened to Jessie, the way she had brushed aside my other questions, her attempts to play down the way Jessie had left everything to the Hereuse. There was only one way to find out and I wouldn't rest until I had the truth. If nothing else I owed it to Jessie.

I was saved from yet another lie to Simon by his coming into the room, saying. 'Would you mind if I went for one last game of golf?'

I dissembled for a few moments, not wanting him to think I was giving in so easily but as if to reinforce his request he said eagerly, 'You could have a restful afternoon with your book. You've had a busy time of it.'

'Good idea. That's exactly what I'll do.' I said, consoling myself with the thought of spending time with my feet up once I'd tried to track down Sylvester.

Simon gathered his golf equipment and hurried off with a cheerful 'See you later'.

When he left I was reclining on the sofa by the window, book in hand. As soon as I saw him walk up the road alongside Kames Castle towards the golf club, I was up quickly in spite of still aching limbs and pulled on my shoes and jacket. A few minutes were wasted scrabbling around for the car keys, hoping that Simon hadn't gone off with them in his pocket, but by a process of emptying everything out on to the hall table I found them at last at the very bottom of my bag.

My heart was thudding as I eased the car through the main gates beside the lodge. I'd no idea what to say to Sylvester or how to find out what he knew. He did know something and that something might help me finally find out not only what had happened to Jessie but also Mrs Bradshaw's role in all this.

The Old Forge was situated on a corner at Straad, once a small but thriving community. Now the village was deserted apart from a few newly built holiday homes, a converted farmhouse well back from the road and the original school building, long since disused. I parked off road, near the hotel, trying to think how best to approach him and how to make a rapid escape should this meeting prove difficult. Should I mention Deborah? Better not. That would only complicate matters.

As I came up to the main entrance, I thought, What if he's not here? The fall out with Deborah might have made him change his plans and he might already have left the island. But I was in luck, though only just. He was standing with his back to me near the hotel loading various items into the boot of a large silver car. Boxes were piled up all round it and he was so engrossed in what he was doing he didn't hear me come up behind him. I moved as quietly as possible, counting on the element of surprise.

As I came alongside him, he moved away to pick up one of the boxes. The boot of his car was almost full of items that he had most likely collected on the island, ready to transport to the mainland for sale. One of them looked suspiciously like a large Chinese vase, even through the bubble wrap encasing it and it was very like the Chinese vase Celia had described to me. I tiptoed over, but this time he heard me coming. He was almost too quick for me, but not quite.

He slammed the boot shut on my approach. Now I was angry, angry on behalf of Celia because the vase he was so carefully putting into the boot of his car was most surely hers, so exactly as she had described it that it was impossible to mistake.

'Going somewhere?' I asked, facing up to him, feeling brave only because we were in such a public place. Surely no harm could come to me here?

He recovered his silky, urbane stance almost immediately. 'Of course. I'm going back to Glasgow.'

'And you're taking all this stuff with you?' A sweep of my arm to encompass the various boxes that still sat on the ground beside his car.

He looked puzzled. 'Certainly. This is my stock.' A pause and then he said, 'I don't know what business it is of yours.' The usually polite Sylvester now looked furious. 'If you're concerned about Deborah, let me say that our relationship and its end was entirely mutual.'

I was about to reply, 'It's nothing to do with Deborah,' but this might be a ploy to distract me, so instead I said, 'Actually, Sylvester, I recognise that vase you've just loaded into the boot. It belonged to someone I knew.' It seemed worth taking a chance I was right.

This seemed to make him hesitate for a moment. 'All my items are legitimate, Mrs Cameron.'

He wasn't going to get off so lightly. 'I didn't suggest they were, but I would like to know how you came about that particular item.'

'I think you should ask Mrs Bradshaw,' he said.

'What has she to do with it?'

'More than you might think.'

So I had been right. Mrs Bradshaw was involved in this murky work. How dreadful that the owner of the Hereuse Nursing home should be the very person to take advantage of the elderly residents. And was she involved in Betsie's death also? Had Betsie found out that the 'stock' Mrs Bradshaw was selling had been obtained by foul means? More than anything I wanted to believe Betsie had also been duped.

I frowned. 'I still want an explanation,' I said, determined to hold my ground and hoping he wouldn't ask what business it was of mine. Mrs Bradshaw might be involved, but Sylvester wasn't blameless. There was no way he could think Mrs Bradshaw had obtained these items legally or at the very least without cheating the residents.

He jingled his car keys. 'Look, I have a couple of things to do here. It will take an hour or so. Why don't you meet me at the Hereuse? Then we can both talk to Mrs Bradshaw. After all,' a pleading look from those liquid brown eyes, 'I don't want to think that I'm involved in anything that's not above board.'

I hesitated. Should I believe him? Then I remembered Simon. He would be a good couple of hours on the golf course yet and in all likelihood would go into the clubhouse after he had finished his round. 'All right,' I replied, making a decision. 'I'll meet you there in an hour's time.'

He gave a little bow and turned on his heel to go back into the hotel.

An hour wasn't long enough to do anything productive, but too long to wait around here. I'd go back into Rothesay for a while before heading off to the Hereuse. I considered whether to phone Simon, let him know my plans, but in the end I contented myself with a text saying where I was going and exactly one hour later, with a mounting sense of excitement, I drove up to the front door of the nursing home. Perhaps at last I would find out what had really been happening here, close this chapter.

Too late I thought I should have alerted the police. But then would they have believed me? I still had no proof of any illegal activity; it was all guesswork and surmise.

There was no sign of Sylvester's car. If I had arrived first so much the better. I might learn more if he wasn't around. I walked over to Mrs Bradshaw's house, musing on what I would say. There was no reply to my first ring at the doorbell so I tried again. Perhaps it wasn't working? I peered through the letterbox but all I could see was a little way into the deserted hallway. As I lifted my hand to the lion knocker, the door swung gently open at my touch. That was very strange.

Very cautiously I went in, calling out in an increasingly loud voice, 'Are you there, Mrs Bradshaw?' as I did so, but there was no answer. I pushed open the door to the living room. Or rather, I tried to push it open. Something was blocking it.

Mrs Bradshaw was lying on the floor at an awkward angle, wedged tightly in the corner behind the door ...and she appeared to be dead.

FORTY TWO

For a moment fear rooted me to the spot. Had Mrs Bradshaw fallen, had an accident? Moving closer little by little, I forced myself to kneel down beside her and gingerly lift her arm to feel for a pulse. There was none. There was a deep gash on her head. She seemed to have fallen off the sofa, taking a couple of the cushions with her, now under her head and slowly absorbing the blood from her wound. This was no accident, no accidental fall and whoever had been responsible might still be in the house.

I didn't wait to find out but turned and fled, panic stricken, out into the garden where I stood bent over, breathing heavily, trying to recover. My first impulse was to leave the scene, but that might only incriminate me. My fingerprints would be everywhere in the house.

I ran as quickly as my shaking legs would allow up to the Hereuse main door and pounded on the knocker.

The door was opened by Sharon. 'Whatever's the matter, Mrs Cameron?'

'Thank goodness it's you, Sharon - it's Mrs Bradshaw,' I gasped, 'she's dead.'

'Dead? What on earth are you talking about?'

'I'm telling you I've come from her house and she's lying there dead.'

Sharon opened the door wider. 'I think you'd better come in.'

'But you can't leave her lying there,' I screamed. 'You need to call the police, like now.'

'I think we need you to calm down a bit.' She grabbed me by the elbow, pulled me inside and ushered me into a side room, the same room where I had heard of Jessie's death.

Suddenly Jason appeared behind her. 'Problem?' he muttered, out of breath, as if he'd been running.

Sharon propelled him outside the door and whispered to him. Strain as I might, I could hear nothing.

I jumped up and went over to the door. 'We can't wait here. We need to do something.'

They exchanged a glance. 'We will,' said Jason. 'I'll go round there now and if Mrs Bradshaw is indeed dead, I'll phone the police. You stay here.'

Sharon nudged me back into the room. 'Leave it to Jason. He'll take care of everything. You've had a terrible shock.'

What a relief. She was right: I was trembling from head to toe. Thank goodness Jason was here. I sat down on one of the chairs as Sharon called one of the staff over to fetch me a cup of strong sweet tea. 'Stay here till this is sorted out. I'll go and see what Jason's doing.'

At first I was grateful for this suggestion. There was nothing I wanted more than to hand over all of this to someone else. I drank the cup of tea slowly, trying not to notice how overwhelmingly sweet it was, but as the minutes ticked by and no one returned my anxiety returned. What was keeping them so long? Had they forgotten about me?

Stealthily, keeping as quiet as possible, I left the room. In the corridor, all was silent, deserted. There had been no sound of a police car, no sound of any activity. There was no one at the reception desk either but though there was a bell marked Press Here, it brought no response to my call. I tried again, listening as it sounded loudly in the silence, but still no one came.

Why wait here any longer? I hurried out of the building, neglecting to close the door behind me. There was no one in sight, no one at this side of the Hereuse. The rest of the staff must be in the residents' quarters: Sharon had been the only one on duty at reception. What had happened to her?

There was a garden bench at the end of the terrace, highly ornate and very uncomfortable. I sat down there to think what to do next. Whatever had happened to Sharon and to Jason? It couldn't have taken them all this time to reach Mrs Bradshaw's house and confirm she was dead. The obvious answer was to leave here, go to the police, explain what had happened and hope they believed me.

As I tried to stand up, somewhat shakily, the thought occurred to me that I might have made a mistake. What if there hadn't been a death? What if her pulse had been really weak and I'd assumed she was dead? And where were Jason and Sharon? There was as yet no sign of either of them. And if Mrs Bradshaw was still alive, surely they would have sent for an ambulance?

Sylvester! He was the one who had suggested meeting here to confront Mrs Bradshaw but he hadn't turned up unless … unless he had come straight here. Of course. I had stupidly delayed for the hour he suggested, had idled away the time in Rothesay while he had come straight over to the nursing home.

Whatever was going on I couldn't remain here any longer. What was the point of waiting? I would go back to Mrs Bradshaw's house and find out what Jason and Sharon were up to.

Slowly and cautiously I walked round to the row of terraced staff houses, all the while watching for them. I couldn't make any sense of this: they must be in the house, waiting for the police. The police station was no more than ten minutes away at most, yet there had been no sound of a police car.

Suddenly appalled, I thought, what if whoever had killed Mrs Bradshaw was still in her house and I'd sent Jason and Sharon into danger? It didn't bear thinking about. I had to go back.

As I slowly approached the door to Mrs Bradshaw's house, every nerve on edge, I noticed it was slightly ajar, as though someone had again neglected to close it properly. Very carefully I pushed it wider, dreading what I would find, but compelled to move forward.

'Hello,' I called. 'Is there anyone there?' I waited. 'Sharon? Jason?'

No reply. I tried again, shouting as loudly as I could, but the house was quiet. The air hung heavy with the smell of lavender, its sweet smell disguising anything else. I breathed deeply, summoning courage to enter the living room where I had found Mrs Bradshaw's body. Sharon and Jason were most certainly not

198

here. I was right: something had happened to them, they had walked into the killer and it was all my fault.

This time the living room door yielded easily to my touch as I pushed it open, my eyes closed, fearful of what might be there. I forced myself to open them, to gaze again on Mrs Bradshaw's body.

The body had disappeared.

FORTY THREE

No one would believe me, would say I had imagined it. But surely Mrs Bradshaw had been lying there dead, the blood oozing from the deep blow to her head, seeping on to the cushions. There was no way she could have survived that. I looked round the room; something was wrong, something was missing. That was what was troubling me. The cushions had disappeared and with them all traces of any blood. It all looked so normal.

My heart started to pound. If I was all alone in the house where were Sharon and Jason? And where was the body? It had been lying here only a short time ago and now it had gone.

I began to move very slowly through the rest of the house. Was I losing my mind? Had I imagined it all? Of course not. Mrs Bradshaw had been lying there dead. Even in my state of shock I would have known if she was still alive.

Everything was in order, with no sign of a struggle. The kitchen was clean and tidy; the small dining room had the air of not being used in a very long time. I stopped at the foot of the stairs, craning to hear any noise. Silence. Why on earth would she be upstairs? Somehow I had to check, make sure. I crept up the narrow staircase step by step, holding on to the banister for support.

There were two bedrooms at the top of the stairs and a large cupboard, its door slightly ajar. I put my head round the cupboard door. It was a linen cupboard and all the sheets, blankets and towels sat on shelves in serried ranks. Nothing here then. As I was about to turn, I felt a sudden push in the small of my back. I was propelled forward into the cupboard and heard the door slam loudly behind me.

'What's going on,' I yelled, trying to push the door open, but my voice was muffled by the quantities of linen in the cupboard. I banged again at the door but it was very firmly locked. I was trapped. I slumped down on the floor, or at least on the little bit of floor available. This was such a stupid thing to do. Why hadn't I gone straight to the police station or called Simon? Who had locked me in here?

It was stuffy inside this cupboard but as I began to feel slightly calmer, I noticed it wasn't quite dark. High above me there was a tiny skylight. Would it be possible to get out through that?

I took off my shoes and eased myself up onto the first shelf, clinging on to the brackets, then up on to the second shelf. It was going to be a long slow process. What if I fell? I climbed down again and pulled all the sheets, blankets and towels I could reach onto the floor. At least if I did fall, these would cushion me.

Another very slow and steady attempt and this time I made it as far as the fourth shelf before stopping to catch my breath, gripping on tightly. This was impossible. There was no way I could make it to the top and if I did there was still a huge gap between the last shelf and the skylight. What's more, this skylight looked as if it hadn't been opened in a very long time.

I moved back down cautiously. My only hope was to keep banging and yelling, hoping that when the police arrived they would hear me. If I could loosen one of the shelves, I'd be able to use it as a way of creating noise. I pulled and pushed at the first shelf, but it was stuck fast with the paint of many years. The next one was no better and I was beginning to sweat profusely as the lack of air affected me. How long could I last in here without fainting? Not very much longer. Don't panic, I told myself. That will only make matters worse.

The third shelf yielded a little as I tugged it and moved it back and forth, pausing every minute of so to take a deep breath. Finally, with a loud crack, it split and I was able to lever off a large piece of the shelf. I sat down, exhausted by my efforts. Now I had this piece of wood, did I have the strength to keep banging on this door for as long as it would take the police to arrive?

I had to try. I began thumping the door, knowing I wouldn't be able to keep this up for any length of time. I strained my ears, listening for any sound. What if the police didn't come? What if Sharon and Jason hadn't called them at all? Why else would Mrs Bradshaw's body have disappeared?

I slumped down amid the piles of linen and began to weep quietly. Was this what it had come to? Trapped in a cupboard in this house on Bute? I thought not. Get a grip, I rebuked myself and steeling myself once more I gave the door an almighty thump, then another and another. Suddenly the panel on the door splintered. Of course. Why hadn't I thought of that? The door might be strong, but the panels were weaker. If I continued battering it, I might be able to knock the panel out. Even if it wasn't possible to squeeze through the gap it would let more air into this stuffy cupboard.

One final thump and the panel ripped away and fresh air flooded in. I breathed deeply, filling my lungs and then began to cough. I wouldn't have been surprised if I'd done myself some permanent damage, breathing in all those fibres from the linen.

Having pushed out the remaining jagged splinters of the door panel, I tried to ease my way through it, but it was far too small. If I turned sideways, perhaps that would be better. I put my shoulder through first, then attempted to pull up my leg to follow, but instead of making it easier this only made it worse and I jammed half way through. Try as I might I couldn't get out and I couldn't get back. What was I going to do?

I stopped, listening intently for any sign that Jason or Sharon might be returning. I had no idea what I would do if they did come back, knowing one of them must have been responsible for my present predicament.

Suddenly I heard the front door open softly and the sound of footsteps in the hall. Having disposed of Mrs Bradshaw was this Jason come back to deal with me? I scarce dared breathe and painfully wrenching my shoulder back through the gap, retreated into the corner among the pile of towels and sheets. Perhaps if I kept absolutely still and quiet, they would see the broken panel on the door and think I'd escaped.

The footsteps began to sound on the stairs, slowly, very slowly. Not for the first time I berated myself for my involvement in all of this. Why had I not accepted that Jessie had died of old age, had been happy to leave her money to this nursing home?

The footsteps stopped at the top of the stairs as though the person was deciding what to do. I couldn't keep still any longer and the dust from the linen was tickling my nose. I thought I was going to explode and let out an almighty sneeze.

There was the sound of the key turning in the lock. Too late now. It was all over.

'What on earth are you up to now?' said a voice. It was Simon.

FORTY FOUR

It was a slow drive back to Ascog, through Rothesay and out to Kames and several times we had to pull over till my trembling stopped. But a determination to find some answers made me urge Simon to keep going. I'd been able to give him only an abbreviated account of what had happened and he said little, but shook his head at regular intervals.

'How did you know where I was?' I said.

'You sent me a text, remember? When you didn't return I went over to the Hereuse and one of the staff there said she'd seen you head towards Mrs Bradshaw's house.' He glanced over at me. 'Luckily there was a taxi available when I phoned.'

I didn't even ask why he had ignored my suggestion about going straight to the police station, as he said, 'Let's get you back and then worry about all of that.'

As the lodge came in sight I almost cried with relief. But as we turned into the gate there was another car parked alongside the front door, a car I didn't recognise. Who could it be? For a moment the cowardly way out seemed the best option: to persuade Simon to take me back to Rothesay and the ferry and the safety of home, pretend all this had been a bad dream. Simon could deal with the police. But that was a mad idea, dismissed almost as soon as it was formed.

He turned off the ignition, sat and waited. There was someone in the other car, but the tinted windows made it impossible to see who it was from this angle. It certainly wasn't Sylvester unless he had made a swift change of car yet again.

I got out of the car and stood beside it, my nerves jangling, a trickle of sweat going down my back as I made ready to flee.

Simon came up behind me. 'You might get some explanation now,' he said calmly, putting his arm round my shoulder.

The door of the other car opened and out stepped Nadine. 'Mrs Cameron, I think I need to speak to you. I've a lot to tell you.'

Incapable of replying, feeling my legs would be unable to support me much longer, I could only nod my head.

We stood there, outside the lodge, neither of us moving, though I had to hold on to the car to stop myself from falling over. Nadine broke the stalemate. 'Perhaps we could go inside and I'll try to fill you in.' Simon stood aside.

Frankly I doubted if anyone could explain what had been happening, but anything was worth trying. 'Good idea.' I fumbled with the key in the lock, my hands shaking so much I dropped it.

Simon picked it up. 'Here, let me do that.'

Once inside, I almost fell onto the sofa, still incapable of speech as Nadine sat on the easy chair by the window and Simon pulled up a chair in the far corner, almost out of sight. Desperate to know the story, but reluctant to be first to speak, I stared at her.

'Mrs Bradshaw's dead,' I eventually managed to croak, 'and I think she's been murdered.'

Nadine acted swiftly, eliciting the details from me in a few sentences and going outside to phone the police.

'Don't worry, it's all under control,' she said, coming back into the lodge.

'You believe me? That I saw Mrs Bradshaw dead?'

Nadine raised her eyebrows. 'Of course I believe you. I'm sorry I was too late to save her. I didn't think she was in danger, not any real danger.'

Relief flooded me, I trembled from head to toe as I sank back. 'What's going on? Why do you know so much about all of this?'

Nadine leaned forward, her voice low, as though afraid of being overheard, even though we were alone.

'It all started because of Betsie and her antiques business.'

Before she could continue, I held up my hand. 'What I have to know, Nadine, is where you really fit into all of this. Are you Betsie's daughter or not? And if not, who are you?'

There was a moment's hesitation, a slight sigh as she shifted in her chair. 'I am Betsie's daughter, but the way I discovered that wasn't quite as I told you.' She at least had the grace to look ashamed.

I could feel myself becoming calmer, the terrible fear ebbing away. 'Well, there's a surprise,' I said but the sarcasm was lost on her.

She opened her handbag and pulled out a photo, passing it to me without comment. It had obviously been downloaded from a computer, taken at some function or other because everyone was in evening dress and as I peered more closely at the background I could see a partly hidden banner *Sterling Antiques Convention.*

What was more astonishing was the group of people in the photo. Betsie was there and on either side of her, laughing for the photographer, were Sylvester and Hilary. 'Where did you find this?'

'I was determined to find out all I could about Betsie before I approached her. I checked her out on the internet and loads of information came up. That photo was particularly interesting, for reasons you can guess.'

'I still don't understand. So Betsie and Sylvester were both in the same business and Hilary knew them.'

She laughed bitterly. 'Hilary more than knew them.' A pause. 'She was Sylvester's wife. They were divorced and then he took up with a much younger woman and not the only one, from what I gather.'

I thought about Deborah. 'But Hilary was the same age as I am.'

'Yes, she was a good few years older than Sylvester. You've met Sylvester?'

I nodded, thinking of his smooth manner, his penchant for flattery.

Nadine went on, 'Hilary was left a lot of money when her parents were killed in a plane crash, money that set him up in business. When he was successful, he left her. I don't think she ever forgave him. So when the business about Betsie happened, she saw an opportunity to take revenge by letting you know what kind of a person he was, though I don't think she knew what he'd done to Betsie. Sylvester had to stop her before she told you about him.'

Deborah might be heartbroken but she had had a lucky escape, luckier than she might ever know. 'And where does all of this take us?'

'Sylvester and Betsie worked together. But times got tight, good antiques hard to come by. Sylvester developed a scam. He would go round the country setting up art exhibitions as a cover for other activities.'

'Other activities?'

'It was Betsie's job to visit as many people in the area as possible and value antiques and then Sylvester would move in and do the bargaining, giving them a fraction of what the items were actually worth.'

Light was beginning to dawn. 'So she was the person who visited the Hereuse, bought Jessie's jewellery, Celia's ceramic pots and Chinese vase?'

She shook her head. 'Not quite. Betsie 'softened up' the owners, if you like, but she was out to make a profit, not rob them. Sylvester was robbing Betsie as well as the owners. Of course the Hereuse was an ideal place because you had to be well off to afford to live there in the first place. But, as you found out, some of the elderly residents weren't as gullible as he would have liked.'

I could feel my temper rising. 'Poor Jessie. So Mrs Bradshaw was involved, she was the one responsible.'

'Mrs Bradshaw?' She looked puzzled at this suggestion. 'No, no. They did have accomplices - Sharon and Jason helped them. Sharon was besotted with Jason, would have done anything for him. She was the one who locked you in the cupboard to buy them time to dispose of the body.'

'Mmm... I understand that,' I muttered, thinking of Deborah and Sylvester. Thank goodness Deborah was made of sterner stuff.

Nadine appeared not to hear me. 'Sharon would let them know when there were new residents at the nursing home and Jason helped get the goods out.'

'How did he do that?'

For the first time in our conversation, Nadine smiled. 'Independent Caterers Limited? What better way to bring the goods out without any fuss. Jason worked part time at the Pavilion and that's where he stored everything till it could be taken off the island. All completely unknown to the other staff there, of course. The building has all kinds of nooks and crannies where the goods could be stored until it was safe.'

I could scarcely take all this in, but now I thought back to all that had happened, it made sense. I had another question. 'But Jessie left all her money to the Hereuse, as no doubt did others.'

'Yes, Mrs Bradshaw was greedy, but she wasn't involved in the theft of items from the residents. How could you imagine she knew about antiques? Did you see her garden with all those terrible cheap ornaments?'

'She had some items that looked antique in her house,' I said defensively.

'Possibly, but because she liked them, not because she thought them valuable.'

'So, let me get this straight. Jason was responsible for Betsie's death?'

For a moment Nadine smiled. 'Sylvester was the one responsible: Betsie was involved in the scam, but she was out to buy the goods cheaply, not to steal. When she found out what Sylvester and Jason were up to, she threatened to spill the beans if they didn't stop.'

'And they couldn't?'

'Exactly. They were in too deep, had been doing this for too long. And owed too much to too many other people.'

All I could think about was Deborah. Would she have been another victim? Would Sylvester have tried to lure her into his crimes? Maybe he had engineered the 'finding out' about his wife, knowing she wouldn't stay with him once she knew.

'I'm still amazed how you managed to uncover all of this.' There was something odd about her story.

She stopped for a moment and fiddled with the top button on her jacket, the colour rising in her cheeks. 'I suppose there's no problem about telling you everything. You'll find it all out eventually. The truth is, I'm a journalist. This all started out as an investigation, a story about the cost of care homes and what the elderly are getting for the enormous sums they have to spend on care. The Hereuse is one of the most expensive in Scotland, so naturally it was on my list. This was going to be a big story for me. I had to use whatever means possible to find the information.'

'But what happened to Mrs Bradshaw?'

'I guess she found out what was going on and threatened to expose Sylvester. So, like Betsie and Hilary, she had to go.'

'And was she responsible for Jessie's death?'

Nadine stared at me. 'What? There was nothing strange about her death. She was old, that's all. Nothing more than natural causes.' Her phone rang.

'You'll have to go outside for a signal,' I said.

Nadine left me alone for a few minutes, trying to come to terms with everything she had said, while she went to the lodge gates to take the call, then returned smiling.

'Sharon and Jason are in custody - caught in the act of trying to dispose of Mrs Bradshaw's body.'

'And Sylvester killed Betsie? His was the other ticket in the glove compartment?'

She nodded. 'Sylvester and Betsie spent a lot of time together, they were partners in business. He went abroad pretty often, stayed with her. It was easy for him to tamper with her medication. Oh, they'll catch up with him, never fear. He's been under surveillance for some time now apparently. Bute wasn't the only island where he was working his scam.'

There was something still niggling me. 'But why was Betsie on that last ferry to Bute?'

'It's only a guess, but I think Betsie insisted that she and Sylvester come over to the island, try to sort everything out with the Hereuse. Perhaps the price of not reporting him to the police? He wasn't worried, of course, because he knew she wouldn't live long enough to cause any trouble.'

It was all too much to take in. Nadine said, 'I can come back and see you later, if you like, once you feel better.'

'Perhaps.' For the moment all I wanted to do was escape from it all.

I walked with Nadine to the door. 'I'm so sorry you didn't find Betsie in time,' I said.

She shrugged. 'I didn't know her, didn't expect to know her. But at least I've managed to find the person responsible for her death. That gives me some satisfaction.'

We shook hands and I lingered at the door as she drove off. The sky was darkening, the stars appearing one by one. Here at this far corner of the Port, without streetlights, their brilliance was undiminished. I shivered and went indoors.

EPILOGUE

Later, much later, we sat by the fire, watching the flames lick the seasoned wood and spurt into life. The evening had turned chilly and the good spell of weather we had enjoyed for the reunion appeared to be coming to an end.

'What I don't understand,' said Simon, 'is how you came to be involved in all of this.'

'I wasn't involved,' I protested. 'It all sort of happened without my permission.'

'That's an odd way to put it, but I believe you.'

'It was nothing to do with me.'

'But if you hadn't contacted Jessie, hadn't gone to the Hereuse Nursing home...'

'It wouldn't have mattered,' I protested. 'It would all still have happened ...because of Betsie.'

'I suppose so. There was nothing suspicious about Jessie's death after all?

'Not at all. Mrs Bradshaw was greedy: she part owned the home, wanted the residents to leave all their money to the Hereuse. I daresay she used a fair bit of persuasion, but there was no more to it.'

'And Nadine? Is she really Betsie's daughter?'

I thought for a few moments before answering. 'I've no idea. I don't even know if that's her real name, but I'm not going to make any more enquiries.'

Simon shook his head. 'I want you to promise me, promise me most solemnly, Alison, you will never, ever take on something like this reunion again.'

'Of course I won't. The very idea.'

He looked at me. 'Promise?'

I crossed my fingers behind my back. How could I know what the future might hold?

ACKNOWLEDGEMENTS

Grateful thanks to the following:

My editor, Katie Worrall, for all her valuable suggestions and her patience, Judith Duffy for editing assistance, Dr Joan Weeple and Dr Patricia Hemmings for answers to medical queries, Paul Duffy for technical assistance, the Rothesay police for advice on procedures (any errors are mine), the Discovery Centre for checking hotel names, Richard Home for agreeing to let me use his photos

...and Peter for his never failing support.

Cover photographs by kind permission of Richard Home

MYRA DUFFY

THE HOUSE AT ETTRICK BAY

An Alison Cameron mystery

Read an extract here

Published by New Generation Publishing

PROLOGUE

At Ettrick Bay, the sun is going down, the rippling light casting long shadows across the water. Along the sand, the oyster catchers gather, shrieking in the gloaming. No boats disturb the tranquillity of the steel grey waters lapping at the shore.

The cattle in the fields beside the long path look up, startled by the sound of plough horses returning home. In the darkening sky, the stars appear one by one as the pale crescent moon casts a ghostly light across the fields ripe with corn.

High above the bay, Ettrick House stands brooding, steadfast against the autumn winds. Couch grass and bindweed choke the once well tended flower beds and the long sweeping drive is pitted and potholed. The windows are shuttered, dark.

Alone in the silence of the empty house he sits nursing a glass of whisky, gazing at the pictures he sees in the flickering flames of the fire set against the chill of the evening.

Now, in his old age, the ghosts come back to haunt him. They give him no rest. And he wonders if tonight will be the night when at last she is found.

ONE

She lay on her side, as though asleep, one arm crooked under her head as a substitute for a pillow. Sunlight filtered into the deep trench at the bottom of the lower gardens, illuminating her outline.

She looked quiet, at peace, in this most tranquil of places high in the hills above the calm waters of Ettrick Bay so far below. If you looked closely you could see a few bits of what looked like pottery in the grave beside her, tiny remnants of a life lost. Her legs were curled up under her like a child's, though even my untrained eye could see she was a fully grown adult.

'How do you know it's a female?' I asked.

Morgan Connolly, the archaeologist in charge of the dig, looked up. It was hard to make out his expression behind the long red beard he sported, an apparent extension of his mass of curly hair. But he seemed happy to answer my questions.

'You can tell by the shape of the pelvis,' he said, bending down to my height as he pointed it out to me. 'And the shape of the skull also helps, though that's less useful.'

How long she had lain there, I wondered, as I watched the team go about their work. It must have been a long time. All that remained now were the bare bones of what had once been a living, breathing person.

Little bits of lichen clung to her feet and a tiny creature or two scuttled away into the remaining darkness, fretting at being so disturbed.

The archaeologists clustered round the trench did not share my concerns as they chattered excitedly about this discovery.

'Stand back.' The order from Morgan was firm. 'It's essential the site isn't contaminated.'

My daughter Deborah moved away reluctantly and came over to join me.

I turned to the slim young woman standing beside me. A terrible thought had suddenly occurred to me. 'Is it a murder victim?' I whispered.

Penny Curtis smiled and shook her head. She pushed back the lock of her long brown hair which had fallen over her face, leaving a little streak of mud on her forehead. Her large grey eyes were shining.

'Unlikely, though Morgan will be able to tell soon. It's much more likely to be an old skeleton.' She waved her trowel around, spattering earth over her yellow safety jacket. 'It's possibly a very old skeleton indeed.' She frowned and consulted a map she pulled out of her back pocket. 'But there's no record of a cemetery anywhere round here, so it is unusual and a great discovery.'

She smiled at me again, 'There's nothing we archaeologists like better than finding something like this. Don't worry.'

She looked over at Morgan who was talking animatedly to the other member of the excavation team. Brian March was still in the trench, standing beside the skeleton. In complete contrast to Morgan he was stout, which made him look smaller than he was and his head was shaven. A single gold earring glittered in the light as he scrambled up out of the trench, hoisting up his faded blue jeans as he did so. He looked more like a professional wrestler than an archaeologist.

Penny said, almost as though speaking to herself, 'Morgan will be incredibly pleased.'

'Why?' I could understand a find like this would be important to an archaeologist, but she spoke as if this skeleton was very special indeed.

She folded up the map and sighed. 'Morgan's been searching for the big discovery for some time now. He's had this theory for years that there was a Roman settlement on Bute somewhere. This high ridge is one of the more likely spots. No one else credits his idea so if he's proved right, it will be a major coup.'

I looked around me. Yes, I could well understand this stretch of land, high in the hills, would be an ideal site for a community to settle and to feel safe.

As though reading my thoughts she pointed over the fields to where the land began to curve steeply upwards. 'You can see the raised beach from here. A great place to build a settlement in ancient times.'

I knew enough about the academic world from my husband Simon to realise that if Morgan was proved right and this was the major find he had so long searched for, his reputation would be made. Papers by the score, conferences in overseas universities: he would be an expert whose opinions would be sought on every occasion. The academic world would be at his feet.

I became aware Simon was speaking. 'What happens next, Morgan?'

Morgan frowned and scratched his head. 'First we have to excavate the skeleton and discard any extraneous material. You often find bits of animal bone in an old site like this. Then we have to date the skeleton and assure the local police it's ancient enough for this not to be a murder enquiry.'

I looked away from the activity of the trench and down the sweep of hills towards the half circle of the bay. It was shaping up to be a perfect West coast afternoon. The sun blazed down from a cloudless sky and the heat was becoming so strong you could almost smell it on the strengthening brine from the bay. But I shivered in spite of the warmth and draped my jacket back over my shoulders.

This might be all in a day's work to these professionals, but it was the first time I had ever seen anything like it. How had the skeleton come to be here, in the grounds of this house at Ettrick Bay?

I heard my husband's voice again, as though from a distance, so engrossed was I in my own thoughts.

'Alison, are you all right?'

I turned to face him, shaking my head.

He grasped my elbow. 'Perhaps we should move away from here and let them do their work?'

I stood still, unable to move. Simon was concerned about this discovery. And so was I.

How could I have known when we agreed to help my friend Susie with this house at Ettrick Bay it would turn out like this?

Lightning Source UK Ltd.
Milton Keynes UK
UKOW051000131011

180247UK00001B/4/P